DeNial

Copyright © 2025 Chelsea Rice
All rights reserved.

Second Edition

ISBN: 978-1-968994-01-3

No part of this book may be reproduced or transmitted in any form or by any means,
electronic or mechanical, including photocopying, recording, or by any information
storage and retrieval system, without written permission from the author.

Published by Immortal Z
Printed in the United States of America

*To Cory: For the loving, yet harsh, push to do this.
Thank you.*

Table of Contents

Prologue 1
Chapter One 7
Chapter Two 20
Chapter Three 31
Chapter Four 38
Chapter Five 46
Chapter Six 60
Chapter Seven 69
Chapter Eight 77
Chapter Nine 84
Chapter Ten 91
Chapter Eleven 100
Chapter Twelve 109
Chapter Thirteen 120
Chapter Fourteen 126
Chapter Fifteen 133
Chapter Sixteen 143
Chapter Seventeen 153
Chapter Eighteen 159
Chapter Nineteen 165
Chapter Twenty 173
Chapter Twenty-One 180
Chapter Twenty-Two 186
Chapter Twenty-Three 191
Chapter Twenty-Four 200
Chapter Twenty-Five 204
Chapter Twenty-Six 208
Chapter Twenty-Seven 215

Chapter Twenty-Eight 221
Chapter Twenty-Nine 229
Chapter Thirty 237
Chapter Thirty-One 247
Chapter Thirty-Two 257
Chapter Thirty-Three 264
Chapter Thirty-Four 269
Chapter Thirty-Five 274
Chapter Thirty-Six 283
Chapter Thirty-Seven 292
Chapter Thirty-Eight 299
Chapter Thirty-Nine 306
Chapter Forty 313
Chapter Forty-One 327
Chapter Forty-Two 341
About the Author 348
Also by C.R. Rice 348
About the Author 353
More From C.R. Rice 354

Prologue

A hooded figure appeared on a moonless night in a small, quiet town. Its citizens slumbered peacefully, oblivious to the heavy foreboding that billowed in like fog down its pristine roads. The soft wind rustled the autumn leaves across the stranger's path as it ambled down the streets in a heavy silence.

Step after silent step, the figure wandered the town, stopping on occasion to peer into a darkened shop window before it pressed on.

The streets were lined with carefully painted and restored buildings, remnants of a town gasping for its last breath, but fighting for its survival. An old ice cream shop, adorned with pink and white striped awnings, was purposefully placed after a quaint cafe. A hint of fresh rose permeated from the blooming flower shop, nestled beside it. Logos were elegantly scrawled against the wide storefront windows with splashes of vibrant colors, hoping to bring wanderers close.

The figure, seemingly indifferent to these attempted draws, passed by unabated.

A small light at the edge of town captured the figure's attention and urged it closer. Something about the warm glow intrigued the being enough to cause a pause in its mission. The old red brick building's small circular window flickered by candlelight, illuminating a bartender, dutifully wiping down the worn, chipped counters while a waitress, swaying to a tune no one else heard, flitted around the room, collecting empty bottles and glasses that had been left from a devout crowd who had long since called it a night. A lone patron sat at the end of the bar, nursing the darkened liquid sitting before him.

For a few moments, the dark figure watched in thoughtful silence before continuing on its path.

As is the standard in most small towns, the end of the main road signaled the end of the town itself. The hooded one gently stepped off the edge of the sidewalk and onto a small gravel path that wound into a dimly lit park. Though it made no sound that humans could hear, the energy pouring off the figure was not so kind to the animals that lived within the park. A rabbit family, once happily asleep, crept from its burrow for a closer look. Birds peaked from their nests, the ruffling of their feathers echoing into the otherwise silent night. Predator and prey alike momentarily set aside their differences in the spirit of neighborhood protection. A brazen owl hooted into the night, eyeing the gracefully silent being with skepticism as it stepped from the park and onto a road adorned with cookie cutter houses.

It was a strange figure, neither resembling man nor woman, seemingly more human than animal, but none could truly tell. There were no limbs or unusual movements, no flash of hair or hint of face to give the possible distinction between one or the other. If someone had seen it pass, which no one had, they would only remember the distinct blood red cloak that seemed abnormally immune to the darkness of night.

Reaching the end of the manicured cul-de-sac, the figure slowed, tilted its hooded head and admired the two-story colonial home. The pristine white color shone, even on this moonless night, leading one to believe it had been painted recently. Its windows were framed with hunter green shutters while a large covered porch held three different colored chairs and a dainty white and glass, wicker table. Flowers hung between the wooden beams, pushing their fresh fragrance into the cool night while vibrant green ivy grew lazily over the railings.

The figure righted itself, drifting forward to follow the siding around the silent house, until it came to a stop and peered up at a single curved window. The figure looked around once, then twice before, somewhat cautiously, it leapt into the nearby tree and evaporated into a fine red mist and slipping through the cracked window. The figure's mist pooled onto the floor and began slinking across the thick, soft, brown carpeting, before finally rematerializing into its cloaked figure once more.

The room was painted a simple white, holding a long distressed white dresser, mirror, and matching nightstands on each side of the queen bed. One held a small clock with glowing red numbers and a book, while the other held a collection of picture frames. The walls were covered in a collage of photos and posters, and a closet that sat partially open beside a bathroom door. The bed was in the middle of the room, holding a multitude of pillows and blankets, the center of which held a disheveled and sleeping figure.

Soft snores filled the room as the hood drifted to the edge of the bed. For a long time, the being looked down at the woman, watching her sleep with her lips slightly parted and her chest rising and falling with deep, even breaths. One of her smooth hands lay carelessly against her chest, while the other was tucked deep into the pillows behind her head. It continued to watch until the lightning flickered across her red-tinted hair, giving birth to fire within the darkness of the night. Her skin held a slight tan from the time she spent in the fresh air and sunshine. She was close enough to reach out and touch and yet still so far. She knew nothing of the true world, of the people that desperately needed her. Or the ones that were waiting for her to fail.

It was time to speed things up. The limbo this world found itself currently trapped in had gone on for far too long. The people of this world ignored the fact that they

Denial

were dying at a higher rate than ever before. In this plane and in the next. Suffering had taken its hold in ways the worlds had never before seen. It was time for it to end.

Filled with a new resolve, the hooded one leaned down, a hand appearing from beneath the wispy material, clasped gently as it clutched a silver-like powder. Moving ever closer to the sleeping girl until it was mere inches away. With a slight inhale of breath, the figure blew the powder from its hand, creating a fine mist that covered the girl's face. The figure watched as the powder took on a shimmering light before finally sinking into her flesh. Her response was instantaneous as she scrunched her face, the hand from her chest coming to rub her nose before she turned on her side and settled once more.

Satisfied with its task completed, the figure righted itself, took one last look at the sleeping girl and the room she dwelled in before it dissolved once more. Settling lightly against the floor, it fluttered to the window before exiting and dropping neatly onto the ground below.

Without sparing a backward glance, the figure quickly crossed the expanse of the grass-covered backyard. Its steps were silent once more as it slid through the gate, navigating the trees beyond with practiced ease. Squirrels peaked out from their homes within the trees as the intruder slid past them. As curiosity often did, it got the best of the small creatures. They quickly crawled from the comfort of their homes and bounced from tree to tree in pursuit. The sun was breaking the horizon, cleansing the darkness of night with its splashes of pink and yellow, before the hooded figure came to a stop before a small cave.

"You shouldn't have done that, Red." The words came on the sickly warm wind to whisper into the figure's ear as it stopped before the small opening. The curious little squirrels halted before darting away at the sudden and deadly sharp voice.

Bowing its head, the figure stepped forward, disappearing into the depths. "You started it."

Chapter One

Averie Hale lay upon the fresh spring grass, a peaceful smile decorating her face as she soaked in the afternoon sun. Stretching her arms high above her head, she lifted her face farther into the warm sun, her smile widening as a dancing wind tickled her nose with a rich wildflower aroma that spread her auburn hair wildly around her. This is where she belonged, surrounded by earth and freshness and peace. The joyous sounds of chirping birds and the trickle of the nearby stream permeated a sense of peace that surrounded the area until a loud clapping of thunder severed the soothing sounds of spring. Birds scattered into the air, taking flight and soaring in the opposite direction of the intrusive sound.

Shocked, Averie bolted upright. With her heart pounding in her chest, she searched her surroundings. Though she saw nothing, another loud boom echoed, bringing her to her feet.

A rolling gray was swallowing the clear blue horizon, luring her closer and pushing her from the center of the field. The sun's warmth against her exposed flesh fought to keep the growing chill at bay as she brushed her fingertips along the swaying flowers. The rich blues, purples, and greens decorating the golden stalks faded as their rich fragrance soured with every step.

Slowly, the sun began to fade, swallowed by the impending darkness. A gasp slipped from her lips as the flowers began to disintegrate beneath her fingers. No matter which direction she turned, the results were the same. Ashy remnants of the once blossoming flowers filled the air, and the stems and blades of grass melted away beneath her feet.

Confusion filled her as her eyes swept across the dying landscape. Quivering, she stumbled back, a scream ripping from her throat as she plopped heavily on the dry and cracked ground. Her eyes burned. She gasped for breath as the world shifted once more. Her stomach rolled as the colors melted together in front of her eyes, twisting and turning over and over again before everything settled on a sickening gray scale. Averie forced herself to her knees, her eyes locked on a distant form. She shoved to her feet and inched closer until the form morphed into the dark figure of a man. He was tall, dressed completely in black, with

Denial

disheveled hair and blood smeared across the serious expression on his face, but the most captivating thing of them all was the piercing teal of his eyes.

Deep inside, Averie knew she recognized him. For years, she had seen the same man drifting to and from her dreams until he had become a constant companion. Whether he was standing in the background watching or sitting on a bench that she could never quite reach, he had always been there but also not. A shimmering mirage showing her she was dreaming. Another step forward, and the chaos of another time and place overlapping with the current, nearly brought her to her knees again as it overwhelmed her dream. Fighting for control, she watched as his lips moved in a familiar pattern.

"What?" Averie called out. "I can't hear you." She stepped toward him, but he stepped back. "Who are you? What do you want from me?"

He remained motionless, continuing to stand there, with only his lips moving in a concise, repeating motion. His eyes pleading, begging for her to understand. She whimpered, growing desperate to understand as the world once more changed around her.

The sky darkened, black clouds consuming the last remaining wisps of white, the gentle wind now a furious and slashing force. Lightning ripped through the dark, sending a foreboding crack that shattered the last shred of silence. Fear gripped her as the ground began to shake and decay. The once vibrant and fragrant flowers wilted further into oblivion, unable to hold their bloom on a blackened stem. Breathless, Averie tried to regain her footing, but the sheer force around her shoved her back to her knees.

Her breath came in quick succession, but the air was dense around her, too heavy to fill her lungs with the much needed oxygen. Her eyes darted back to the man. "What's going on?"

He stood in silent resolution; his eyes fixed on her. The ground, unable to keep up with the constant motion, began to crack open. Once again, Averie tried to stand, but the quaking ground forced her back down. Still, the man did nothing but stand and stare, his lips twisting with the unheard words.

"Please! Help me!" she begged, her fingers digging into the dry, cracked earth. Her nails tore as she gripped desperately at the landscape while it continued to self-destruct around her.

The dark figure tilted his head, the first movement she had seen since this hellscape had unfolded. A sadness entered his downcast eyes. Following his gaze, she watched in horror as a deep crimson fluid oozed from the cracks beneath his feet. It pooled around him, bubbling at his feet, then rising to consume his ankles before engulfing his entire lower body. The man flailed, trying to pull himself free from the thick, blood-colored liquid. In soundless horror, the ooze exploded up around his entire body before pulling him below the cracked surface.

"No!" Averie screamed, lunging for the man. She tore at the cracked earth, her flesh tearing from her fingers as she screamed out in pain.

Denial

* * *

Averie jolted upright, awake, with a sweat-covered brow and panic thundering in her chest. Gasping for breath, she searched her shaking hands for any evidence of her endured pain. She frantically looked around, but instead of the horror-scape she was just in, she was laying safe in her plain, cream-colored bedroom. "It was just a dream," she breathed in relief. "Just a dream."

She fell back against her bed, her sweat-soaked head falling with a soft *thud* on her pillow.

This time, he was so close; he had felt so *real*.

Her door swung open and a half-asleep, her mother, Karen, burst into the room, her head on a frantic swivel. Averie watched in amusement as she fought back her sleep tangled, slightly gray hair. Karen fumbled along the wall before finally finding the light switch. The sudden burst of light forced a groan from Averie as she blinked the white spots from her vision. She pulled her old cream-colored blanket over her head in an effort to fight off the invading brightness and growing spots.

"Averie, are you okay? I thought I heard a scream," she asked, striding toward her bed, while trying desperately to tie the light pink robe into a bow at her waist. She sat beside Averie and pulled the covers off Averie's head. Karen placed a hand against Averie's forehead for a moment before rubbing the backs of her hands down her cheeks. Karen looked down with kind, yet worry-filled, brown eyes.

Taking a deep breath, Averie forced a reassuring smile. "Yeah, Mom, I'm sorry. I didn't mean to wake you. It was just a bad dream."

"Are you sure you're alright?" her mother repeated, taking Averie's hand into her own. "You don't seem to have a fever, but you're drenched, and this room is freezing!"

Nodding, Averie held her smile. "Just a dream. I shouldn't have watched a scary movie before bed."

Karen frowned at the lie; she knew they had watched a comedy together before Averie had fallen asleep, but knew there was no point in discussing it right now. She glanced at the clock: 4:13. "It's still early. You should try to get some more sleep before everyone shows up later."

Averie knew full well she wasn't getting anymore sleep tonight but instead of saying such things, she simply smiled and nodded her head at her mother in agreement. Satisfied, Karen stood and closed the open window before hesitating at the door. She turned and smiled. "Happy birthday, Averie." She paused for an extended moment and, when met with nothing but silence, closed the door.

Settling herself back into the bed, Averie listened to the retreating footsteps end with a distinct clicking of a door. She sighed deeply, staring up at the ceiling, her mind racing with images of those piercing teal eyes. How was it she had never seen him before, but she had also seen him so often? How could a dream feel so real? Her body still hummed with the chill of pure terror. She could still feel the pain of her fingers digging into the dry earth, still feel herself falling.

Averie recalled reading a story about dreams and how everything in a dream represented something the dreamer was going through. But what did this all mean? Averie tossed her arm over her face in dismay. Maybe it was showing just how much she dreaded her birthday. After all, dark omens had always marked her birthday. None of them ever had a purpose, but something bad always happened. *But what about those eyes?*

Averie took a deep breath, peaked from beneath her arm and groaned. 4:43. She kicked her kicked against the mattress in annoyance. *There's no point lying in bed and dwelling on dreams*, she thought as she threw the blanket aside and heaved herself out of bed. She had a long day ahead, and though it was absurdly early, she may as well get ready and face it.

Hoping to dispel the lingering effects of the terrible dream, Averie drew out her shower, her face lifted to the hot water until the chill of fear slipped from her body and disappeared down the swirling drain. She stepped from the shower with a renewed feeling tingling in her veins. *It's going to be a good day.* She promised herself as she readied herself to make sure that it was just that. A good day.

"Happy birthday, Fox!" bellowed a big, burly man, ambushing Averie the moment she entered the small kitchen.

Averie smiled a genuine wide smile and shoved him away to adjust her carefully braided hair. "Thanks, Thane.

You got any of that wonderful, lifesaving coffee left for me?"

Thane Matthias was large for his nineteen years. With a trim waist, broad shoulders, light brown hair and striking crystal blue eyes, he was nearly heart stopping. For anyone that wasn't his sister and had to deal with his annoying, overbearing brother attitude, crass humor, and pranks.

Thane smiled down at her with a huge smile that covered all the parts of his face that weren't concealed by his neatly trimmed beard. He grabbed her normal large black and gold striped mug and filled it, added a tad bit of cream and sugar, and slid it down the long counter to her. She barely had time to grab the mug before a plate of giant pancakes, smothered in syrup and whipped cream, came sliding down the counter behind it. Averie held the mug to her lips for a brief moment before drawing that first magical sip. She took a moment of contemplation, savoring the simple brilliance of her favorite hot beverage, and let out a sigh. Regarding Thane in appreciation, she smiled and danced a little jig of happiness. Feeling she had shown enough appreciation for the drink, she sat down on the bar stool before her, then took a giant bite of blueberry pancake.

She groaned. "You are a god among men," she praised, closing her eyes and relishing the delicious flavor as it melted in her mouth.

Thane crossed his thick arms and leaned against the counter, arching a brow at her. "I don't know about that, but I'll take the compliment," he said, grabbing a fork and taking a bite for himself off her plate. Averie glared at him and, with exaggerated force, stabbed her fork into the pancake for a giant bite.

"So where are Lucas and Sera?" Averie asked as she chewed on her over-sized bite.

"It's a little early for them, don't you think?" He asked with an arched brow.

Averie shrugged. "Maybe for Lucas, definitely not for Sera."

Thane looked down at her diminishing plate and snagged another piece. "Can I ask you something?"

"Sure."

Thane lifted his eyes to hers and, for an uncomfortable moment, his big, warm blue eyes darkened, before clearing once more. "Is it really over this time? Or are we continuing this cycle?"

She had expected this. Thane wasn't happy to find out she was dating Lucas in the first place, add in a vicious cycle of anger and betrayal, lies and screaming throughout the house, in had to stop. "It's really over. It has to be. I'm eighteen now, Thane. I can't do this anymore. I have goals and a life to live that doesn't involve eternal relationship roller coasters. This year will be different; you just watch." Averie lowered her gaze to her plate and stabbed her fork into the dwindling stack.

Thane nodded, dropped his fork to the plate, and returned to the stove, removing the last few pancakes. "Is it because of your dream man?" he asked, his back turned, holding syrup high above his plate.

Averie slowly lowered her fork to her plate, then took a long sip from her cup. "He told you?" she finally asked.

Thane shrugged, glancing over his shoulder. "Well, between the nightmares, sleep talking, and Lucas's unbearable jealousy and babbling during workouts, I kind of figured it out."

Averie rolled her eyes, thinking of Lucas.

"So," Thane sighed, bringing his plate to the counter. "Who is he?"

Averie's thoughts jumbled and scrambled as she tried to formulate an acceptable answer. She bit her lip for a moment, then took the last sip from her mug. Readjusting her braid, she picked up her plate and mug and deposited them in the sink. Anything to buy time. "I don't know," she whispered.

Thane coughed behind her. Whether he choked on her words, the pancakes, or his own coffee, she wasn't sure. "Excuse me?" Thane asked, shock lacing his voice.

Averie flinched at his tone, her stomach clenching as she turned to face him.

"What do you *mean*, you don't know?" Thane demanded. His fork clamored against the plate as he stood. "Are you seriously telling me that Lucas has been causing hell, literal *hell*, over an imaginary man?"

Averie frowned. "What do you mean he's 'causing hell'?"

Thane stopped, mouth gaping as he tried to find the words. Finally, he reached down, grabbed the fork, and

Denial

shoved an excessive amount of pancake into it while shaking his head and shrugging. "Mumm sunm nom."

"Mmm, did anyone ever tell you what a horrible liar you are?"

Laying the fork down once more, Thane clasped his hands together and swallowed the food in his mouth. "Look, Lucas is my friend, but you are my best friend—my *sister*, and as your *brother*, I am telling you that when it comes to you two, no one wins."

"I know, and I'm sorry. Really, I am, it's just—"

"Happy birthday, darling!" Karen announced, throwing the front door wide and strolling in with two armfuls of groceries. She gave both Averie and Thane a kiss on the cheek before dramatically dropping the grocery bags to the floor. Releasing a heavy sigh, she turned with forlorn eyes to face them. "Is there no one willing to help this poor old lady get the rest of the groceries?" she asked sweetly.

Thane bowed. "My apologies, Queen Karen," Karen swatted playfully at his arm. Thane dodged and let out a boisterous laugh, and with exaggerated movements ran out to the door.

"You're not old, Mom." Averie grinned, picking up the bags and placing them on the counter. She hovered over a particular sparkling bag "Anything for me?" she asked, her finger gripping the side to get a glimpse of inside.

"Shoo, get out of there! Don't be nosey." Karen nudged Averie away as she lifted the bag onto the counter. "Don't you have something to do?"

"Nope," Averie smiled and jumped to sit on the counter. "Classes are out for the day."

"Oh, really?" Karen asked suspiciously.

"Special delivery," Thane muttered, his arms full of the remaining bags.

"You know you can take more than one trip, young man," Karen scolded, taking several from him.

Thane and Averie shared a collective eye roll.

"Hello, lovelies," Sera announced, her arms spread wide. Her face perfectly porcelain and rich blue eyes gleaming with delight. Her classically blonde hair and matching attitude fulfilled every conceivable movie stereotype. She was perfectly bubbly, flirtatious, and spoiled rotten. But even so, she and Averie had been best friends since they were seven, complete opposites, and yet somehow, they made it work.

Averie flinched at the terrible fake English accent, that for some unknown reason to everyone but her, Sera was putting on. Sera pulled Averie in tightly and kissed each of her cheeks before holding her at arms length. "Watching English TV again, Sera?" Averie grinned.

"Oh, pish posh," she giggled. "Happy birthday, Avi." Sera beamed and held out an outrageously pink bag. Averie smiled back and, careful of the glitter, took the bag.

"Thanks Sera."

Sera waved away her thanks and began tapping her fingers together as Averie opened it. Putting aside the excessive amount of pink tissue paper, Averie withdrew a small white box.

Denial

Averie gave Sera a bemused half smile. "What is it?"

"Open it, silly," Sera said, rolling her bright blue eyes in feigned annoyance.

Delicately, Averie pulled the box open and gasped. Nestled on a small black pillow was a crystallized silver omega encased in a golden inlay, with an onyx above and a diamond below. The intricacy and delicate etching of it was breathtaking. "Oh, my god, Sera, this is beautiful," she gushed, hugging her friend tightly. "Thank you."

"Yay! I am so glad you like it. I have one just like it!" Sera beamed, pulling the same charm from beneath her plunged neckline. "Friends forever, love. Friends forever."

"Alright, girls, why don't you go out and find something to wear tonight?" Karen asked, holding a bright blue card aloft.

Averie and Sera shared a smile, then turned toward Karen. "Well, if you insist," they chimed in harmony. Averie grabbed the card and kissed her mother's cheek. "We will be out of your hair in no time!"

Chapter Two

An agonized silence blanketed the night. They had been forced to retreat after creating a desperate opening, their numbers dramatically lowered, the wounded still being brought back to the hideout. Soft, anguish filled moans echoed in the wind, mingling with the hushed and huddled discussions of their losses. For now, the physical battle was over.

Radnar Lockin laid his head against the smooth, cool stone wall. *I'm getting too damn old for this.* Running into battle time after time like a madman was a quick way to end one's life, or at least it was supposed to be. He ran his fingers over various scars covering his exposed flesh, each one a solemn reminder of the different battles he had survived.

He took a deep breath and adjusted himself more fully against the stone. The movement released more of the warm life blood to stream heavily down to his fingertips. This seemed like the perfect moment to consider the road that had led him to this moment. His mind wandered in and out, head swimming from lack of blood, while a small girl worked tirelessly to remove his chain mail and suture the wound. Radnar, without thought, shifted himself, causing the girl to throw him a glare that could cut him like the deep wound running down his forearm. He locked eyes briefly with her, seeing the blend of contempt and reverence reflected in her bright eyes. "Bring me Silas," he ordered flatly.

Confusion flashed across the girl's petite face. "Radnar, I must staunch the bleeding, otherwise—"

Radnar shooed her hands away, reached into his breastplate, and removed a flask. He looked at the small container of joy and at his own crimson blood sliding down the side before he took a long draw from the flask and sighed with exaggerated contentment. "Much better. Now, do as I say and bring me Silas."

The girl stood with a flourish, disgust and frustration etched on her face. "If you die, it's your own bloody fault, you old goat!"

Chuckling to himself, Radnar took another swig, the slight metallic taste of blood mixing with the burn of the contents of the flask. He scanned the room, acknowledging the familiar panoramic of his surroundings. Not even time could change the portrait of war. The young soldiers carried in the last of the wounded through the small cave entryway. Though their hearts were heavy with loss, their spirits *knew* they would avenge the fallen.

Radnar chuckled again. That was a young man's game. The older soldiers had long since had that kind of spirit ground out of them; instead, they sat around the flickering fire, exchanging hearth tales of the vanquished and their day's heroic deeds. Radnar couldn't help but let his mind take him back to one of his first battles. Even then, when he should have been one of the young and naïve, he had sat by the fire and regaled as though he had been through it a thousand times before. He closed his eyes and smiled. Yes, this was the perfect path for a man like him.

A rich black smoke rose, filling the cave, but this wasn't the standard, wispy and thin smoke that dissipated after a moment, forgotten. This smoke was thick and black, twisting and twirling like dense morning fog captured by the wind. This smoke had a meaning, had a purpose, and it would not give up until it was complete. This smoke released the fallen from their mortal coils and guided them to the heavens.

Radnar opened his eyes when the familiar scent reached his nose and solemnly watched the scene. Loved ones stood at the fire's edge, tears streaming as they readied their fallen kin. How many times had he stood there, readying his friends and loved ones for the same ceremony? He shook his head. Too many to count and, at this point, too many to remember. For longer than he would admit, even to himself, he had been alone, and he preferred to keep it that way.

Denial

The soft rhythm of song rose into the air. The ceremony had begun. As the song rang out, those outside, and those gathered at the cave entrance joined in, their voices combining, drowning out the soft cries of agony from the wounded. The ancient words surrounded them, wrapping around the wounded and grieving like a temporary salve to their torment.

Radnar laid his head back against the stone and closed his eyes, allowing the words to transport him back to a happier, more peaceful time. The smell of wildflowers reached his nose, bringing a smile to his face. He sat, enthralled by the power of the ancient words as they echoed throughout the cave. No matter how many times he had heard them before, as they were always sung after the battle, they never failed to lift the spirits of the lost ones to the sky and bring peace to those left behind. The brief salvation those ancient words gave almost made the blood and death worth it, almost.

A kick against his foot pulled him from his own thoughts as pain vibrated through his aching body. "Damn you!" he roared, forcing his eyes open.

"Still alive, old man?"

Radnar glared up at the grinning man. He was young, yet not so young he didn't wear the shadow of a growing beard. His eyes were blazing with purpose and his skin smooth with youth. Sweat wet his black hair, making it seem somehow darker. He stood over Radnar, his arms crossed over his broad chest, and for a brief moment, Radnar wondered if he had the energy to knock the boy on his ass just for old times' sake. Radnar, the majority of his body in a constant ache, decided he would save that idea for another day.

"Silas, I should have known. Only you would kick a defenseless old man while he is down."

Silas tipped his head back and laughed. "No soul alive, except me, would dare call you defenseless or old."

"I am defenseless at this moment, no thanks to you." Radnar watched Silas's features flinch with guilt. *Good,* he thought. *He feels his mistakes.*

"Agnes said you refused to let her heal you," Silas said.

Radnar grimaced, then grinned. "I prefer my own method of healing, boy," he said, lifting his flask. "Perhaps, when you reach my age, you will understand that this works much better for healing the body and spirit than medicine."

Silas crouched low, his frown deepening as he brought himself to eye level with the older man, the scent of smoke heavy in the air. "You must let Agnes help you before you have no choice but to leave this world." Silas turned and motioned the woman forward. Radnar made mocking faces at his back, stopping only for a moment to take another quick nip from his flask before returning to his juvenile display. Silas, seeing the corner of Agnes's mouth start to twitch, snapped back to look at Radnar, who looked up innocently and held the flask out.

"Itching for a taste, boy?"

Silas shook his head, and Radnar shrugged, bringing the metal to his lips.

Denial

Agnes knelt beside the pacified Radnar and started pulling at the bent buckles of his armor. "Is this what you called me for?" Silas asked, his frustration audible in his tone.

"Of course not," Radnar said, shaking his head in disagreement as he watched the woman finally defeat the bent buckle, allowing her to peel the armor from his body. With his breastplate pulled back and his shirt mostly cut away, the gash covering his chest came into full view. The thick, jagged wound forked through his blood smeared chest. "Well, isn't that something? Gonna leave a ghastly scar on my otherwise perfect form," Radnar said in fake sorrow, for his chest was already marbled with scars of the past. The rest of his visible chest, that wasn't covered in scars or blood, had deep hues of black and blue bruises. "Give me just a few minutes to let this lass do her thing, then we can chat," he said, grunting as Agnes poked at his seeping wound.

Agnes looked up at Radnar's expectant face and narrowed her eyes. "If you need me to leave, so you can share your bloody man's secrets, then don't be a coward. Just say so!" she snapped, releasing the chest plate to slap against Radnar's already bruised chest.

"Dammit, woman!" Radnar roared. "Can't you treat a dying man with better care?"

Agnes stood up, her entire body tensed with rage, and shoved a small vial into Silas's hands. "You deal with him," she snapped, turning on her heel and storming away.

Silas looked to Radnar, who was grinning like a schoolboy after the frustrated woman. He knelt beside his old friend, knowing the old man pretended as though his life wasn't draining by the moment, even though it was. Silas gently reached up and pulled the breastplate back, re-exposing the wound to the world.

He sucked in through his teeth at the gnarly sight.

"I will not be as delicate as Agnes would have been," Silas stated matter-of-factly.

Lifting the flask once more, Radnar shrugged. "Get on with it then. Can't you see I am dying here?"

Silas leaned closer, pulling the blood-soaked fabric from Radnar's body. He pinched the sides of slashed skin together with his fingertips, with less tenderness than he typically would have used, causing Radnar to grimace and pull away.

"By the Stars, boy! Have you such little care in your brutish hands that you harm a poor, dying old man?"

Silas rolled his eyes and took the vial top between his teeth. With his one free hand, he jerked the bottle loose and removed the lid while the other hand kept Radnar's raw skin pinched together. "What is it you want from me that requires such secrecy that you would so harshly dismiss Agnes? It will take more than flowers to bring her back this time."

Radnar stayed silent, teeth gritted, as the first drops of the green liquid hissed against his pinched flesh. "I've located the Key, the Lost One, and you must go retrieve it."

Denial

Silas's hand shuddered at his words, causing a drop to miss the wound entirely and hissing against clean skin.

"Easy, boy, before you cause more damage than there already is!"

Silas mumbled a half-hearted apology under his breath and moved his fingers slowly down the wound, releasing small droplets as he went. "We don't have time to go chasing fairy tales, Radnar. If you haven't noticed, we are at *war*."

"We have no other choice. If you haven't noticed, we are losing. You must go now. Tonight. Find her before they do," Radnar spoke with the tone that said this was not a request, but an order.

Radnar watched Silas's brow furrow at his words. "Her?" Silas laughed. "You want me to leave now, when I am needed most, to not only search for a person who no one can confirm even exists to begin with, but now this person also happens to be a girl?"

"We don't have time for this!" Radnar hissed through clenched teeth as more of the liquid bubbled and smoked as it penetrated and sewed the deeper parts of the gash. "The stories are true, and she is who we need. Whether or not you are happy it is a girl is something for you to deal with on your own time. Right now, your people need you to do this."

"We still have other options. We haven't reached desperation yet," Silas countered, the words a brittle shield against the mounting pressure.

Radnar clenched his jaw harder as the man poured the last of the vile green liquid, fighting back a scream as it filled the deepest depths of the wound. With a puff of green smoke, a rich and dark red flame spread across Radnar's chest, creating the last seal and stopping the bleeding, leaving behind a fresh and slightly sizzling scar.

"There is no time to argue! You failed to listen to me once and have suffered a great loss because of it. Now, *now* you will listen," Radnar's voice dripped with the heat of leadership.

Silas looked up briefly from his crouched position by his elder's side. It had been a long time since Radnar had given him an order. The man flitted from one battle to the next as though he were begging for the Reaper himself to claim his soul. "How are we even supposed to find this, maybe real, girl?" Silas asked, unrolling a large bandage and crudely wrapping it around the man's side.

"Silas, listen to me, boy," Radnar urged, gently pulling himself up. While his wound was sealed, the muscle and tissue underneath took at least half a day to mend completely. He inhaled a deep, pain filled breath, pulled a small golden dagger hidden within his belt and gently placed it on his lap. "Come closer, I'm growing tired and must get this out before the medicine puts me to sleep." Silas shifted closer to the old man's scarred and weathered face. Radnar motioned to the far wall. "Gather the men and return them to the stronghold. Once you have secured them, return alone. Behind that gray rock, you will find a

Denial

small crack, slide this dagger into it without nicking the wall."

"I don't understand what this means, Radnar. How does stabbing a wall solve anything?" Silas confessed.

The older man waved a dismissive hand, his eyes fluttering with exhaustion. "No, boy, the wall will separate just enough for a hand to reach in. You must retrieve the package the wall hides. It will show you the way."

"Package? Show me the way to what?" Silas questioned. Radnar's eyes fluttered shut, leaving Silas without a reply. Silas grabbed him by the shoulders and shook him. "What package? Where am I going, old man?"

Radnar tried to force his eyes open but his eyelids were too heavy and they closed once more. He blindly pulled the flask to his lips and swallowed deeply.

Silas shook the man, rougher this time. "Dammit, old man! Stop wasting energy on the damn flask and answer my questions!"

"It is a map to her location," he answered in a tired whisper. "Go and bring her back before he finds us. We don't have the manpower nor the drive to finish this fight alone. We need hope, boy, and it's up to you to bring it to us."

Silas squared his jaw. "We don't need to chase stories; I can do this. The men look to me to guide them. We can take the castle!"

Radnar shook his head, a humorless chuckle tumbling free. "We can't and you know it. We have no other choice."

Two young soldiers walked up and nodded at Radnar, though he couldn't see them through his closed eyes. "Sir, we are here to help you back," the blond one announced.

Radnar's lips curved into a slight grin. "Well, soldier, earn your salt and help me up. Oh, and don't forget the flask, boy! It's essential to my healing!"

Silas rose to his feet and watched the two young men, one under each of Radnar's shoulders, help the old man deeper into the mountain, their conversation revolving through his mind. Slowly, a dirt covered soldier approached Silas. "How many?" Silas asked, not looking away as the trio disappeared into darkness.

The other man looked sheepishly at his feet. "Too many."

Silas nodded stiffly. "Find Callen and bring him to me. Tell him it's urgent."

"Urgent, sir?"

"We have plans to make."

Chapter Three

"Let's go, woman! We have people waiting for us," Sera cheered, carefully reapplying the bright pink lipstick and smacking them together and giving herself a flirty smile in the mirror.

"Are you sure it's okay we're here? I really don't want to get into trouble, Sera," Averie called through the bathroom stall.

Sera rolled her eyes. "It's fine! It's your birthday, and you deserve something special."

"I know, and it's not that I don't appreciate you getting us in. It's just we told my mom that we were having a party at your house. What if she stops by and notices we aren't there?" Averie asked, nibbling her lip in worry as she secured the belt around her waist.

"Oh, Avi, poor sweet, naïve Avi. Everything will be fine. Just relax and enjoy your birthday," Sera reassured.

Averie sighed. There was no defeating Sera when she set her mind to something. "Alright, alright," she conceded and with one last breath to gather her courage, stepped from the stall. "What do you think?" she asked, spreading her arms wide.

Sera tilted her head, made the turn motion with her fingers and finally nodded. "It'll do."

Averie's shoulders dropped as she looked down at her outfit. A slinky black dress that barely grazed her knees, tied with a ruby red belt around her waist and perfected with a pair of glossy black heels that were higher than her comfort level. "It'll do? That's it? That's all you have to say? We spent three hours looking for this stupid dress, Sera, and two hours ago, you said it was perfect."

Sera laughed and stepped forward to brush the fallen strands from Averie's eyes. "You look perfect, I promise. I wouldn't lie to you about this. I mean, I can't be seen with someone who doesn't look at least as amazing as I do, now can I?"

Averie gave a half-hearted grin and looked at herself in the mirror, adjusting the black shimmering top. "Alright, let's do the damn thing."

Sera groaned and dramatically threw her head back. "Can you *please* be a bit more enthusiastic about this?"

Averie's lips twisted in contemplation before she threw her hands into the air and cheered, with exaggerated enthusiasm, "Let's go party our asses off!"

Denial

Sera clapped her hands together excitedly, choosing to ignore the blatant sarcasm in her friend's voice. "Now that's better!"

They left the bathroom laughing, their arms locked together, and entered the strobe lit darkness of the club. The light, lively music beat and atmosphere was intoxicating. Before she could fully register the swirling chaos around her, Averie found herself strangely captivated, a smile tugging at her lips as the unexpected joy blossomed within her. They danced through the thick crowd. Averie lost herself in the moment as the music wove itself through to her core, temporarily washing away her haunted dreams. Like one covers their eyes from the bright light with sunglasses, a fix that only lasts as long as the glasses stay on and the music keeps playing.

The crowd closed in around them as group dancing began to break out and the crowd morphed into a single mass. Averie let herself get taken away with the beat as she moved across the floor, circled by lighthearted people looking to enjoy each other, even for just the time of a song.

She turned to say something to Sera, only to find her friend was not beside her anymore. Averie scanned the crowd, finally finding her friend in an angry discussion with a man she had never seen before. Worried, she started toward Sera when an arm looped around her waist and she was pulled into the dancing body of a handsome, dark-haired, coal-eyed man. Averie smiled politely and glanced over her shoulder to where Sera had stood to find it consumed with other dancers. Shrugging, she let the music take hold once more.

When the music finally slowed and the lights stopped their bright pulsating, dimming into a light glow, Averie excused herself from the dark-haired man and went in search of Sera. She scanned the boisterous, growing crowd, the music a pulsing thrum in her ears, finally spotting Sera finishing a dance with a tall, powerfully built man. Reaching her eyes, Averie made the drink motion to Sera, who smiled and nodded in return. Sera leaned forward and said something to the large man, who frowned slightly before nearly running away.

"I thought I'd lost you!" Sera teased, as she reached Averie's side.

Averie laughed. "Oh, please, you were dancing between those guys quicker than anyone could catch you!"

Sera laughed and curtsied sarcastically. "Thank you. I do love being fought over."

Hands clasped, Sera danced Averie through the crowd, trying to reach the crowded bar. Her words brought the image of an angry Sera to Averie's mind. "Speaking of which, who was that man you were arguing with before?" Averie asked, squeezing around couples who were grinding more than they were dancing.

Sera's head snapped to Averie before turning back with a plastic fake smile. "Just some random, trying to get a little more than a dance," Sera explained.

Averie frowned. She had known Sera almost her whole life; she'd never seen her get this angry over a simple reason before, but more than that, Sera had never lied to her face. "Are you sure? Do you want me to find security and get him out of here?" Averie asked.

Sera stopped in the crowd and waved a dismissive hand. "Don't worry, Birthday Girl. I can handle myself. This night is all about you." Before Averie could say anything else, Sera began pulling her across the room once more. The music grew to a crescendo, sending the dancers into frantic movements that knocked Averie and Sera's hand apart. The bodies gyrated and blocked her view. Averie opened her mouth to call out when a thick, warm arm wound itself around Averie's waist and spun her about. Panic gripped her, her heart pounding deep within her chest, threatening to lurch from her throat when a rough, familiar voice reached her ears.

"Happy birthday, Evie!" a voice boomed in her ear.

"Jesus, Thane! I thought you were some creep trying to snatch me away!" she snapped, smacking at his chest in mock disgust. Thane smiled down at her, flashing a set of perfect white teeth. He wore a pair of dark blue jeans and black boots, paired with a white tee shirt and fitted black vest. His face was a mask of amusement at her attempt to harm him.

His booming laugh echoed along with the music. "Silly girl," Thane laughed, wagging his finger and tapping her nose. "No one would want to take a girl like you away into the night."

"Some would beg to differ on that one," a rich, velvet voice objected.

Averie looked up and her smile instantly faded, but ever quick to recover, she plastered a sickly sweet and fake smile to her features and looked to the tall thinly built, but overly-muscled blond-haired, blue-eyed, sun-kissed man that stood beside her. He truly was a walking cliché. Perfect smile and artistic features that made anyone stop and stare. This was Lucas Saint, all American golden boy throughout high school, as a rising baseball star. With several colleges trying to woo him to join their teams, his ego had grown to astronomical proportions. Smart, athletic, completely full of himself and Averie's freshly ex of a boyfriend.

"Lucas! I am so happy that you could make it," Averie forced herself to say, stepping in for a quick hug.

Lucas's arms were firm behind her, locking her into place. His smell was the same intoxicating thick cologne he always wore, though his grip held just a little too low and a little too long for an ex-boyfriend. Stepping away, he caught her hands in his own and brought them to his lips. "What kind of boyfriend misses his own girlfriend's birthday?" he asked sweetly.

Averie released a heavy sigh and caught Thane's darkened expression as he lifted a beer bottle to his lips and took a long and deliberate draw. After a momentary pause, she withdrew her hands from Lucas's and looked into his sea-blue eyes, suddenly struck by the realization of how different he was from the man haunting her dreams. "Lucas, we—"

"There you are, woman!" Sera's voice tore through the sea of noise, immediately derailing Averie's sentence.

Denial

Averie stopped and searched the crowd of poorly dressed gyrating crowds to find the lively, brightly dressed Sera coming toward them with a pair of women in tow. Both were bottle-blondes with thick, dark, glitter eye makeup and neon lipstick on their plump lips. Their bodies, adorned with wide, stark white ribbons twisted artfully to obscure key areas, vanished beneath the elegant lines of their strappy heels. The scent of expensive perfume lingering in the air. Each woman wore the identical pretty and practiced smile while carrying a silver tray with six shots on each.

Sera beamed as she joined them. "I brought shots!" she said, throwing her hands into the air victoriously. Her eyes took on a mischievous glint. "Who's ready to play a game?"

The rest of the group exchanged brief, worried looks.

Chapter Four

Silas stood at the cave's edge, captivated by the black flames as they rose to the sky, symbolizing the release of souls for the ones they've lost. It was his fault; their blood dripped fresh and burning from his hands. It was he who had been the foolish one that believed he could win against the Deceiver. It was he who had stood before them all just yesterday, and lure the fear from their eyes with promises of victory, leaving them fresh and begging for excitement and glory that the battle would bring.

None of the legends and heroic tales that were told to children ever mentioned the loss, the gore, the blood that battles brought. The legends only spoke of glory and honor. Never showing that those who survive to see that glory and honor are the few who actually survive. No one told these young, eager children that it was a rare thing to make it through these vicious and unforgiving battles alive, let alone unscathed. Yet, knowing all of this, he had stood before them and promised to bring these men back to their families, the day and war having been won. But he had failed miserably to keep those promises because he wasn't strong enough.

Radnar had tried to explain; *Gods,* had he tried.

For days, Radnar had fought him, telling him he was not ready for this mission, for the consequences that came with leading such a reckless attack. But the lure of victory was intoxicating. It would have tasted so sweet, like the first crisp bite of an apple. But the loss ... There were no words to describe the bitter sensation, the pain, and the complete mental destruction that came with such a loss. Silas had not even contemplated the notion of losing.

Silas shook the thoughts away. It didn't matter if they had won. Either way, he was responsible for so much death, so much pain. No one won in a game of war. There was a price to pay, no matter the outcome.

Radnar's lectures circled his mind, laced with unforgiving regret. His warnings about not being ready to lead the attack, that he needed to plan more, strategize better, all rang in his ears. But Silas had been too stubborn and still reveling in his previous glory to hear it. Now his men were gone and their families were left to pay the ultimate price.

One by one, he watched the loved ones of the fallen pay their respects. They dropped flowers, goods, and personal memorabilia into the flames depths, drying their tears in its heat and whispering their goodbyes into the smoke. To die in battle was a great honor, but that honor would not fill the empty seat at the dinner table. No, it would now sit forever empty. The spectrum of emotions on each face was complex and yet so clear. The tears of happy memories, the silent stare of sorrow, the smiles of stories exaggerated for laughs and honors. Through it all, Silas stood resolute and strong, waiting for the moment when they would finally turn against him.

"I heard you called for me," beckoned a baritone voice.

Silas turned toward the familiar sound of his friend's voice. They had matching black hair, both still damp and caked with mud and blood from their battle, and were matched in height, but that was where the similarities stopped. Silas was slighter in build and less broad than the mountain that was Callen. Where his eyes were a stunning teal, Callen's were a frightening silver that rivaled the full moon. Silas eyed the fresh cut Callen bore across one cheek. Callen's steel eyes never faltered as he approached.

"At dawn, I leave to find the Key. The Lost One," Silas said, returning his attention to the dwindling flames. "I need you to look after the group."

Callen arched a brow. "The Lost One? And just how do you plan on doing that?"

"Radnar—"

"Radnar? Have you lost your senses?" Callen interrupted. "That old man has been consumed with the Lost One for years. I would not be surprised if it was him that had started the rumors himself. Countless people have searched and found nothing. The Lost One is just that, lost. Just like the old king and queen. The Deceiver destroyed the entire family. There is nothing left to find. The Lost One being the Key to end this war is a story spun by those of the old world to keep hope."

Silas unsheathed the small dagger from his belt and handed it to his friend.

"Where did you get this?" Callen asked, running his finger over the golden crest. "This has the Royal insignia."

"Radnar. He gave it to me. He said the old king had entrusted it to him to use to find the Lost One when the time was right."

"Entrusted? It is an old, bloody dagger, Silas." Callen ran his finger along the tip. "And a dull one at that."

Silas snatched the dagger from Callen's large hand and re-sheathed it at his side. "The dagger doesn't matter, and this isn't up for debate. I need you to stay here and keep an eye on everyone. Can I trust you?"

Callen looked over at the gathering and nodded. "How long before you return?"

Silas took a deep breath. "A week, maybe two."

Callen made a clicking sound through his teeth. "We may only have a month before the retaliation. We can not stay in one place for too long." He looked from the group to his friend. "We leave from here in a week. We can not let the Deceiver to find us."

Silas locked gazes with his friend. "I know what you must do, and I know what that means. But I also know what I must do." He patted Callen on the shoulder, gave him a final smile, before walking into the cave. "We leave at dawn."

* * *

"Is everything okay?"

Averie looked up to find Sera staring, a worried expression etching her porcelain features. Averie forced a smile. "Yeah, of course. Everything's great. Thank you so much for this, Sera," she said, motioning around them. She hugged Sera tightly and, in one quick movement, grabbed the random drink from in front of her and downed it in one gulp. Sera's eyes widened in surprise.

"Is it Lucas? I can tell him to leave if you want," Sera asked, glancing at the collection of empty glasses.

Averie shrugged. "No, it's fine. Just a little weird, for one of us at least." She motioned for another glass that hadn't been emptied.

Sera shooed the man sitting beside her at the bar and moved to the stool closer to Averie. "Alright, Avi, talk to me. What is going on with you? You and Lucas are perfect together. What happened?"

Averie bit at her lip, twirling the straw between her fingers as she collected her thoughts and debated the words before finally caving to the foot-tapping, eyebrow-arching, bubble-blonde perching beside her. "Have you ever had a dream just stick with you? A dream that haunted your every thought?" Averie asked finally.

Denial

For a long while, Sera watched her friend before shaking her head. "No, I can't say that I have. Is that what's bothering you, Avi? A dream?"

Averie shrugged and smiled at the bartender, who began making another round. "It wasn't just any dream, Sera. It's more than that. It felt so real and *strange*, unlike anything I have ever experienced before. Even when I woke up, I could still feel it. I could still smell it. It was like it was still there with me for a moment before it faded."

Nodding thanks to the bartender, Averie picked up the two drinks and handed one to Sera. "It doesn't matter now, let's get through this party before the curfew crew breaks it up," she said, motioning to the older group of men wearing black shirts that had 'Security' printed across them in yellow letters, gathered at the entrance.

Sera slammed the shot back, the liquid burning down her throat to warm her belly, before placing the empty glass on the bar and looking at Averie. "What exactly is this dream you keep having?"

Averie slowly sipped the shot down, enjoying the warm burn it made as it slipped from her throat to pool in her stomach. Tossing back the remnants, she carefully wiped the corner of her mouth before looking at her friend. Sera's eyes held a cautious glow, and Averie suddenly felt self-conscious of sharing her dream, almost as if something deep inside was warning her against saying anything. Waving her hand, Averie changed the subject. "Tomorrow. Tonight is for celebrating another year around the sun!" She motioned for another round.

"Hey now, I hope you have some for us, too, or are you just taking it all for yourselves?" Lucas smiled and leaned against the bar.

"Easy, Fox. I don't want to explain this whole thing to Karen tomorrow," Thane warned.

Sera tore her gaze from Averie to smile at Lucas and Thane. "Don't worry, boys, you are just in time for another round of my world-famous drinking games!" Turning, she waved the bartender over. "We are gonna need a bottle of your finest tequila, a couple of your limes, and fresh shot glasses." Turning back, she motioned to the corner table that had miraculously emptied. "Shall we?"

The trio eyed each other worriedly before silently before following Sera and settling into the booth as another scantily dressed waitress dropped off a tray with a large, clear bottle and several shot glasses. She leaned in low, showing off parts of her that her small outfit left little to the imagination, raising the brows of the young men with a suggestive smile.

Lucas returned a wide smile, while Thane looked skyward.

Averie gave a disgusted sigh.

Sera made a shooing motion towards the woman. "That will be all, dear, be gone now," Sera said forcefully, taking a seat opposite the group. "Alright, now we can get this thing started!" Sera cheered as she grabbed several of the shot glasses and began generously filling them.

Denial

"Sera, I'm not sure this is such a good idea," Averie admitted, her head already buzzing from the drinks she consumed.

Grinning tightly, Sera lifted her gaze to Averie, then to Thane, ending with Lucas. The music pulsated, each beat shaking the liquid in the glasses slightly while the lights flickered and flashed. "What do you boys think? Are you ready for a more cheerful and excited Averie?"

Thane shrugged, playfully rubbing his elbow against Averie's rib cage. "To each his own, I suppose. She seems plenty cheerful and exciting to me," he snickered.

Lucas lifted his glass. "To the rarity of a cheerful Avi!"

Sera beamed with her win. "To Avi," she chimed.

Thane lifted his own, watching Averie. "What do you say, Fox?"

With a deep sigh, and preemptively filling with regret, Averie lifted her glass. "Tomorrow is gonna suck more than … finals?"

The group exchanged a brief look, tapped their glasses off the table, then threw back the first of what would end up being too many shots.

Chapter Five

How the hell is this thing supposed to work? Silas was pissed, tired, and disgusted with the world he was being forced into. Pushing his way through yet another loud, drunk group of obnoxious young men that stumbled against him, Silas lifted the medallion and gave it a small shake. Nothing. The slow breaths he was forcing himself to take in an effort to remain calm were becoming less effective with each drunken collision.

Silas grit his teeth and continued to work his way through the convulsing bodies, narrowly sidestepping a lanky man who was emptying his stomach contents over the railing and into the street below. How this world was surviving, let alone supposedly thriving, was beyond his comprehension.

Shaking the small metal medallion in his hand again, he waited for the damn thing to light, vibrate, or anything to give him another clue as to where he should go next.

Denial

But no matter how much he shook it, it remained stubbornly silent. Silas refused to believe the savior of the Realm, the Key, the Lost One, would ever be in a place like this. As Silas continued his trek through the crowded space, he thought over the last eighteen hours since he had arrived in this dreaded land.

* * *

After the camp had settled down and everyone had drifted to sleep, Silas and Callen met with Radnar to form a plan. Callen would take his place leading the army, giving Silas one week to return before the army would move on to a new location. If Silas failed to come back by that time, once a week, Callen would send a message only Silas could understand, revealing an alternative meeting place.

Callen sighed. "This is a terrible idea, Silas. We do not have time to search for a legend."

"It is not just a legend, boy. I was there. I have seen the child with my own eyes," Radnar defended.

"Yes, in another time and place, but who has seen her since? Who is to say that Marcus's story is not true? He has killed women and children, his own family. What makes you think he would stop at the Princess? How do we even know the Princess is the Lost One? How do we know that Key is the Princess?" Callen demanded.

"We don't," Silas admitted. "But if any piece of what Radnar says is true, we have to try. If she is the Princess and the Lost One, I'll know when I find her. And I will bring her back, and she will help us fight against Marcus. You can't say it wouldn't help to have someone with the Key on our side."

"None of this makes sense and we are wasting our time, our lives, and resources. But since you have no interest in listening to me, fine. Let continue down this uncertain path," Callen said with a new level of annoyance in his voice.

Just before the sun was due to rise, Callen and Silas scaled down the side of the mountain and disappeared into the thick forest. Callen led the way while Silas had followed close behind, careful to keep from disturbing too many of the slumbering animals, lest they be working for Marcus.

It didn't take them long to reach one of the few remaining portals. Callen stopped a few feet away, pulling the overgrown vines and fallen limbs from the entrance, careful not to slip any of his fingers inside.

"Are you sure that you want to do this?" Callen asked for a last time.

Silas nodded. "Yes."

"You know that if the portal resists you, because you are not a Traveler, it could tear you to pieces."

"Yes, Callen, I am painfully aware of that," Silas responded, his eyes fixated on the portal before him.

"Can you imagine? Coming this far, getting this close and bam! Ripped to shreds. Do you think it waits until you are fully inside, or do you think it happens piece by piece?" Callen asked, his questions more curious than instigating. "This is not a standard portal after all. It was made specifically for Travelers, by Travelers," Callen rambled, lost in thought. "The Travelers are not known for willingly making them for casual passage."

Denial

"I don't know, Callen, and I really don't want to think about that right now!" Silas snapped.

"Right, right. Sorry. I was just thinking I would want it to happen quick once I was fully inside. Not knowing that part of me is being pulled apart, but—" Callen continued.

"Shut up, Callen!" yelled Silas, making a half-hearted swat at Callen.

Callen's mouth snapped shut. His eyes noticing the worried lines on Silas's face. "I am sure it will be fine. It is not really my problem either way. Now, repeat it once more," Callen ordered.

Silas released an anxious sigh and recited his task. "Once I enter the portal, I'll use the dagger to lead the way to the Realm where the Lost One resides, where Cleo and Armand should be waiting for me. After that, I use the medallion," Silas lifted the palm sized, golden disc etched with an intricate sun on one side and the face of a roaring lion on the other. "To hopefully lead me to the actual Lost One, if they even exist. The rest is easy enough, convince her that she is from a world that she has never heard of, then get her to come here and save the world. Easy." Silas smiled.

Callen rolled his eyes. "You should hope you are going to a Realm with magic to make your task easier."

"Right." Silas faced the portal and took a deep breath. "Fingers crossed."

"Silas," Callen said, his voice stone cold.

"Yes?"

"Do not trust them," Callen warned, his face an emotionless mask.

Confused at this last minute, seemingly dire warning, but trusting his friend's instincts, he nodded once and stepped forward.

Callen watched the outline of Silas get swallowed by a whirling blue-black darkness. A darkness so thick, it looked like thick liquid as it enveloped his form, before finally absorbing him completely. Callen sent a silent prayer of protection up as he carefully placed the vines and limbs back, making sure to fully hide the portal before starting back toward the cave.

Silas stepped forward through the continued black abyss. Every muscle in his body writhing in pain, as though they were being torn from the bone, just as Callen had predicted. His lungs, seeming to be filled with fire, burned in his chest. He grit his teeth against the pain and forced one foot before the other as he pushed through the molasses like air. Each step he took, harder than the last. Though deep down he knew it had only been a moment, it felt like hours. He was not sure his body would be able to hold up. Gathering the last of his strength, Silas threw himself forward in one final push.

His body burst through and collided with the other side with a breath stealing thud. His ears popped and static flooded his vision. Silas blinked against the dots bursting across his vision and rose unsteadily to his feet to look around. The ground, more solid than the dirt in his Realm, was covered in a strange, dark rock with an odd double yellow streak running straight down it. There were few trees, and even the ones that were there, he didn't recognize. They were not the tall and strong forest trees he knew so well, but looked like seedlings that had somehow grown out of the large, orange bowls that sat under them.

The worst part was the air that overwhelmed him. It was dense and filled with too many things to decipher. There was the slight scent of cooking food mingling with a sooty and dank fragrance that reminded him of the toxins that the disfigured and grotesque

Denial

Shadowed emitted. This was the smell that overpowered all else and made his stomach churn. Had the Shadowed made it here as well?

Movement caught Silas's attention and sank him into a fighting stance as he whirled to face a pair that stepped from the shadows. The man was tall and broad, much like Silas, wearing a plain white shirt and standing beside a tall and thin blonde-haired woman, her blue eyes contrasting with her short, pale, pink dress. The couple unwaveringly fixated their stare on him.

"Silas?" the woman asked, her voice almost musical.

Silas, his head and senses still reeling on overload from his journey through the portal, straightened his stance and forced a slight nod. The woman stepped forward, putting her hand gently on his shoulder. "I am Cleo, and this is my husband, Armand. We have been expecting you," she smiled.

"Where am I?" asked Silas, still trying to gain control of himself.

"Third Realm, we call it the Dream Realm," the man, Armand, answered.

"Main Street, to be exact," Cleo clarified.

"Main street?" Silas repeated, his lips moving more out of automation than thought.

"Come, we will explain everything. We get your clothes changed before someone sees you," Cleo motioned to a large, black metal and glass box that, for some reason, had what looked like small cart wheels on it.

Silas looked down at his attire and took in the notable differences. The couple's clothing was simple and light, and though it would give them the ability to run away easily, it would provide no help in a potential ambush. While Silas adorned his charmed chain shirt and thick wool pants with his trusted long swords strapped to his back, it was plain to see he did not belong in this Realm. His clothes shimmered in the moonlight, throwing small fractions of light, casting a soft glow around him. Though he understood he would stand out, Callen's warning echoed fresh in his mind. He gave the couple a long and purposeful stare before finally giving a confirmation nod and followed the couple. He had no choice but to follow, with his guard carefully in place.

* * *

Now, many hours later, here he was, carrying a pointless medallion and the dagger Radnar had given him, which gave him at least a shred of comfort, hidden safely away, waiting for something wonderful to happen. Silas was sincerely attempting to remain positive, but found it to be quite difficult the longer he was in this Realm. Much to Silas's surprise, the medallion had, for at least a moment, been useful when it led him to this noisy and crowded room before falling uselessly dormant once more.

He moved through the strange crowd, their bodies convulsing in unusual and disturbing ways. Though nothing was stranger than the noises coming from the giant boxes around the room. It sounded like music, if the music had been made by people who did not know what proper music was supposed to sound like. It was only because of the bodies that swayed and jerked along with it,

Denial

in what he could only assume was dancing, to this travesty blaring from the boxes that he concluded it must be their music. None of it made sense and only served to make him long for home even more.

A sudden and violent tremor from the medallion yanked him from his thoughts. Shocked, he held the medallion out in his hand. A bright white glow eliminated from the center, looking like a single bright star on a dark night. He scanned the crowd, twisting to look in all directions, but not a single soul there could possibly be the Lost One.

Silas held the medallion before him and wove through the collection of scantily clad young women, each of them flashing him a provocative smile as he passed. A pair of girls covered their mouths to hide their shy giggles when he threw them a quick half-hearted grin. A short, raven-haired girl wearing a tight blue dress tried to pull him into her, urging him to join her in the strange gyrating dance. He arched a brow at the display of her rolling body, then politely smiled at her before shaking his head and excusing himself. Frustration brew beneath his skin as he struggled to make his way through the never-ending crowd. *Damn it*, he didn't have time for this. He had to focus.

His hope of finding the Lost One was dwindling quickly when finally, the light in the medallion flashed, its bright light etching itself into his eyes. Silas blinked away the spots, a feat between the pulsing lights above him and the blinding in his hand. He lifted his gaze and found an average-sized, long red-haired, green-eyed enchantress swaying in front of him.

She wore a short black dress that barely grazed the top of her thighs as she danced alongside a petite, stunning blonde girl, dressed in a bright pink dress that reminded Silas of the star berries they enjoyed in the spring time back home. His mind wandered for a moment back to the simple days of playing in the forest and searching for the berries, whose scent was as intoxicating as their juice was toxic. He shook his head. Was it possible to be homesick this soon?

Silas watched the red-haired goddess dance with careless abandon and something primal in him almost urged him to join her, almost. Her smile was intoxicating, contagious to the point that Silas found himself smiling along with her. *So*, Silas thought, *this was the one, this was the savior of their kingdom, the Lost One, the Princess. The Key to them winning the war.* It simply had to be.

Something deep inside thrummed to life, and there was no question left in his heart. The Savior, the one to win the war against the Deceiver, was a woman. *This woman.* A stunning and entrancing woman at that. He took a few more long strides forward until he was a foot away, standing amid all the chaos, waiting for her to stop.

His sudden stop drew the attention of the girl in pink. "Hello," she purred and stalked toward him like a prowling panther. "What's your name, handsome?"

Averie stopped dancing and turned to follow Sera's slinking body. She froze, finding herself locked in a staring

Denial

match with a pair of haunting teal eyes. As her gaze broke, she finally saw his whole face. Shock rippled through her body. This was him! The man from her dreams and he was standing in front of her! Or, wait, was he? Averie narrowed her eyes, swaying slightly on her feet as she tried to steady her vision. She had had quite a few drinks, maybe even a little more than she realized, considering the ground was still twirling under her. Ignoring the shifting ground, Averie pushed Sera to the side and took his face between her hands.

Silas stood in stunned silence. His mind had moved past her beauty and back into his jaded standard. She was so fragile looking, as if the wind itself would break her in two. How was this flower of a girl supposed to save anyone from anything? A pair of cool hands against his cheeks jarred him from his thoughts. Snapping back from his mind, he found himself a breath away. He wasn't sure how he had missed her move, but before he could even blink, her lips were against his. Her soft, lush lips tasted of fruit and something spicy that entranced Silas in an instant.

As suddenly as their connection was made, it was severed. The heat of her body and the taste of her lips were replaced with a large hand slamming against his chest. His back collided against a rough stone wall, forcing the air from his lungs.

Dazed and surprised by her own boldness, Averie slapped her hands to her mouth, dissolving into giggles as Sera helped steady her. "Did you see that, Sera? I told you he wasn't a dream!"

Sera looked from her drunk, and giggling friend to the storm cloud that stood in front of them. Lucas stood with his hands clenched into fists, his body shaking and jaw ticking. He ground his teeth and glared with unadulterated rage into the face of the tall stranger. Never in Sera's fourteen years of friendship with Averie had she ever seen her act so recklessly.

"Lucas!" Sera called over the music. "Knock it off!"

Lucas ignored her plea as he let his red-hot fury take hold. Stepping toward the stranger, he reared back, swinging his fist upwards toward the stranger's face. Silas casually lifted his arm, neatly blocking Lucas's attack, and slammed his own into Lucas's stomach with a sickening thud.

Sera's heart thundered against her chest as she searched the crowd. "Thane!" she cried desperately, catching sight of the larger man laughing at the bar.

The fear in her voice rose above the thready beat and put Thane instantly on alert. His head snapped in her direction, his brow drawn down in confusion until he caught sight of Sera who held Averie in a loose embrace. With her open hand, Sera pointed frantically to the ensuing brawl. Thane took in the fury of Lucas's face, with his clenched jaw, narrowed eyes, and hands fisted as he stood partially doubled over from the blow he had taken. Where Lucas was shaking in his rage, the unknown man stood watching with a calculating calm that absorbed Lucas's every move, like a predator watching its prey. Thane

Denial

recognized that calm. It was the same that he had before facing each opponent he had fell.

With an annoyed sigh, Thane drained the last of his whiskey, then pardoned himself from the smiling brunette. Cracking his neck and stretching his hands, he made his way through the oblivious crowd.

Recovering from the blow to his stomach, Lucas straightened, his eyes flashing with deep contempt. He lunged forward, only to be ripped back by an unforgiving grip that dug like a vise around his shoulders, throwing him back against the wall.

"Enough!" Thane bellowed into his face.

"Thane!" Sera shrieked. He glance over and found her eyes pleading for him to stop. "Don't hurt him!"

Silas tilted his head in curiosity, and he eyed the new arrival. The one the blonde woman had called Thane. He watched as Thane dropped his head with a sigh at the woman's words. *This man was built for battle*, Silas thought to himself. *Maybe this Realm did have warriors after all.* At last, there was something that felt like home.

Thane turned toward the stranger, trapping Lucas against the wall with his forearm. "Are you alright?" he asked.

Silas nodded with a subtle indifference to what had transpired.

Lucas struggled against Thane's grip, his nails scraping against Thane's skin, drawing small droplets of blood to the surface of his rippling forearm. Rolling his eyes, Thane slammed Lucas once more against the wall, creating a sound like a bag of flowers dropped to the floor. "Stop it," Thane ordered, as he would to a petulant child. Turning, he looked back at Sera and Averie. "Are you guys okay?"

Sera nodded, her eyes wide.

"What the hell happened?" Thane demanded.

Sera shrugged; her arms wrapped around the giggling Averie. "She kissed him."

Thane jerked back, blinking in confusion. "Kissed who?" he asked.

"Him," Sera answered, nodding toward the dark-haired stranger.

Thane's mouth dropped in apparent shock. "Why the hell did she do that?"

Sera flinched, the echo of Thane telling her not to give Averie anymore after the last game ringing in her ears. "She may have had more than the recommended amount."

"Dammit, Sera! What did I tell you? Get her out of here," Thane ordered.

"No," Silas said deeply. He couldn't lose her now, not when he was so close. He didn't come all this way just to fail now. "I need to speak with her."

"Over my dead body!" Lucas spewed, attempting to lunge past the giant body holding him back.

Thane slammed him once more, jarring his teeth hard enough that Sera cringed in sympathy. "Enough!" Thane shook his head, glancing at Silas. "Not tonight, buddy." Shifting his stance, he motioned toward the door. "Take her home, Sera."

Denial

Sera nodded frantically. "Come on, Averie, let's get you home." Wrapping an arm around her friend's waist, she began the slow process of guiding the drunk and wobbling Averie to the club's exit.

Though Averie had heard every word, her mind wasn't in the state to comprehend what was happening. As they began making their way across the room, Averie stopped and turned in Sera's embrace to glance over her shoulder to meet the stranger's eyes. "You were in my dreams," she said, a broad smile crossing her face.

Thane shook his head and groaned. "Okay, Fox, that's enough of that. You are going to have those two killing each other!" he snapped.

"Let's get another round!" Averie yelled drunkenly at Sera.

Sera recoiled as her friend screamed into her face. "No, no, let's not. We are going to get you home before you start a war," Sera said warmly.

"I love you, Sera. You are just the bestest in the entire world!" Averie declared.

Sera cringed at the heavy scent of alcohol on her breath. *Thane's going to kill me.*

Chapter Six

"Wake up, sleepyhead!" Thane boomed, his overly chipper voice grating against Averie's aching head.

Averie groaned and yanked the blanket over her head. "What happened?" she croaked. Her throat dryer than ever before.

Thane plopped himself, none too gently, beside her on the bed. "You don't remember?" he asked, feigning shock.

Dread pooled, rolling her already nauseous stomach. "Remember what?" she asked, peeking over the blanket with burning, bloodshot eyes. Thane smiled down, one hand holding her black and gold cup while the other shook a triple chocolate chip muffin tauntingly. Averie looked longingly at the coffee and muffin, reaching out a hand just to have it pull it out of reach at the last second.

Thane released an exaggerated breath. "Oh, well, where do I start? Ah, I know! How about we begin with

Denial

how you had way too many drinks, especially for a beginner such as yourself. Which went against my loving and thoughtful advice, might I add. After having too many of said drinks, you made out with a random dude that then caused a fight to break out between Lucas and said guy. Making it so I had to leave a lovely woman drinking alone at the bar so I could go play referee," Thane explained, taking a long and deliberate sip of the coffee.

Averie groaned and pushed the blanket from her head. Dragging her tired and sore body up, she leaned against the headboard. Thane offered her the mug with a knowing smile. Averie took a long draw of the rich and sweetened caffeinated liquid before answering. "I did not. Thane smirked down at her and held out the muffin, which Averie snapped up as though he would pull it away if she waited too long.

Thane's grin grew wide, and his eyes sparkled as the night ran through his mind. Leaning his head against the headboard, he crossed his arms over his chest, suppressing an amused chuckle. "Ah, but you did, little Fox, and more than that, you forced me to intervene and put this wonderful gift to the ladies in danger," he said, motioning to his face in mock horror.

Averie took a small bite from the warm muffin and thought back to last night. Most of it was a blur of music, lights, laughter, and drinks. Except for a pair of striking teal eyes. Licking the chocolate from her lips, she stole a glance at Thane. "How bad?" she asked, preparing for the worst.

The smile she was quickly growing to dislike appeared once more, nearly glowing with excitement. "Well, Lucas took quite a beating and—"

"Thane! How could you?" she demanded, jerking upright and forcing the steaming coffee to splash out of the mug and onto his arm.

"Hey, watch it! It wasn't from me. Trust me, the little bit of force I did have to use on him saved him from a whole lot more of a beating, I'm guessing. Whoever that guy was you'd decided to kiss," Thane shook his head and rubbed the liquid on his arm against his shirt. "He was intense."

Confusion furrowed Averie's brow. Thane was known for his strength and his size. It was what had gotten him so far on the boxing scene. He was tall and built, which made his opponents think he couldn't move as quickly, only to find out too late he could move swifter than men half his size. More than the physical, though, was his confidence, and aside from the man that had trained him, Averie had never heard him speak of someone in such regard.

"So, what's the damage? I mean, does…" Averie's words trailed off as she dropped her eyes to her mug.

Thane watched Averie struggle in her own mind, letting the silence stretch between them before grabbing her muffin, then taking a large bite. "Are you asking if mommy dearest was a witness to the greatness that was drunk, Avi?"

Averie flinched at his words, then tipped her head.

Denial

Shoving the remaining muffin into his mouth, he licked the remnants of chocolate from his fingers before finally giving her the reprieve she sought. "Nope, Sera got you in here, free and clear. Not sure how she did it honestly, sly one she is."

Averie sighed in relief, her body sagging back against the bed, and sipped from the mug. "You owe me a muffin," she mumbled.

Thane's eccentric laugh echoed off the walls, causing Averie to writhe and grab her head. "I believe we are even, my little Fox, for it was I who saved you!" Thane proclaimed, jumping from the bed with a flourish as he dropped to one knee and threw his arms wide.

Averie struggled to hold the smile tugging at her lips as she placed her cup on the smooth, white nightstand before she slid from the bed. Averie stood before him, her hands clutched to her chest, the ends of her bright green, fuzzy sweatpants pooling at her feet, giving her a childlike appearance. Lifting her chin, she bestowed on him the greatest of smiles before placing a hand to her forehead and closing her eyes. "Oh, my hero! My knight in…" She peaked down at him before snapping her eyes shut once more. "In cotton-blended armor! What would I, a mere woman, do without a man as strong as you?"

Thane leapt to his feet, lifted her into his arms, and spun her about, sending her laughter to echo off the walls, the ache in her head momentarily forgotten. "Oh, my lady, what honor you have—"

"Ah, hem," a displeased voice interrupted.

Thane turned them toward the door with Averie dangling in his grip and found a mixed audience. Karen stood with a wide smile and shimmering eyes while Sera hid a giggle behind her hand and Lucas stood glaring, his hands crossed over his chest in contempt. Thane and Averie exchanged a brief, wide-eyed look. "Alas, my lady, I must go. Damsels await!" Giving her a resounding kiss on her forehead, he dropped her to the bed and turned to the group. "She's all yours," Thane announced with a deep bow.

Lucas glared as Thane passed him in the doorway. "Do you always have to be so friendly with her?" he hissed.

"Someone's gotta be." Nudging him aside with more force than necessary, Thane descended the hallway, disappearing into the kitchen.

Averie sat up among the disheveled blankets and pushed her hair from her eyes. "Good morning," she said with more cheer than she suddenly felt.

"Good morning, honey, I hope you slept well and don't have too bad of a headache," Karen smiled, shooting a knowing parental look at the three of them while they exchanged nervous glances. "I may be a mother, but I'm not stupid. Do *not* do this again," she warned.

Sera dropped beside Averie on the bed. "Of course not, Karen. We appreciate everything you did to help us with Avi's party." The words hung in the air, the unspoken apology and guilt leaking from the three of them.

Karen shook her head. "Happy to help. Now, you guys, play nice while I make up some more breakfast. I'm sure

Denial

Thane has cleared it all out by now," she finished with a loving sigh.

The room fell into silence as they waited for Karen to get farther down the hall. It wasn't until Karen lecturing Thane about eating all the bacon that Sera broke the silence with her squeal of laughter. She threw herself back against the bed, pulling Averie into a heap against her. "You should have been sooo dead!" Sera laughed.

Averie chuckled as the wind blew the curtains apart, grabbing her attention. As she gazed at the sun piercing through the clouds, a tight force tugged at her chest and the smile faded from her face.

Every twinge forced a cold shiver down her spine as she remembered the first time she'd experienced it. It was the first day of her sophomore year, her sixteenth birthday to be exact. She could still remember the jolt of being woken to the strange pulling that was building inside of her. It wasn't physical, but as if her very soul was trying to force her out of her body. Her world had changed that day, in more ways than she ever could have imagined. The pain, that had once been a slight itch, had slowly increased to the slight twinge of pain but has since grown exponentially.

"Avi," a voice beckoned. "Earth to Averie."

Snapping from her reverie, she turned to find both Sera and Lucas staring at her with mirrored expressions of worry. "Sorry. I got distracted. What were you saying?"

"Just reliving moments from last night," Sera said, waving her hand at the thought. "Are you okay? Your mind seems somewhere else."

"Yeah, I'm fine, just thinking. Wait. Why are you both here?" Averie asked as her eyes shifted from one to the other. "Is something wrong?"

Sera shrugged, pulling at a loose string on the comforter. "Lucas brought me while my car is in the shop."

Averie looked between the two of them, giving each a long stare, trying to read into what was going on. Something wasn't quite right. Sera was fidgeting, something she never did, and Lucas was leaning against the door frame with a scowl. *Though*, she thought to herself, *that part was probably to be expected, especially if that Thane said was true...* "What happened to your car?" Averie asked, eyes locked with the scowling Lucas. Her question was met with a responding stare and a resounding silence. "Are you just going to stand there and glare all day?" she demanded.

Lucas grunted, looking away.

Once more, Sera waved a dismissive hand. "Oh, nothing. I just had a little fender bender is all."

"Another one?" she asked, her head snapping back to her friend. "You didn't drive last night, did you?"

"Of course not. But this time I had an excellent reason," Sera replied, flipping her hair off her shoulder as she rose into a sitting position.

"Really, and just what was that reason?" Averie asked, crossing her arms, chuckling. The fact that Sera still had a license, or a car at all, was a shock to everyone. Her car spent more time in the auto shop than on the road.

Denial

"Well, there was this really cute guy at the coffee shop this morning and oh my *god*, Avi! He had these eyes—"

Averie held her hand up. "Spare me," she said with a grimace. "How could you possibly still have insurance? What will your parents say?"

Sera shrugged as she dug through the purse at her side. "Well, when your parents own the insurance agency, it's kind of hard to get kicked off of the policy. Besides, they are out of town for the next week, and by the time they get back, it will be like it never happened."

"Mmm," Averie murmured.

Sera pulled out her compact and her signature pink lipstick, quickly applying it before snapping it closed and looking excitedly to her friend. "So, what is the plan for the day?"

"Well, considering I have one hell of a headache and desperately need a shower, I really haven't thought past that. Why? What do you have in mind?" Averie asked.

"Well, we have a whole day, and the fair isn't in town for another couple weeks. What do you say we have some good old fashion fun? Movies and the mall today, then when the fair comes, we can pretend we are seven all over again?" Sera offered excitedly.

"Sure, sounds go—" Averie clutched her chest, losing her breath as her head swam from a searing pain that struck her insides like lightning.

Sera leapt to her feet. "Hey! Are you okay?" she asked, grabbing Averie's arms. Lucas pushed from the door frame; his face masked with panic.

Averie took a deep, steadying breath, and nodded. "Yep, all good," she said, forcing a smile. Her eyes drifted to the window, as another burst of pain tore into her, threatening to split her in twain. She took another deep, shaking breath, closed her eyes, and focused on pushing against the pain. It was getting worse, but more than that, it was starting to feel like something was tugging on a rope tethered to something inside of her.

"Averie? Are you sure you're okay?" Sera repeated, panic engulfing her face.

"Yeah, I'm fine." Averie sat up in bed, forcing a smile. "I'm going to take a quick shower. Why don't you two go eat? I'm sure my mom has made plenty."

Sera and Lucas exchanged worried glances as Sera forced a smile. "Yes indeed, then we will be off!" she beamed in her terrible English accent.

Chapter Seven

"Averie! You're going to be late again if you don't get up!" her mother announced, swinging Averie's door wide, the sound of the shower pulling Averie from her slumber.

"Get up!" Karen ordered, pulling the blanket from Averie's head and slipping from the room.

Releasing an irritated whine, Averie sat up and wiped the sleepy seeds from her eyes. The weekend was a fine haze of shopping, food court food, and romantic comedies with short bursts of much-needed study sessions. Stretching her arms high above her head, Averie slipped from her bed, walked to her bathroom, and stepped into the cool shower.

"Averie! It's seven-twenty!" Karen called again, her voice etched with annoyance.

Releasing an aggravated sigh, Averie jumped from the shower and loaded her toothbrush. After a quick brush, she spit the gob of minty toothpaste from her mouth, rinsed it out, and darted quickly to her room. Just because she was late didn't mean she should neglect her teeth. She slipped into her closet, pulled on a green t-shirt, and shimmied into her favorite torn skinny jeans. After a moment of contemplation, she grabbed her favorite pair of black Converse, and hopping from one foot to the other, she put them on and shook the extra water from her hair. No time to make it manageable today. Looks like it will be up to the Hair Gods.

Karen sighed. "You'll have to take the bus," she said, holding out a silver backpack.

"What?" Averie asked, throwing her foot on the counter to tie her shoe.

"Thane took your car this morning. He said he had an early workout, and Sera's car is in the shop," Karen explained.

"Why didn't he take his bike?" Averie demanded, tying the other shoe.

"Now, don't be angry. I told him you wouldn't mind. Plus, Sera will be on the bus this morning, too," Karen continued, as though a senior taking the bus was completely fine and would not immediately plummet her social rank.

Averie groaned, throwing her head back, her wet hair sending droplets all over the floor. "That's not fair! It's my car! Do you have any idea how ridiculous it is for a senior

Denial

to ride the bus? Can't you just take me? I would rather be dropped off by my mother than take the bus."

Karen shook her head. "Yes, but you can't even drive it without Thane, because you *still* haven't passed the test to get your full license. So, even though I am so very thankful you find it less embarrassing for your darling mother to take you, I can't. I should have already left by now," she said, checking the dainty silver watch on her wrist. "Besides, Thane will meet you at school, and you guys can drive home together. No big deal. Now go. Before you miss the bus."

Averie rolled her eyes and placed a quick kiss on her mother's cheek. Taking her bag from her mother, she pushed through the front door and began to quickly descend the driveway. Her heart thumped against her rib cage, her lungs filling with the cool dewy air, limbs stretching and muscles unwinding from the early morning sprint. She slid to a stop in the loose gravel, just in time to see the bus rounding the corner. She waited patiently until the bus came to a sudden stop beside her.

Flashing the bus driver a large and toothy smile, she climbed the stairs. Mrs. Hammond, an old lady that probably should've retired five years ago, was still the sweetest woman Averie had ever met, even if her driving was more of a hazard than it was safe. With her silver hair neatly piled on her head and bright, freshly applied makeup on her face, Mrs. Hammond gave the appearance of a cliché grandmother that would welcome any stranger with a hug and a fresh plate of cookies.

Mrs. Hammond smiled. "I didn't know you would be riding today," she said. "I almost missed your stop this morning, Averie."

"No kidding," Averie returned the smile, still struggling to catch her breath.

Averie made her way down the old bus until she reached the back. Sitting down heavily onto the tattered and torn blue-gray seat, she rested her head against the cool glass window, letting the silence of the sleeping bus envelop her. With a deep rumble, the bus awoke, and with a slight jerk and bounce, continued its journey down the road. The smell of the girls wearing too much perfume and the guys not wearing enough tickled her nose as the outside world passed quickly by. An occasional tune would reach her ears from someone playing their music too loud before the silence came back, the deep monotone groan of the bus acting as a natural white noise.

As she stared listlessly out the window, the sun pierced through the clouds, causing the tight force to tug at her chest again. The pain was quickly becoming a constant companion. It was starting to happen more often. *Should I be worried?* Maybe everyone was right; she probably needed to tell Karen before it ended up being something serious. Perhaps she should go to a doctor and get checked out; after all, being adopted meant she didn't exactly have the most informed medical history.

"Avi," a familiar voice beckoned. "Earth to Avi."

Denial

Shaking herself from her thoughts, Averie turned to see Sera holding out a large coffee and a small brown paper bag. "Oh, hey, Sera, when did you get on?"

"Just a few minutes ago," she said, waving her hand at the thought. "Are you okay? You seem distracted."

Averie took the cup and bag, peering in to see a perfectly made chocolate muffin.

"You are a goddess, you know that? How do you always know when I need a boost?"

Flipping her hair back, Sera sat a little straighter. "Well, first of all, it's Monday, so who doesn't? Second, it's you. You are always running late and can always use a pick me up."

Sipping gratefully from the steaming cup, Averie felt herself begin to unwind.

"So, when do you get your car back?" Averie asked, eyeing her friend. Sera was one of those people that always appeared perfectly composed and happy. If her dog died, Sera would smile and suddenly everything was somehow okay. Tornadoes could go through and make you and everyone else look like they have been electrocuted. Not Sera. She could stand in the middle of a windstorm and the wind would blow around her, afraid of moving a single strand out of place.

Sera peered into the small compact. "When will you get your license? Or tell Thane to stop taking your car?" she retorted.

Averie narrowed her eyes. Did she technically still have her permit yes? Why? Because she thought it was stupid to waste an entire afternoon at the DMV just to take the driving test ... again. Was she going to do it? Yes. "I don't really mind, but it would be nice if he would actually tell me beforehand once in a while. I mean, who really needs to work out as much as he does? He's such a pain," Averie chuckled. Thane really did workout too much and the constant complaints he made about being sore and hungry made her want to smack him.

"You are such a weirdo," Sera smiled, rolling her eyes.

"Yep." Looking back out the window, Averie was overwhelmed by another shocking burst of pain. She took a deep, cleansing breath and closed her eyes against it.

"Avi? Are you okay?" Sera asked, her hands gripped tightly over Averie's shoulders.

Averie took long, labored breaths. Finally, after several lungfuls, she looked into Sera's eyes and said, "Yeah, fine."

"This is getting ridiculous. Look, I know you don't like talking about this, but I really think you need to see a doctor, Averie. That has been happening all the time lately and being adopted ... you don't really know your family history. Maybe heart conditions, or something worse, runs in your family," Sera finished softly.

Averie flinched as she heard her thoughts repeated aloud. "Well, would you look at that? We're at school already." Averie evaded, leaping to her feet and making her way down the aisle just as Mrs. Hammond slammed the bus to a stop. She caught herself against one of the seats, a slight pain tingling down her wrist. Shaking her hand and twisting her wrist back and forth, Averie straightened, bouncing on her toes in anticipation as she waited for the door to open.

As she climbed down the step, she glanced at the back of the bus, watching as Sera struggled to get through the crowded walkway. Averie had to admit, she truly did feel bad for leaving Sera behind like that, but she couldn't hear another lecture about how irresponsible she was being by not telling her mother or going to a doctor. Besides, she wasn't really leaving her behind. She was just going to get off the bus and wait by the entrance for her to catch up. Maybe.

The bus doors opened and Averie darted down the stairs into the crowd of students congregated around the curbside. "Excuse me … sorry… coming through… move!" Averie snapped, shoving people aside.

"Wait! Avi, wait for me!" Sera called as she started pushing through people that had already stood in the aisle to get off the bus.

Averie stared up at the stone, slate gray building. It was a sad-looking building that had carefully placed banners, advertising the next sporting event and fundraiser, in an attempt to hide how old and decrepit it truly was. The broken exterior was surrounded by a metal fence with the main purpose of stopping any crumbling rock from hitting any students that happened to be wandering by. Averie likened it to a low rent prison. The building was one of the original buildings in the small, rural town, and even though they had tried to fix it over the years with various cosmetic upgrades, it never seemed to take hold, finally leaving them with the last option, the fence.

A hand caught her elbow, halting her forward progress. "There you are, Avi. I never thought I would get through!" Sera said with a satisfied grin. "Wow, there are a lot of people here."

"Yeah, are you just now noticing that?" Averie snapped, the words coming out much harsher than she had intended. She wasn't sure where the sudden burst of hostility had come from, but she felt the immediate urge to apologize when a voice stopped her.

"Are you normally this hostile so early in the morning?"

Chapter Eight

The girls stopped, their brows drawn together as they exchanged a look, before turning to face the unknown intruder. A vague but undeniable feeling of déjà vu fluttered through Averie. He was tall, with broad shoulders and black hair that was cut shorter on the sides than it was on top. But it wasn't his heart stopping looks or deep voice that made Averie's breath catch. No, it was the nearly glowing teal eyes that had stolen the air from her lungs and made the hair rise on her arms. Her mind scrambled as she stared up at his tall frame. Standing at least six foot three, he towered over her average five foot five frame and looked down upon her with amusement.

Averie cleared her throat and narrowed her eyes at his smirk. "Do I know you?" she snapped.

"Well, you seemed sure the other night." The man chuckled, giving her a wink.

"Excuse me? Just who the hell are you?" Averie asked. Though something inside her wiggled to get out, she felt deep down she knew him; like a word trapped on the tip of your tongue, her memory scrambled to place him.

Sera snapped her fingers. "It is you!" she shrieked in excitement as she turned to her friend. "Avi, he's the guy you were kissing the other night!"

Averie's eyes widened, and her jaw dropped. "Wh-what?" *Oh, gods, Thane wasn't lying.*

The boy smiled a wide, face-covering smile, his perfect teeth gleaming in the early morning light. "Good to see you, too."

"What are you doing here? Are you stalking me? I will call the police," Averie glared.

The boy looked between the two girls, slight, possibly fake, puzzlement crossing his face. "Stalking? I am here for the schooling," he said, motioning to the building behind them and shrugging the bag strapped over one shoulder.

"*The schooling*? You are a weird one, aren't you?" Averie quipped.

"Well, it appears you are a tad bit of a rude one, aren't you?" he countered.

Sera laughed, her hands clutching her sides, as she looked from Averie's glowering face to the boy's smiling one.

Denial

Averie's hands fisted at her sides, red creeping up her neck. "You don't even know me. How dare you say something like that?" she demanded.

"Oh, I have heard quite a lot about you," he said flippantly, his bright eyes surveying around like someone watching for an attack at any moment.

"Yeah, well, don't believe everything that you hear," Averie spat, and taking Sera's arm, she spun on her heel and walked away before Sera could start in whatever come on was brewing in her head.

Sera slipped her arm from Averie's grip and whirled back to smile at the newcomer. "Have you heard anything about me?" Sera asked, practically purring.

Averie rolled her eyes. "Sera! Let's go already," she sighed, talking her arm once more. "You don't know the guy, for goodness sakes," she hissed, pulling Sera along. "Keep it together."

Silas held his smirk as he watched Averie drag her friend away from him. *This might be more fun than I thought.* Trailing after them, he shoved his hands in his pockets and listened to the exchange between them with growing amusement.

"True, but who said I don't *want* to? He seems really nice," Sera smiled, watching the boy over her shoulder. "And he's really hot."

Averie shook her head. "You don't even know his name, let alone his character. For all we know, he could be a complete nut job. Or a serial killer stalker."

"A serial killer stalker? You made out with him without even knowing his name!" Sera pointed out.

"She has you there," Silas chuckled at Averie's stiff movements. Her irritation with him was clearly visible.

"Why are you following me?" Averie demanded, refusing to stop or look back as she weaved them through the crowd.

"Who said I was following you?" he asked.

"Yeah, Avi, maybe he's following me," Sera said with a smile as she grinned back.

"Alright, that is it!" Averie stopped suddenly, causing Sera to stumble into her back. "Sera, go to class!" she ordered, pointing toward the far building.

Sera frowned, her bright pink lips pursing in disappointment. "That's not fair. I still have ten minutes until the bell rings," she said, pouting.

"Go!" Averie snapped in a motherly tone.

Sighing in defeat, Sera reluctantly agreed. "Fine." Turning to the boy, Sera gave a large, inviting smile as she held out her hand. "The name is Sera. If you need any help, with anything, I'm here."

"Silas, pleasure to meet you." He smiled, bowing over her hand and giving it a slight kiss.

Sera gave Averie a wide-eyed look as she fanned herself, causing Averie to roll her eyes in annoyance.

"Yeah, yeah. Sera, just go already," Averie ordered, crossing her arms.

"Alright, see you at lunch, Avi." Waving, Sera disappeared into the meandering students.

Denial

"One down," Averie mumbled and released a pent up breath before turning to find that the one was actively watching Sera walk away. "That is so going to be a problem later," Averie groaned, turning to leave.

"Wait!" Silas called, grabbing her arm and spinning her to face him. "I need to talk to you."

"About what?" Averie asked, torn between pulling from his touch and her curiosity.

"Your chest," Silas answered.

Averie's jaw dropped. "Excuse me?" she demanded, jerking her arm from his grasp and crossing them protectively in front of her.

Silas frowned at her reaction before his own words replayed his mind. With wide eyes he shook his head and held up his hands. "No, no, wait, that came out wrong," he stammered. "I mean the *feeling* in your chest."

"What?" Averie had to admit, he did look adorable as he fumbled with his explanation.

Silas ran his hands through his hair in exasperation as he struggled to find the right words. "Okay, have you felt—"

"What's going on here?" a familiar voice demanded from behind her.

Averie stifled an irritated groan and turned to find Thane and Lucas standing behind her, intently listening to the conversation. *Today is definitely not my day.* While Thane found the entire thing extremely amusing, based on the smile cemented to his face, Lucas had gone the opposite direction, his lips were twisted into a scowl that oozed disgust and contempt.

"Hey," Averie greeted them both with a forced smile, hoping to distract them from the current situation.

"What the hell is he doing here?" Lucas sneered, jerking his head to Silas before possessively wrapping his arm around her waist.

"This is—" Averie tried to answer but was promptly interrupted.

"Silas," Silas answered simply, contempt dripping from his words. "And you are?"

"Lucas Parker, Averie's boyfriend," Lucas sneered.

Silas looked from Averie to Lucas and back in confusion. "You're with him? First, you have no idea how out of his league you are, but more importantly, the other night you kissed me."

Averie removed Lucas's hand from her waist and adjust her shirt back into place. With the situation quickly getting out of hand, she looked to Thane for help, receiving an amused smile and arched brow in response. "We're not together anymore, Luke, you know that," she snipped. "And the other night was an accident," she shot, looking back at Silas.

As she looked from one to the other, she found they reminded her of peacocks, standing with their chests puffed out, staring at each other as if daring the other to do something.

Denial

Silas straightened; his eyes still fixed on Lucas. His body was tense, but radiated a wave of calm. "I must get to class. I take it, that is the bell?"

"The bell hasn't rung yet-" Averie started, but as she spoke the bell sounded loudly. She paused for a moment, shrugged, and started off toward her classroom.

Silas flashed Lucas a quick grin. "Until later then," Spinning on his heel, he headed into the building.

"I don't like him," Lucas said, following Averie through a set of double doors.

"You don't even know him," Averie corrected.

"I don't care. I don't want you hanging around him," Lucas voiced.

Stopping, she turned on Lucas. "Look, it has already been a hell of a morning and I don't have time for your ego. I am sick and tired of you telling me who I can and cannot hang out with. We are not together anymore. Do you get that? So lay off already! And you," she said, turning to Thane, who was still beaming with amusement in the entire situation, "You are absolutely no help at all."

Thane shrugged. "It's your mess to clean up, Fox. I'm just here to ensure another brawl doesn't break out."

Averie rolled her eyes. "Men."

Chapter Nine

The morning passed with an unusual stillness that left Averie nervous and jumpy. First period went by smoothly; being a fabric design class, it was designed to be relaxing, but there was something in the air that made Averie uncomfortable, like the reassuring calm before the worst storms.

For Averie, that storm started to rumble as she made her way to the second period. It was slow rolling at first, like the silent gray clouds that bruised the sky with a hushed breeze. Averie felt eyes follow her as she walked down the hushed hall, only when she would turn to see where the stare came from, all eyes would be quickly averted.

Averie stepped into the blinding, fluorescent-lit classroom and made her way to her seat. "So, did you hear?" Thane asked from the desk beside her.

Averie's gaze narrowed as she took in his too wide smile and mischievous glint in his eyes. "No, what?" she asked, plopping down onto the hard metal and plastic chair.

"Apparently, there's a new guy in this class, and all the girls are fawning over him already," Thane mused.

Averie grimaced. "Have you seen him?" she asked.

"No, but I can make a guess at who it is," Thane chuckled. "And it appears he has a *thing* for you. Apparently, he has been asking everyone about you."

"No one knows me, so he should probably just stop asking," Averie snapped, slamming her books on the desk.

"True, but now almost everyone is trying to, so that they can talk to the new guy," Thane chuckle. He was getting too much enjoyment out of the current situation for Averie's liking.

"Knock it off, Thane. This isn't funny."

"Maybe not for you. But - oh, incoming," he finished in a whisper, nodding toward the door.

Averie frowned and turned toward the door, already knowing what she was in for. As she waited for the inevitable, there was a deep intake of breath from just about every girl in the room, confirming her fear.

"Oh no," she groaned, sinking into her seat.

"Hey Avi, isn't that the guy from the other night?" Thane asked, too loud for the distance between them. Averie shot him a glare that would burn a hole through a table at the audible amusement in his voice.

"Alright, everyone, take your seats," Mr. Hall ordered as he walked in and set his coffee on his desk. He was an average man, of average height and build, with thin black-wired glasses and short brown hair that was always just a little too disheveled for a teacher. Lifting a paper from his desk, he pushed his glasses up his nose and looked over the room. "We have a new student. This is Silas Frost. Today is his first day and I hope everyone will make him feel welcome," Mr. Hall motioned to Silas with a wave of his hand.

"Where would you have me sit, sir?" Silas asked politely, looking pointedly at Averie.

"Um, are there any open seats?" Mr. Hall asked, his eyes scanning the nearly full room.

The room erupted. The sudden burst of exclamations and Silas's name overpowering the teacher's comment. Hands flew into the air, pointing to nearby chairs in a dizzying flurry of motion. Some, mostly girls, began trying to force others out of seats to empty the ones closest to them, while others took the opposite approach of moving to an empty seat, waiting for another to open up. Averie watched in unabashed fascination. The erratic movements had her comparing her classmates to wild animals fighting for domination.

The reality of her situation began to weigh heavily as she realized the desk behind her remained empty, none of the jostling classmates seeming to notice what was right in front of them. While everyone was trying to get the teacher's attention, Averie only sank farther down in her chair, dreading the possibility of the teacher placing Silas in the chair directly behind her, while knowing that with her luck, it was inevitable.

Denial

"Ah. There is one. Averie, please raise your hand." Mr. Hall asked. A statement, not a question, as he raised his voice against the students' continued wave of sound. The room went silent before erupting once more.

Several female students shouted their objections, covering Averie's miserable groan. As she fought the urge to smack her head against the desk, she caught Thane's muffled laugh. Averie begrudgingly raised her hand slightly, hoping maybe if the teacher didn't see it, he would move on, but knowing he wouldn't.

"Oh, no need Mr. Hall. I know who Averie is," Silas smiled with a smug smile. He tucked his hands tucked into his pockets and sauntered down the small aisle, oblivious to the glares Averie was getting as the girls huffed their disapproval. *Great,* Averie thought. *Just what I need.*

"Alright, now that that's settled, let us begin. What was it we were working on last class?" Mr. Hall asked as he shifted the disorganized papers around his desk.

"The American Revolution," Averie reminded.

"Ah. Yes, that we were." Mr. Hall nodded in agreement, lifting a wrinkled stack of papers from his desk.

As Mr. Hall turned to the board, Thane slid a folded paper across to Averie.

Hey are you okay? You seem a little off and not because of your new seatmate.

I'm fine.

Is it weird, knowing you made out with the new guy?

Averie heard Thane snicker before she read the last line. Shaking her head in disgust, she balled the paper and shoved it into her bag. The class droned on and Averie struggled to pay any attention as her mind kept drifting to the boy sitting behind her. Every movement he made and every breath he took reverberated through her. Even the scratching sound of his pen skimmed across her skin.

"Please finish the end-of-chapter questions, all of them." Mr. Hall instructed, creating a collective groan to cycle the room as the bell rang out.

The echoing ring sent Averie into motion, snapping her notebook closed. She ignored the fact that she had missed the entire lecture, including the notes, and shoved the book haphazardly into her bag as she jumped from her seat.

"Hey, I'm not sure if you remember, but we met the other night. I had my hands a little full thanks to you, though. I'm Thane. You're Silas, right?"

Averie froze, her jaw dropping as she turned and watched Thane hold his hand out and introduce himself with a smile.

"I remember you," Silas gripped it before giving a small shake.

Thane grinned. "So, what class are you going to?" he asked, throwing his bag over his shoulder.

"Oh, um, hold on," Silas reached inside his pocket and pulled out a perfectly folded piece of paper. "It says here my next class is math."

Averie, who was putting her bag across her back, froze once again. "Which math class?" It was a whisper, but seemed like a scream in the empty classroom.

"Ah, Mrs. Frees," Silas answered, giving her a polite smile. "Do you happen to know where that is?"

"Today is just not my day," Averie mumbled, heading to the door.

"Hey, Fox, isn't that *your* teacher?" Thane teased.

"Yeah, Thane, it is," she fired back.

"Why do you call her 'Fox' when her name is Averie?" Silas inquired curiously.

"Oh, well, when Karen first brought me home, Averie used to follow me around all the time; thought she was being sneaky, but she would always wear this fox eared headband that would stick out of wherever she was hiding and give her away. As a joke, I called her Fox one time, and it just kind of stuck," Thane explained, smiling at the memory.

"What does she call you?" Silas questioned.

"Bear," Thane said proudly. "Can you guess why?"

"Because you're a giant oaf," Averie snapped and stormed from the classroom.

Thane exchanged a glance with Silas before shrugging and trailing after her. "She isn't normally this grumpy, I promise. You see her boyfriend is a real piece of work-"

"*Ex*-boyfriend," she amended through clenched teeth.

"Yeah, this week, maybe," Thane answered, rolling his eyes.

"Does he hurt her? Is that why she is so grumpy?" Silas questioned.

Thane laughed heartily, his deep laugh booming off the walls. "Someone hurt little Avi here? You really don't know her. If anything, she has a real temper on her. No, he doesn't hurt her. Even if he tried, I would be more worried about her hurting him."

"Maybe you should be with her," Silas said, a touch of hostility in his voice.

Thane's jaw dropped, his feet coming to a quick stop. "Averie's my sister. Biological or not, gross," he said with disgust sticking his tongue out and scrunching his face.

Silas looked momentarily embarrassed but quickly recovered and smiled. "To class," he stated flatly.

"Ah. Yeah. Follow me," Thane said, frowning at the sudden change in tone.

"Are you in this class, too?" Silas asked, as they made their way down the hall.

"Um, yeah." Thane found himself taken back by the whirlwind that had been the last two minutes. Silas's quick glide from hot to cold and back was hard to keep up with.

"Good," Silas nodded, back to cold again.

Chapter Ten

Her next class went very much like the previous. Averie had taken her seat, pulled her notebook back out from her bag, smoothing down the bent edge, when everything shifted again. The room was full of gossiping girls sharing the latest rumor while the boys sat talking about the upcoming game. Then, just like before, everything fell to a hush when Thane and Silas walked in. Smiling first at Thane, she then pierced Silas with a vicious glare before dropping her gaze to her notes.

Silas was once more placed in the empty seat behind her, earning her another round of glares and whispers from the disappointed girls. Averie sighed and promised herself she would ignore the boy behind her this time and focus on every word the teacher said.

Much like the last class, her attempt at focus failed. When the bell rang twenty minutes later, signaling it was their turn for lunch, Averie practically ran from the classroom hoping to get as far away from Silas as she possibly could. Why was she letting someone so annoying distract her so much?

"Where are we going?" Silas asked Thane, looking at his schedule trying to figure out his next class.

"Lunch," Thane explained.

"She must be famished," Silas said, watching as Averie fled the room.

Thane chuckled to himself. "Yeah, I'm sure that's exactly what it is."

For Silas, lunch was an entertaining affair. Thane led him to a line where they stood waiting for food to be placed on a plastic tray. The whole affair reminded Silas of waiting in line for food at a battle camp where the camp cook spooning out a random bowl of slop to eagerly-waiting soldiers. From there, Silas followed Thane through the room lined with tables that reminded Silas of the giant dining halls from home, only where his were hewn from stone and wood, these appeared to be plastic painted to look like wood. On their walk through the large room, Silas had been asked to sit at seven different tables, politely declining each offer with a charming smile.

Thane finally stopped at a long table against the wall. They each sat in what Silas considered to be a tiny, uncomfortable, and overly small chairs. After a moment, they were joined by an annoyed-looking Averie, a bubbly and smiling Sera, a glaring Lucas, and several other random faces that Silas had yet to meet. While Thane and Sera started to banter, Averie kept her eyes fixed on the random piece of gray meat, covered in gravy, she was stabbing and sliding across the plate. Silas couldn't help but watch her. After all, she was the reason he was here, though he could go without the constant glare that Lucas was sending his way.

Shifting in her seat, Averie wondered if she was the only one that could feel the tension at the table. Sera babbled on per usual, fluttering her lashes, tossing her hair and twirling it between her fingers while the other guys at the table watched like she was an enchantress and they were all under her spell.

"You know, if you two take a picture, it will last a great deal longer," Averie finally muttered.

"I'm sorry, but I wouldn't waste a perfectly good camera," Silas said with an innocent smile.

"Alright, that's it!" Lucas stood and pushed his tray from the table, spilling food across the tiled floor.

"What is?" Silas asked cheerfully, taking another fry from his plate.

"You know damn well what I mean!" Lucas shot back. "You think you can make out with my girlfriend then show up here and act like nothing happened?"

The cafeteria fell into complete silence. Everyone's eyes on them as Lucas stepped forward to tower over the sitting new arrival. Averie's face burned with embarrassment beneath the weighted stares from the cafeteria. Stiffing a groan, she hid face in her hands.

"From what I hear, she's not your girlfriend, and if you want to get technical, your girlfriend made out with me," Silas responded calmly, taking a bite of the fry. He was quickly growing to enjoy the way this Realm utilized the simple vegetable.

Thane sighed and set down his burger, gently wiping his hands on a napkin, as he waited for Lucas to cause an even bigger scene that he would eventually have to intervene in.

Movement brought Averie's eye to the collection of teachers and students that were slowly making their way closer. Trying to avoid an even more embarrassing moment, Averie stood and leaned over the table. "Come with me," she whispered angrily to Silas.

Lucas's jaw dropped at her words, seething with loathing, when Averie walked away with Silas. "Are you kidding me!?" he shouted, kicking over the chair Silas had been sitting in.

"Sit down, Lucas," Thane snapped.

"Are you seriously just going to let her leave with him?" Lucas demanded.

"Yeah, actually, I am. She can do what she wants, and it's not up to you or me to decide where she can go or with who. Now sit *down*." Thane had reached his limit with the current situation, and it pushed him from anger to fury

Denial

when he looked back down to his burger and found he no longer had an appetite.

Lucas glared down the hallway, battling against the urge to follow them before sitting down with a huff.

"Show's over, everyone." Thane announced. "Go back to whatever you were doing," he said, waving a dismissive hand at the group of teachers and students.

Averie dragged the rather compliant Silas down the hallway by his arm, ignoring the scathing glances from the girls they passed. Pushing the hall door open she stepped into the stairwell and motioned for Silas to follow. As she waited for the door to close behind them, she crossed her arms and began tapping her foot.

"This is starting to get ridiculous," she decreed as the door snapped shut.

"What is?" Silas asked with wide-eyed innocence.

Averie took a deep breath and sent a quick prayer for patience to the gods above. Clasping her hands together, she forced a smile. "Alright, here's the deal: I need you to leave me alone. So, if you agree to forget about the other night, I will tell you anything you want to know about me," she offered.

Silas smirked. "But if I am to leave you alone, how is it that you will tell me what I want to know, that is, if I want to know anything?"

"Stop talking in riddles!" she demanded.

"Royalty," he mumbled under his breath

"What?" Averie asked.

Silas sighed. "Nothing. Everything will come clear in due time."

"What will?" Averie asked again. She was getting nowhere, and she could feel her anger building up inside her with each question that he danced around.

"I just hope it is before the end of the fallen moon," Silas mused.

Averie threw her arms up. "Alright, I give! What the bloody hell are you talking about? Quit giving me stupid answers. I know something strange is going on. I can feel it inside and have for a while. Then you just show up, out of my dream, which is weird enough by the way, and annoy the hell out of me and instead of giving me a single answer, you just keep saying your dumb riddles!"

Silas was taken aback. "Wow, I never would have thought you would have asked so soon. I mean, I know Cleo said that I should take this slowly, but if you are asking, then it means you must already have some idea. This will be easier than I had expected."

Averie sat down on one of the stairs, resting her head in her hands, exhaustion overtaking her rage. "Can you please just say what's on your mind before we have to go back to class?"

Silas crouched down, lifting her eyes to meet his own and Averie watched the cheer fade from his face and morph into seriousness. "What I tell you is no lie and is of the utmost importance. Do you acknowledge and understand this?" he asked.

Averie sighed, reluctantly nodding.

Denial

"Alright then. I have come here from the Heart Realm. Now ruled by the betrayer Marcus. I was… a boy when the Day of Betrayal took place, and I had no idea that my— that he would cause the Realm to split. I was sent here by Radnar, who was a longtime friend of the old king, your father, in hopes that you, the Key to ending this all, the Lost One, will return and defeat Marcus the Betrayer, and restore the Realm back to its former glory."

Averie sat there staring into Silas's serious expression struggling to process his words. She opened and closed her mouth several times before a frown settled.

"Averie? Do you understand what I am telling you?" Silas asked, searching her face.

Averie's mind raced. Was he kidding? Did he think she was stupid? What the hell kind of person comes up with something like that? Was he a stalker? How did he know she enjoyed fantasy and sci-fi? Did he really think this was a workable pickup line?

"You need more," Silas nodded in understanding, reading the questioning look on her face. "Alright, no problem. Before Marcus could finish what he'd started, taking over the whole Realm, it is said that the queen locked the Heart of the Realm inside a young child, her child, and sent her out into the blank space to search for a home of stability and peace. Why that child, you, chose this place, I have yet to figure out."

Averie stayed silent, struggling to comprehend what he was saying when suddenly it all made sense. Silas was mental. Absolutely out of his mind, just escaped from the psych ward, bonkers. "You think that this bizarre story, that you concocted, is supposed to somehow mean something to me? Did you find out I was adopted and thought this would be a funny joke? You honestly want me to believe that I am this lost child, sent from a different world. Oh wait, and yes, I'm a princess," she laughed. Averie knew that somewhere in the back of her mind she had read or heard something about keeping crazy people calm until you could get away or alert help, but she couldn't seem to help herself. He had annoyed her and ruined her day, so her compassion, and apparent sanity, was nonexistent.

Silas's face fell, reminding Averie of a lost puppy. "Of course, it is. You have no knowledge about what I'm saying? You don't remember anything?"

"There's nothing to remember!" Averie said, leaping to her feet. "Now, leave me alone!"

As she went to walk away, Silas caught her hand. "You must remember," he said softly, his voice emotionless, as he pressed something into her hand.

Glancing down, she found a warm, golden disk shimmering in her palm. A flash crossed Averie's mind at his touch, a woman with long hair, dark as night, was singing a beautiful melody to the small child in her arms. The tune felt so familiar, yet so far away. Like a long forgotten memory that had finally been unearthed. The woman's face was as pale as marble with eyes as golden as the sun, the same golden eyes that Averie herself had.

Denial

Where had the vision come from? Was Silas's insanity contagious? Or was it from her past? Or was it something from a movie she had watched when she was a child? Whatever it was, all she knew was that she must find out the woman's identity, what was really going on, and where had she come from. Averie's head swam, a deep dizziness spinning her around and sinking to the ground. Her final feeling was strong arms wrapped around her before everything went black and silent.

Chapter Eleven

The world was dark, empty, suffocating. She was lost in a spiraling void, falling. *No*, she thought, *that didn't make sense*. How could she be falling into nothingness? Stories played out before her eyes, as if she was watching television, only instead of pictures flashing by, there were feelings, flashes of colors that filled the darkness around her. Warmth surrounded her, happiness radiated and she swore she heard a laugh echoing in the distance. She smiled at the cheer and warmth that swaddled her like a newborn baby. Then suddenly, a vicious cold wave washed it all away in an instant.

Despair and a sick, warm wetness covered her. She struggled against it, the sticky liquid holding a metallic smell surrounded her, making her stomach roll and jolting her awake. Her eyes opened to a bright light. Groaning, she pulled the blanket over her head.

Denial

"Oh, thank the heavens you're okay," came her mother's concerned voice.

"Mom? Why is it so bright?" Averie asked, her eyes tightly shut under her blanket, the light still pouring in from beneath her lids.

"Because you're in the sun room. That new boy, now what was his name? Oh, yes, Silas—he brought you home from school," Karen mused, pulling the blanket from Averie's head and holding out a glass of water.

Averie shot up at the mention of his name, knocking the glass from her mother's hand. "Silas? How did he know where I lived? Where is he?"

"The school told him. Somehow, he managed to convince the school to let him bring you home instead of bringing you to the hospital. He said something about a flash?" Karen turned back to her daughter. "What kind of flash did you have, honey? Are you sick? Do you need to go to the hospital?"

"No, I'm not sick and I definitely don't need to go to the hospital. But, mom, where is he? Where is Silas?" Averie asked.

"He's sitting on the porch. I told him I'd get him when you woke up," Karen answered.

"No, no, don't worry about it," Averie threw the blanket from her body and swung her legs over the side of the bed. "I'll get him."

"Are you sure that you should be walking around?" Karen asked with a worried look.

"Yep," Averie answered sternly.

Averie's steps wobbled slightly as she hurried toward the porch. She flung the door open and stared down at Silas.

"You're up," Silas stated, looking up from his phone.

"Yes, now you can leave," Averie answered curtly.

Sliding his phone into his pocket, a mischievous glint entered his eyes when he opened his mouth to speak. "I'm not leaving."

"What do you mean, you're not leaving?" Averie demanded.

"I live next door. So I could leave, but I would already be where I am going," he smiled.

"But I thought you just said that you're not from here," Averie mocked.

"I'm not, but I can't go home without you and you won't come with me until you understand what you're supposed to do. So, until then, you are stuck with me." His smile grew with every word and with it, Averie's frustration.

"And just where is that?"

"You know where," he said longingly, looking skyward. "You must return and reclaim your throne. We need you to restore order, and I would really like to go home."

"How do you expect me to take you seriously when you say crazy things like that?"

For several moments, Silas gave her a blank stare, his glowing eyes locked on hers. "Meet me tonight, in the field just beyond that fence."

Denial

Averie looked to where he was pointing. She knew that just beyond her backyard and through the trees there was a large field. Every year, it would fill with wildflowers of every color anyone could possibly imagine. It had been her secret place since she had moved into this house. Averie thought on it for several moments, weighing what she was thinking in her head against what she was feeling in her heart, before finally relenting. Besides, what could really go wrong? Silas was odd but he didn't seem dangerous, at least not toward her.

She nodded. "Fine. Tonight, but this is your last chance. No stupid stories, only the truth."

Silas smiled. "No lies, only the truth. I'll meet you when the moon is high."

Averie waved her hand in dismissal. "Yeah, whatever."

Silas stood, and took her hand in his own, bowing slightly before kissing it. "You shall see tonight, my Princess, " he turned, stopping on the stairs. "Oh, and please bring the medallion."

Moving her hand to her chest, Averie felt a strange twinge of excitement stream through her. He was so much sweeter to her than Lucas had ever been.

"Wait, what? Princess?" Averie asked aloud to Silas's back, too far away for him to hear.

* * *

Later that night, Averie sat at the table, biting the end of her pen as she thrummed her fingers on the table, her leg shaking her chair. Thane's hand flew out, catching hers, the look on his face immediately stopping the shaking of her leg.

"What is wrong with you?" he asked.

"What do you mean?"

Thane tilted his head, narrowing his gaze at her. "What are you about to do, Averie?"

"N-nothing. What, ah, what do you mean?" Averie squirmed under his gaze, like a poor snail trying to flee as it's captor slowly rains the salt down.

"Mmm. How long have I known you, Fox? Hell, how long have I lived here?"

"A while," she murmured.

"And you are still going to sit there, acting like I don't know when you're lying? Especially when it's to my face?"

Averie bit the inside of her bottom lip and looked down the hall to the kitchen where her mother was dancing to some music as she made their dinner. "Okay, fine. I'm going to meet Silas after dinner. Happy?"

"*No*, I'm not happy. How would any part of that make me happy? Have you not noticed the impending doom you are raining down on me?" Thane snapped.

"I can do what I want to, Thane. I am not a child asking for your protection or your permission," Averie countered.

They stared at each other in silence, waiting for the other to cave when Thane finally turned his head away.

Denial

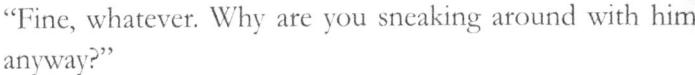

"Fine, whatever. Why are you sneaking around with him anyway?"

Averie scoffed. "I'm not sneaking around."

Thane quirked his brow, and leaning back in his chair, crossed his large arms over his chest. "Oh, yeah?"

Averie scowled.

"Hey, no judgment here, I just thought you were still all goo-goo eyes for Mr. Douchebag."

"Lucas isn't a douchebag, Thane. He's just…"

"Douchey? Self-absorbed?" He snapped his fingers. "Narcissistic! That's the word."

"Oh, stop it, I thought you liked him," she asked, fiddling with the end of her destroyed pen.

Thane's booming laughter made Averie jump. Their mother turned with a smile and shook her head at them before returning to the stove.

He shifted his hands behind his head. "You're kidding, right? The only reason I even tolerated him is because I thought the asshat made you happy. Hell, the only reason I broke the fight up was because Sera was practically crying and you were way passed the point of being okay. Don't get me wrong, he is a great guy as long as he's not dating your sister and you're into being friends with a douchebag."

"Why didn't you ever say anything?" she asked.

Thane shrugged, bracing his broad frame and elbows on the table. "What was I supposed to say, Averie? Hey, the guy you're clearly infatuated with is a bigger tool then I am? Yeah, that would have worked."

"You are not a tool, Thane."

He sat back in his chair again, looking offended. "Excuse me? Do you think I have these glorious muscles and perfect face for any other reason than to be a complete and utter tool master? Hell, I pride myself on being the mechanic."

"The mechanic?"

He smiled his perfect toothy grin. "Absolutely. Do you know what mechanics do? They fix things for people using their ... variety of tools." He wiggled his brows and Averie laughed.

"You, sir, are disgusting." Averie laughed, discrediting her words.

A brief moment passed before Karen declared dinner ready. Thane kept the chatter up, as he always did, while Averie sat fighting an internal battle of whether or not she should really go and meet Silas. After all, he was a stranger. Was it really that smart to meet up with a guy she didn't know, in the middle of the night, when only Thane knew she was going anywhere? Even he didn't know where they were meeting, just that she was going.

"Hey, Mom?" she asked suddenly.

Karen looked away from Thane. "Yes?"

"Um, I'm heading to bed early tonight, is that okay?" she asked, keeping her eyes at her plate, feeling Thane's smirk bore into her.

Karen frowned at Averie's strange behavior. "Alright, honey, I want you to get some extra sleep anyways, especially after the day you have had. Silas said that he would bring you to school tomorrow," her mother added, the last words with the tone of order not choice.

"Did he now?" Thane chucked behind his cup. "What did you think of the kid, Karen?"

The older woman practically glowed, "Oh, he was just the sweetest most thoughtful thing. Did you know he is the one that brought Averie home? How considerate was that!"

"Oh yes, just the sweetest," Thane said in a tone dripping with sarcasm as he held his hands up to his face and tilting his head mockingly.

Karen swatted his arm. "Oh, you! Don't you pick on me. I am an old woman and I appreciate a gentleman when I see one."

"You are not old, Mom, and you don't even know him. Maybe he's crazy," Averie chimed.

"Yeah, Karen, you never know. He might be a serial killer, just biding his time until he invites you over in the middle of the night and chops you into a million pieces," Thane added, his eyes locking on Averie's slack expression.

Karen watched her children exchange a secret conversation with looks alone. "Are you working out tonight?" Karen inquired, hoping the change of subject would diffuse the situation.

"Yep, I'll leave in a little while," Thane said, sending Averie one last concerned glance when she rose from the table.

The table talk faded as Averie made her way down the hallway and disappeared into her room. After hesitating for a moment, she locked the door and moved to her closet. Most of her attire consisted of darker colors which would certainly help her sneak out into the night. She slipped on her second favorite pair of black leggings as there was no use in risking ruining her favorite ones, slid a tank top over her head, and pulled on her black hoodie before grabbing her combat boots from the bottom of her closet. With her outfit ready to go, she sat down on the edge of her bed and waited.

Chapter Twelve

As it turned out, she didn't have long to wait before the light under her door disappeared and the sound of the shower starting echoed through the wall. Averie sat, waiting, counting slowly in her head as her heart thudded against her chest. It wasn't that this was the first time she was sneaking out; quite the contrary. She and Thane had snuck out so many times that they knew their mother's nightly schedule down to the minute. This, though, was the first time she had done it alone.

Averie jerked from her bed when the buzzing of her phone caused her already thumping heart to skip a beat. Clutching her chest and releasing a sigh of relief, she opened the new message.

I don't like this. It goes against everything I believe in.

But I trust you.

Be safe.

Call me if he gets weird.

Averie smiled at Thane's concern as the sound of his motorcycle starting broke through the night's silence.

Always am, Bear.

She slipped her locked phone back into her hoodie pocket and sat back down to wait. Averie heard the water cut off and waited another fifteen minutes. By now, her mother would be tucking herself into bed with a book or watching one of her guilty pleasure reality TV shows. Averie watched the minutes tick by, her leg starting to tap against the soft carpet as she patiently waited for the opportune moment.

Ten minutes passed with no movement, it was now or never. Averie reached down, grabbed her boots, and slipped them onto her feet. Another silent breath and she moved to the cracked window. She deliberately slid the window up, ensuring it did not make a sound, then slid one leg, followed by the other, out before silently dropping to the ground.

Averie could have told Karen she was meeting Silas tonight—Karen trusted Averie and had faith in her to make the right decisions—but she didn't want her mother

Denial

thinking something was going on that wasn't. Even if her mother didn't know exactly what was going on, she knew her mother's mind would run carelessly down the road of what it wasn't. Karen had taken to Silas the instant he had brought her home and the last thing she needed was her mother expecting something to come to fruition that would never happen. She wiped her sweaty hands down her pants as she crept along the house, avoiding the floodlights, and darting to the shed.

Averie sighed in relief at her ability to dodge the lights as she slowly made her way to the backyard fence. She sent a hushed thank you to the full moon above at the success of her mission and let her eyes wander the night sky. The stars seemed to shine extra bright against the dark, velvet night. Before she turned away, she muttered a quick, silent prayer, in the hope that there were no snakes or bugs hiding anywhere nearby, ready and waiting to attack her as she reached the old fence outlining the property. Averie ran her hand along the old wooden surface in search of the latch and closed her eyes. As she opened the gate, her mind prepared her for the inevitable loud creaking that always accompanied opening the old door, instead the gate opened with a resounding silence.

"Hey," a chipper voice whispered in her ear.

Squealing in terror, Averie fell into the bushes, her hand covering her mouth in horror as she watched a large shadow separate from the darkness.

"Shh!" the shadow whispered, stepping into the moonlight. "Do you want to get caught? You are sneaking, aren't you?" Silas asked, reaching out a hand to help her up.

"Dammit, Silas," she screamed silently, pushing his hand away.

"Of course, were you expecting someone else?" he asked, disappointed.

"No, but I didn't think that you would stalk up behind me in my backyard. What the hell is wrong with you?! You don't sneak up on people, *ever*, and definitely not at night," she lectured, climbing to her feet and brushing the dirt from her legs.

"Maybe you should be more aware of your surroundings," Silas retorted. "Plus, I couldn't trust that you would make it on your own."

"What makes you think that I couldn't make it across my own yard?"

Silas frowned in confusion. "I just thought—"

"You just thought that I was a girl and that I can't find my way out of a wet paper bag," Averie supplied.

"No, of course not. I have no doubt you can find your way through anything. If even half of the stories of the Lost One are true, you can navigate through every Realm with your eyes closed," Silas amended quickly.

"And you seem to have it in your head that I'm this Lost One, that you claim you need to find?"

"Correct. Also known as the Key, the Lost Princess, and our last hope. Now, follow me and I'll prove it."

Averie hesitated.

Denial

"Are you coming or not?" he asked, turning around and walking off into the dark.

Averie stood, unsure, as she watched him begin down the small trail. It was, after all, how many of the horror movies Sera liked to watch started out. Girl wanders out to meet a handsome stranger in the middle of the night, with no one knowing where she is or what she is doing. Averie took a cautious step forward, searching the tree line as she followed.

"You know, Thane knows I'm here." She mentioned the lie, giving her some type reassurance.

Silas stopped, tilting his head sideways as he glance at her over his shoulder. "Mmm, I don't think he does."

"Of course, he does," Averie sputtered, her self-assurance quickly beginning to fade away. "Who wouldn't tell someone where they were going before they decide to wander in the woods with a complete stranger?"

"Do you think I intend to hurt you?" Silas questioned.

Averie shook her head. "Of course not. That is what a crazy person would do, and you don't seem like a crazy person. Although, I guess most crazy people don't exactly seem crazy to those that they end up … you know," Averie rambled as she brought her finger up to her throat and made a slicing motion. "Not that you plan to do that because you are not crazy and that just wouldn't be, ah, nice," Averie cleared her throat, shifting her feet.

Silas watched her frantic movements, captivated by her attempt to soothe her own fears while simultaneously helping them grow. "I am not crazy. Nor do I plan on hurting you in any way," he offered, continuing down the slightly overgrown path.

Averie hesitated a moment again before following. If Silas thought she was going to be an easy target, he was mistaken. She hadn't taken years of self-defense and kickboxing classes for no reason. Sure, she might be making a huge mistake by following him and sure, she hadn't told anyone where she was, and okay, with his size she didn't know if she could even do any real damage to him, even after years of Thane teaching her self defense, but she had walked this path hundreds of times as a child; if he tried anything she would quickly stun him and run.

The path they walked came to an end, opening to the large sprawling field. Silas continued forward, only coming to a stop when he reached its center. Averie was slow to follow as she took in the stunning scene. High in the sky, the full moon cast its silvery light on the summer flowers, giving them an ethereal, almost metallic glow as they swayed gently in the cool midnight breeze, their perfume thick in the air. If Averie had come for any other reason, it would have felt like she had walked straight into a dream. The irony of the fact that she was with the man she had seen in her dreams was not lost. Her hands fell loosely by her sides, brushing against the moon-kissed petals as she crossed the field. Stopping a few feet from Silas, she took a deep breath.

"Alright, Silas, I'm here. Now it's time for you to tell me why it was so important for me to meet you," Averie exasperatedly said.

Denial

Silas inhaled deeply, his mind rebelling against the idea of his entire life, his very survival revolving around this girl. "Alright, what I am about to tell you is going to sound absurd, especially coming from a world with limited magic and even less belief in it, but I need you to promise me that you are going to keep an open mind."

"Sure," Averie agreed, crossing her arms over her chest.

"Good. I should start by saying I'm not from around here."

"No kidding," Averie said in sarcastic shock.

"I am afraid not. I know I could blend nearly seamlessly, but alas, I am not from here."

"I take it sarcasm isn't something you have back home."

"Of course we do. I'm very fluent in sarcasm. I am even able to fool Callen into thinking that I am truly interested when he starts rambling on about his newest theory."

"Right ... so you aren't from here. Is that what you wanted to say?"

Silas shook his head. "Apologies, I got caught up in something else. Now, where was I?"

"The beginning, you made it one sentence."

"Yes, well, here we go. Where I am from, where you are truly from, is a place that was filled with light, magic, and hope, until one day Marcus, you know, the bad guy, couldn't take it anymore and he plotted to overthrow your birth father hoping to claim the Realm as his own. In an effort to stop him, your father used his power to divide the Realm, sending it into pieces. Literal pieces. The Realms have been spread out far and wide, trapping Marcus in my Realm, thereby stopping him from taking complete control. This world, the one that you are currently residing in, is known to us as R3."

"R3? What does that mean?" Averie asked, her curiosity begging for more information.

"R3 is the third Realm. The Dream Realm," Silas explained. His body buzzed at her question; she was believing him.

"The Dream Realm," Averie parroted.

"Yes. Those in this Realm walk around as though in a trance. Working themselves to death, their only one true desire is to have everything, even though you can never bring any of it with you into the afterlife. It's actually rather silly if you think about it."

Averie scoffed at his words. Sure, they sounded true, but that didn't make them true, right? "That is ridiculous."

Silas raised a brow. "Oh? Am I wrong? I have been here for approximately four days and I have seen countless individuals walking through as though they are racing death himself. I have yet to see someone truly experience the world around them, to stop and take in the vast sky or smell the blossoming flowers. Do you guys even stop and just take a deep breath? Well, it would be understandable if you don't, the air here is just … it's weird if I am being completely honest."

Denial

Silas looked over at Averie and cleared his throat. He could sense she was running out of enthusiasm and desire to be here. He knew if he didn't explain this just right, she would walk away, leaving his entire Realm, all the Realm, to suffer.

"Anyway, after the Realm was divided and Marcus came to power, the Key or Heart Realm, my Realm, fell into despair. Marcus rules with an iron fist, allowing no one to speak against him and those that do lose their families before their eyes. Magic is torn from the bodies of those that still possess it, leaving them to live a half-life, a husk of the person that they once were. It's falling apart, Averie. People are dying and the only hope we have … is *you*."

"Me?"

Silas nodded. "There is a story in my Realm, one that tells of the old queen placing the Heart of the Realm, the piece that holds it all together, inside a young girl just before she cast her out. It promises that one day she will return and bring the Realm together once more. Ridding Marcus of his throne and reclaiming it as her own."

Silence stretched in the air between them. Silas prayed to the stars for their help, while Averie was currently struggling with finding an effective way to get as far from him as she possibly could, and fast.

Releasing a slow, heavy breath, Averie gave a tight smile. "Wow, Silas, that was … an incredible story. However, I'm leaving, um, maybe grab a shower and get some sleep. I really think that you should do the same. Maybe call one of those hotlines or something."

"Wait!" Silas called, catching her wrist. "That's it? You don't have any questions? Don't you want to know more?"

"What the hell did you expect me to do, Silas? Thank you for coming here and dragging me out of bed in the middle of the night, just so you could tell me some weird story about another world and that I am supposed to save by dethroning some evil ruler?"

"See! I know you wouldn't truly give it a chance!" Silas accused.

"Are you kidding me right now? That's the most ridiculous thing I've ever heard in my entire life."

"I thought you would understand. That something inside you would explain what I'm saying is the truth."

"Well, you were wrong. Goodnight, Silas."

"You can't just run away, Averie. There is a world of people that have nothing left, they need you."

Averie dropped her head and took a deep breath before turning back to Silas. The same man who she was starting to believe may have escaped a psych ward. Giving a small smile, she clasped her hands in front of her. "Look, I know you believe this and that's great, I get it. Sometimes life deals us some really crappy stuff and people retreat into their minds to get away from it. Cool, I am all for that, but I won't let you drag me into it with you."

"Damn it, Averie! Why is this so hard for you to believe?" Silas demanded.

"Seriously? Are you seriously asking me that right now?" Averie asked in disbelief.

Denial

"Yes, of course. I just asked you," Silas explained, confusion creasing his face.

"How about we start with the fact that I met you less than twenty-four hours ago? Or maybe that different worlds—"

"Realms," Silas corrected.

"*Realms* don't exist, Silas. This isn't some sci-fi show. This is my life, and I would appreciate it if you left me alone and out of your crazy fantasies."

"People are dying, Averie," Silas tried, his voice taking a softer, more desperate tone.

"People die every day, Silas. Here in the *real* world."

"Are you really going to lie? Ignore the things going on around you because you don't want to be different? In my Realm, the gift you have is praised, not hidden. Anyone who truly uses their eyes can see who you are."

"What are you even saying?" Averie asked, exasperated.

Silas shook his head incredibly. "It is so clear you might as well scream it to the stars! The Earth moves around you Averie, trees part to keep you safe and shielded, flowers lean into your words, and the ground softens under your feet. I came here not believing a damn word of this story and in the span of a day, in a single moment, everything I thought I knew was wrong."

"I don't know what you're talking about," Averie defended, turning on her heel she started back through the darkness, searching for the trail she had been led down, when she heard words that froze her steps.

Chapter Thirteen

"It started around sixteen," Silas started, his heart pounding against his ribs. *This is my last chance.* "You were ripped from your sleep as your body felt like it was being set ablaze from the inside. It lasted a moment but it felt like years and ever since that day things have been different for you. When you feel things, you truly feel them and the world feels them. It rains when you cry, thunder booms when you are mad and the sun shines so brightly, the days so perfect, when you are happy."

Averie's breath was coming in sharp bursts as she stood listening to Silas spill her deepest, darkest secret. Her greatest fear came to life as she turned to face him. Panic threatened to take her as fear shook her limbs. She looked Silas in the face, his emotional level did not match hers. He wasn't angry, not a single trace of hate or judgment in his voice. It was almost as if he was retelling his own story, not hers.

Denial

"At first it was easy to control, a few deep breaths here and there and you would be fine, but lately things haven't been going as smoothly." As he spoke, Silas had closed the space between them. She could see the desperation in his eyes for her to believe him.

"How do you know that?" Averie's voice was barely a murmur, shaking with fear.

Silas released a breath he hadn't realized he was holding and smiled. "Where I'm from, the magic that is so rare here, thrives everywhere. More people are born with gifts than without them. I have seen the same thing happen to many powerful people in my Realm and the story of your power dwarves them all."

"Okay, prove it," Averie said, crossing her arms.

"What do you mean?" Silas asked.

"I mean prove it. Prove to me that you are not some crazy person, that you have some type of 'gift' like you think I do," Averie explained.

"I can't," Silas answered, his shoulders drooping.

"Exactly. Just like I thought."

"Averie, please wait! I can't because I was one of the few in my world that was born without a gift, but that doesn't mean I'm lying to you."

"No, of course not. Who wouldn't believe the insanity you are spewing, especially without any proof?"

"So you believe me?" Silas asked, relief creeping into his voice.

"No! You said you knew sarcasm," she stated incredulously. "You know, you almost had me going there for a second."

Silas scoffed. "Of course I do, I just didn't realize…" Clearing his throat, he shook his head. "That's not the point. I do have something I can show you," he offered.

Averie chewed on her lip, pondering what he said. Did she really want him to prove anything? Regardless of any truth he might have spoken, did she really want to give him the chance to change everything she believed? What was there to really lose? She knew deep down he was just crazy, so why not let him prove it? "Okay, show me," she relented.

Silas reached behind him, withdrawing a long, curved dagger. Even in the moonlight, Averie could see the intricate swirls carved in the hilt, the large black stone glittering under the night light. Averie took an involuntary step back. So, he had brought her here to kill her. Shaking her head, she held her hands up in surrender.

"Look, I know I may have been a little meaner than I should have, but I was only kidding. We can absolutely go to your world and—"

"Realm," Silas repeated.

"Right, right. Of course, Realm. We can go there right now. Just let me run home, pack a bag, and we can go."

Silas watched her, confused by her blatant lies and defensive actions. "Why do you lie?" he asked.

"I'm not the one holding a dagger," she defended.

Denial

Silas looked down at the blade in his hands, his eyes widening in understanding. "Oh, no, I'm not going to hurt you. I am going to prove my story to you," he explained, stepping forward.

Averie matched his step by taking one back. "Stop! Stay right there," she warned.

"You are being ridiculous, Averie. If I wanted to hurt you, I would have done it when I snuck up on you in the woods."

"So you did sneak up!" Averie shook herself. *That isn't important right now.* "What do you want, Silas?"

Silas wracked his brain for a way to explain what needed to be done without scaring her any further. "How about this? I am going to place this on the ground and take a step back. I need you to pick it up and make a small cut on your palm, like this." Silas demonstrated by drawing the blade down his palm, piercing the skin before placing the blade on the ground and stepping away. Averie watched in shock as blood sprang to the surface, flowing freely down to his wrist. "Then we will place them together, and it will show you everything."

"Yeah, I'm not doing that. Have you never heard of communicable diseases? And with your level of crazy with these other worl ... Realms ... you would probably think it means we are married or something," Averie explained slowly, shaking her head.

"Averie, *please* do this, and if it doesn't work, I will walk away and leave you alone forever."

She had to be insane for considering his offer, but here she was, standing in the middle of a field, in the dead of night, doing just that. Averie eyed the dagger as it lay on the ground shimmering in the moonlight, the tip flashing red with Silas's blood. "You don't go around cutting open your hand and just rubbing blood together. I don't know what you have, but I certainly don't want it."

"I have nothing. Disease is something long banished from my Realm. As for the cut, it will close soon after I show you what you wish to see," Silas explained.

Averie shook her head. *Don't do it, Averie. Absolutely not. You will not reach down, take that dagger, and slice your own palm open. Nope, not happening.*

Even as those thoughts echoed in her head, she found herself doing the exact opposite. The metal was warm in her hand, and though the dagger was large, it was surprisingly light in her grasp. She wasn't sure what had come over her; one minute she was staring at the swirling lines, her eyes drawn to the mesmerizing gem, and the next she had sliced her palm open and stood barely a foot from Silas, her hand outstretched, palm facing up. A sick feeling settled into the pit of her stomach as she watched the blood—her *blood*, fill her palm and stream between her fingers.

She lifted frightened eyes to Silas and only briefly caught his smile before his hand slammed tightly against hers. With no time to react or pull away, her eyes widened and her mouth fell open in shock. A deep warmth started to fill her like a bath, starting from her hand and spreading

Denial

until her whole body radiated with the heat. A small glow appeared between their clasped hands and drew her attention. It started faint but quickly grew under her gaze until it forced her eyes shut. Even with her eyes closed, she could see the light, glowing like the sun before her. Silas's grip tightened as Averie fought to separate them. The warmth and glow more than he had ever experienced, hardened his resolve to not let go.

Averie's heart began to race as blood pounded in her ears, her head swimming in the unfamiliar sensations. Her body swayed like an undocked ship in a storm when the first flashes crossed her mind. A distant ringing sounded, its intensity increasing until it became a living creature inside her. Images flashed before her like a slow-moving filmstrip. The images passed by faster and faster until it looked like a movie she didn't want to see, being shown on fast forward. Her breath was shallow and thin. Her head throbbed, and just when she thought she couldn't take it anymore, blissful darkness took her away.

Chapter Fourteen

Thunder roared and lightning slashed the sky with its sharp luster. A murky room was filled with the sound of relentless rain battering against glass while a white-haired man nervously paced its length. His voice muffled as he pulled at his hair, his eyes frantic as glared skyward.

A light breeze swept through the room, sending the already disorganized papers scattering across the floor and halting the man's steps. Hands fisted at his sides; he turned his eyes flashing in anger. "What?" he demanded through clenched teeth.

A woman stood an arm's length away, her hands clasped neatly together at her waist. Her long dark hair was pinned into a neat braid that trailed down her back. With a serene smile covering her delicate features, she appeared otherworldly, dressed in a flowing white gown that billowed behind her as she moved to a perch in a chair. "Marcus, I have come to see why you are upset," she explained, taking the end of her thin scarf between her fingers. "What is it that has created such an uproar among the town and castle?"

Marcus narrowed his eyes and took a menacing step toward the smiling woman. "Do not sit there and pretend you are oblivious to the events transpiring."

The woman sat, a puzzling look crossing her face before it lit up once more in realization. "Oh! You speak of the girl."

"Yes, the *girl*. The girl you claimed was dead. The girl that you have been lying about for years. The girl that you are hoping will destroy everything that I have spent years building!" With each word he spoke, his voice rose, and his steps carried him closer until he was gripping the arms of her chair, a breath away. Their eyes shot daggers at one another.

"Everything you have was stolen!" the woman said sharply. "You are only here because of your betrayal. The bed you lie upon has been sewn together with your lies and deceit. Now, the devil has come to tuck you in."

"You—" A knock sounded, and his ire reached its peak as he swung toward the door. "What!"

"Sir, there has been a summons," the guard called, his voice quaking.

The woman watched curiously as Marcus immediately stiffened, blood slowly seeping from his features as his hands took on a slight tremor. She continued to watch as he clenched his fists in an attempt to still his shaking and relaxed his stance into one of indifference.

"I will be there shortly," he answered firmly.

"Is something frightening you, oh great and powerful ruler?" the woman inquired.

"You will stay here; you will speak to no one, and you will do nothing. When I return, we have matters to speak of." Marcus strode from the room, the door slamming behind him. While he was gone, she was trapped. Left to wander the room in silence, with nothing but her thoughts to keep her company, leaving her to wonder what it was that he was so afraid of.

Marcus stormed down the darkened corridor, trailed by two rather nervous-looking guards, his stomach churning at the knowledge of the summons. He stopped at a dead end and motioned for the guards to turn around before tracing his finger across the stones, bringing forth a glowing collection of symbols. After a moment, the symbols expanded, creating a door made entirely of an eerie light that brought a shiver to the guard's spines.

"Stay here. Let no one pass," Marcus ordered. The guards stood straighter, their hands resting against their swords.

Darkness slammed the door closed with a hiss the moment Marcus stepped through. His cloak smoking as he began his descent down the spiraling staircase. The air, while plush, echoed his steps and harsh breaths. A deep chill crept into him, soaking through his clothes and leeching into his marrow. Suppressing his body's impulse to shiver, he continued his trek into the growing darkness, eyes scanning the old familiar stone until it faded into pure darkness.

The stairs ended, opening into a large circular room. Marcus moved toward its center, as he had countless times before. Stopping in the middle of a small stone circle, he lifted his chin in defiance, straightened his shoulders and waited. Minutes slipped by slowly and with a stillness. He stood rigid in the darkness, not knowing whether it would be minutes more or hours longer before he would be greeted. But his resolution, much like his posture, would not waver.

The air was frigid in the dark; his fingers and toes had long since gone numb as the temperature continued to grow colder. His nose had begun to run as his eyes continued to scan the darkness. A twitch in a darkened corner finally caught his gaze. He released a slow breath and watched the thick tendrils slink through the darkness toward him.

"You're late," Marcus said, flinching as the words were wretched from his mouth and met with a low, vibrating chuckle, rumbling from the passageway. The sound of approaching steps echoed around him, growing closer until he was surrounded and a sick warmth covered his face.

"Tell me how you *really* feel, Marcus."

Marcus cleared his throat and forced himself to his full height. Around him, inky, darker than night, tendrils parted the darkness before him and revealed a shadowed figure.

Marcus, still unwavering, formed a glare. "You summoned me?"

"Tsk, tsk, Marcus. You should never be rude to the carrier of your soul. Have you no manners?"

Grimacing against the whip of words, Marcus tensed as a light began to flow, pulsing to life as it grew larger, from behind the shadowed figure. They were so close, a foot or less separating them. Marcus' stomach clenched as the light revealed dark, snake like coils inching closer to his face. Like fingers, they pressed forward, itching to scratch as they slinked toward him. Forcing his eyes away, he moved to lock his gaze with the hooded figure instead.

"What is this meeting about, Shadow?"

The Shadow's body vibrated from side to side before settling itself against the wall. "She has been found."

Marcus nodded, forcing his thoughts to focus on maintaining the escalation of his rising heart rate as the snake like veins encircled his legs, their touch sending short bursts of electricity through his body.

"She has," Marcus agreed.

"What do you plan to do?" The Shadow asked.

"Nothing." Zap. "She will never step foot into this Realm," Marcus promised.

The Shadow stepped from the wall. "How can you be so sure?" it asked.

"I have a contingency plan in place," Marcus informed with pride swelling in his voice.

"And just what might that be, Marcus?" The Shadow asked, slinking forward as chills overtook Marcus's body.

Denial

"I have an inside man who will be there to pick her apart piece by piece. He will rip the Heart from her body and bring it to me. She will never see it coming."

"And if you fail?" The Shadow asked.

"I will not fail," Marcus affirmed.

The Shadow sighed, swiping a long, black-tipped finger along Marcus's jaw, his body convulsing beneath its touch. "I have given you many gifts."

"As I have you."

The light pulsed harder in anger as The Shadow tilted its head to the side. 'Have you now? Just what would those things be?"

Zap. Zap. Zap. The continued thread of electricity forced Marcus to his knees.

"Even after defying me, I have let you keep your kingdom, the object of your desire, and all the power you could ever control, and yet you stand there and presume to say that you have done the same for me?" The Shadow's voice echoed off the walls, sending tremors throughout the darkened cavern.

Marcus threw his head back in a silent scream as The Shadow squatted before him, an inky tentacle circling his fallen body. "You know our bargain, Marcus. If you fail me in this, I will take everything that I have given you, slice by slice. And when you are nothing but a skin sack, begging for mercy, I will take what is left and devour it whole." With each word, the tentacle slithered its way further up Marcus' body before plunging into his mouth.

The darkness descended once more as he collapsed to the floor, sweat covering his convulsing body.

"I'll be waiting for you, Marcus. Don't fail me."

Chapter Fifteen

Averie couldn't sleep that night, her mind raced with the weight of everything she had seen. Even at the late hour that she had crawled back into her bed, her body exhausted, sleep had still been far from her reach. Her mind was awake, alive and buzzing with things she had only ever read about or seen on television. It had only taken her two hours before she had finally given up, crawled free from the warmth of her bed to shower and ready herself for the day.

She walked to the kitchen with her hair pulled into a high ponytail, dressed in her signature hunter green tee, paired with her favorite black jacket, jeans, and Converse. The comfort of the favorite clothes gave her a sense of normalcy that she currently lacked.

Averie filled her favorite cup with the steaming coffee and sat heavily at the breakfast bar. Absentmindedly, she ran her finger down the center of her smooth palm. Silas had been telling the truth about it healing, though he hadn't mentioned the thin golden line that would take its place. Her mind replayed the night over and over again in her mind, like a song you couldn't escape. Sipping the brew, she flipped the small kitchen television on in hope of distracting herself.

"*Police are asking for anyone with information on the incident to please contact the police immediately.*"

Averie looked from the well-dressed reporter to the small image they were showing in the top right corner. A blurred image of a boy about her age, with mussed jet-black hair and glowing red eyes, looked back at her.

"*The suspect is wanted for questioning regarding a variety of fires that have been happening across the county. Officials are also asking that if you see him, to not approach but to call the police immediately, as he may be armed and is considered dangerous.*"

The reporter droned on, but all Averie could see was the boy with the glowing eyes. In the picture, he appeared to be running from something or someone. The remorseful expression he wore twisted her heart. For some unforeseen reason, Averie felt sorry for him.

The world was changing as daily reports of the police searching for 'suspects' in connection with a variety of strange crimes. They were slow to come at first, the police looking for a man responsible for totaling someone's car when he walked out into oncoming traffic. Only the car

Denial

hadn't been totaled because it had swerved to miss the man but had actually collided with him. This story was quickly discredited days later, and the man was never seen or heard from again. Conspiracy theorists were thriving as similar stories began popping up all across the world.

One day would start with a story claiming a young girl had electrocuted her foster parents by touching them, then was later explained away by saying she had hidden a supercharged taser in her sleeve before attacking them. Others were not quite as easy for the public to ignore, like when a woman walked into the middle of Times Square and water started shooting from fire hydrants after they exploded one by one. Sure, the media and police had tried to say that she was just a sick woman who had taken advantage of a malfunction at the water plant, but did anyone really believe that? Then, just as the world hit the point of hysteria, the news would instantly shift to an overdosed rapper or new celebrity couple, and it was as if the world was pacified once more, forgetting all the strange events.

Averie's mind wandered back to the time when she had first noticed there was something different about her, the time that Silas had first spoken of. She was sixteen when she was awakened in the early hours by a pain unlike any other. It felt as though molten iron had been poured into her chest and hardened around her heart. She had twisted and flailed on her bed, fighting to get away from the pain with no hope of escape. Her flailing had thrown her from her bed. The sheets had twisted around her ankles, tripping her and causing her head to slam against the ground.

Averie struggled to breathe, scream, and shout, but to no avail.

She wasn't sure how much time had passed, seconds or hours, of her rolling into herself, a silent scream on her lips, but just as suddenly as it had arrived, it disappeared. Her breath had caught in her chest, her body prepared for the next assault. When it never came, she had finally started to breathe again. Slow at first, short, strangled wisps of air in and out of her bruised lungs. Sweat had coated her skin in a cool, sickening film.

The sun had started to rise before she was able to make it to her feet. Her legs shook beneath her weight. Using the wall to steady herself, she slowly crept her way to the small adjoining bathroom.

Resting her hands against the cool sink, she had tried to slow her racing heart. *What the hell was that?* If the soreness in her body hadn't still been pulsing through her, she could almost have believed it had all been a terrible dream. She shook her head as she glimpsed her reflection in the mirror.

A gasp ripped from her trembling lips as she fell back against the wall.

Averie had blinked in stunned silence, then forced herself slowly to her feet, her breath stopping altogether at the golden orbs staring back. Her eyes fluttered in a fury of blinks, tears starting to fill her eyes. "No, God, please no. No, no, no," she whispered.

Pushing from the sink, she bit back the impending sob in favor of turning the shower on. She had stripped off

Denial

her clothes, her mind racing as it replayed the news stories she had seen, the theories she had been told and wondered what it meant for her. Was she one of those freak stories from the news? Should she go to her mother? Thane? What would they do? What could they possibly say to make it all better? Averie had quickly resigned herself to keeping the secret to herself. She didn't know what it meant, but she knew it would bring nothing but trouble to the people she loved.

After her decision of secrecy, she climbed into the shower, sat herself down, and hugged her knees to her chest. Several moments had passed before she had realized the water hadn't reached her quivering form. Steam filled the room around her as she stared deftly at the falling spray, a wavering orb flowing from her, serving as a shield against the water.

Before allowing the panic to take complete hold, she had drifted to every television show, movie, and comic book she had ever seen. They all had one thing in common: the only way to keep control was to remain calm. This may all be a dream, but for now, until she awoke, she needed to handle this situation. She forced herself to take three deep breaths. *One*, holy shit, *two*, this is insane, *three*, I can't do this. With each exhale, the tension released a little more until the water freckled her skin before raining down completely.

Her world had changed that night, not just because she had turned sixteen, not just because she had woken up to some insane body-melting pain that she still couldn't explain but because in that moment she knew without a doubt, she was different. In one moment, she had gone from being the typical sixteen-year-old girl, obsessed with boys and shopping, to a girl that needed to be hidden in the shadows, someone living a life of lies.

So much had changed since that night. She had forced herself to give up her possible gifts, to focus on protecting herself, her mother, and those that she loved most. She threw herself into schoolwork, kickboxing, yoga, and meditation. School helped her maintain a feeling of normalcy, while kickboxing helped with the ever-growing aggression she was feeling, and the yoga and meditation helped keep her calm and focused.

Shaking the unnecessary thoughts from her mind, Averie shook away the dark turn her thoughts were taking, sipped her coffee and flipped through the channels. The reporter switched from the suspected arsonist to a fluff story about the upcoming fair. The piece droned on until she had drank the last of her coffee before rising to refill it. Today was going to suck.

"Good morning, Averie," her mother greeted with her typical cheery smile as she entered the kitchen, the morning paper under her arm. Averie smiled back, handing her mother a fresh cup of the morning brew. "Thank you, honey," she said, moving to her usual seat across from Averie.

Averie found herself inspecting her mother as she sat back down. Karen was an average woman in every way. She was average in every way, height and weight. She had average brown hair and normal brown eyes that never lit up for any other reason than happiness. She had an average home and an average job, and yet as Averie continued to watch her move, her mind began to wonder, was she really just this perfectly normal person?

Karen looked up with her brow drawn together in amusement. "Is everything alright?"

"Yeah, sorry. I didn't get much sleep last night," Averie answered, running her finger around the cup rim.

"Mmm, well you're up unusually early, even for you." Karen inspected Averie while sipping from her steaming cup. "Is something on your mind?"

"Do you think I'm weird?" Averie asked.

Karen frowned. "Of course not! Why would you even ask something like that?"

Averie shrugged. "No reason."

"Is this about that boy?" Karen asked, grinning.

"What boy?" Thane interjected as he walked into the room, yawning loudly.

"No one," Averie quipped while her mother simultaneously said, "Silas."

Thane turned his sleep-mussed head to look at Averie. "I thought you weren't interested in him."

"I'm not," Averie defended.

"Yes, well, I have to get ready for work. You two make sure that you make it to school on time, please." Karen excused herself, giving Averie a knowing look before slipping from the room.

Averie chanced a glance in Thane's direction and found him glaring back as he leaned against the counter, with his arms and legs crossed. "What?" She asked, sipping from her now-chilled cup with a grimace.

"You know what," he shot back.

"I can assure you, that I don't."

Averie moved to the sink and dumped the chilled coffee down the drain. She watched the water swirl and mix with the emptied contents as she took her time to rinse and place the cup in the strainer, before finally turning to him.

"Fox, please don't do this," Thane begged.

"Do what? What are you talking about?" she demanded.

"You are shutting me out. You never shut me out, not unless you're doing something I wouldn't approve of."

"I'm not shutting you out," Averie promised.

"What happened last night?" Thane asked.

"Nothing. We just talked."

Thane sighed as he pushed away from the counter. "If you say so."

"Thane, wait," Averie called, following him from the kitchen.

Thane ignored her plea, swinging his door open and climbing the stairs. Averie jumped, narrowly catching the door before it slammed against the wall, and closed it behind her.

"Will you talk to me, please?" Averie asked, taking a seat on his already made bed. For a teenage boy, Thane tended to be excessively tidy. There were never clothes on his floor, his bed unmade, or dust anywhere to be seen. His deodorant, cologne, and gel sat on the far right side of his black dresser, with their labels all facing out. His clothes were hung neatly, color-coded, in his closet with his six pairs of shoes lined perfectly beneath.

Averie watched him tap his fingers against the hangers before pulling a plain navy tee shirt and white-washed jeans from the closet, and carefully laid them over his computer chair. Maintaining his silence, he bent down and withdrew a matching pair of blue shoes and placed them to the right of the chair.

"Is that a no?" Averie asked again.

"Look, I'm trying really hard here not to judge you, but what you did last night. It was dangerous," Thane said, looking over at her. "You don't know him, and if anything had happened …" He shook his head, his words trailing away.

"Thane, you know better than anyone that I know how to defend myself, you trained me. I still go every week with you."

"He's still a man, Averie! He can easily overpower you, then what?"

Averie flinched at his use of her name. He never called her Averie unless he was upset with her, which seemed to be happening a lot lately, but there were still parts of herself she wasn't ready to share. Not even with him. Averie sat in silence as she struggled for words. "I'm sorry," she whispered. "I didn't mean to worry you."

"Don't apologize. Just be smart, okay?" Thane pleaded.

"I will," Averie promised.

Chapter Sixteen

Silas hadn't shown to bring her to school, and after three unanswered texts, Averie decided to stop waiting around like a girl obsessed, swallowed her pride, and went inside to find Thane. He stood leaning against the same counter; his mouth full of colored cereal with milk running down his chin.

Averie looked on, disgusted. "You know, for such a neat freak; you eat like an animal."

Thane wiped his chin with a towel before shoveling another bite into his mouth. "Can I help you with something, or are you just here to insult me?"

Averie shifted her stance, then sighed. "Can you drive me to school, please? Mom won't let me after yesterday, and Silas was supposed to pick me up, but he hasn't shown or texted me back."

Thane's spoon halted in the air. "He's ignoring you?"

A slight shrug was her only answer.

"What a dick," Thane growled, disposing his bowl, then swinging the bag over his shoulder, he nodded to the door. "Let's go."

As Thane pulled up to the school, Averie's heart did a little flip as she scanned the parking lot. To Averie's shock, Silas wasn't there. It wasn't as though they had made any plans to meet, but Averie had just assumed that after what had been done, he might have wanted to check on her, especially after not showing up this morning. Swallowing back her disappointment, she climbed from the car and took a deep breath. As she stood in the cool breeze, the warmth of an arm spread across her shoulders. Thane smiled down at her, squeezing her tightly.

"He's an ass, Fox. You don't need him."

"Yeah, you're right. I've already forgotten all about him." She smiled.

Averie lied. He wasn't forgotten, not even close. The moment she and Thane had separated for their first block, she searched the halls, even stopping to walk past his locker twice. Every door that opened had her head snapping up to look to see if it was him. Her heart jumped every time someone said her name or brushed against her in the hallway.

Averie sat silently, picking at her lunch. The buzz of Sera rambling about her ideas for prom was white noise compared to the heat of Thane's stare. After walking three blocks with a crushed look, Thane had tried to talk to her, asking her over and over again if she was alright. Apparently, her fake smile came across as more fake and less smile to him.

Averie shook herself; she was being ridiculous. She was better than this, better than him. She sat up straight and gave Thane a genuine smile. It didn't matter that Silas wasn't here, or that she felt a little used, or even that she was genuinely hurt that he hadn't even bothered to reply to a single text. She decided she would be fine if she never saw him again, it would surely make things less complicated.

"So what do you think, Avi?" Lucas asked shyly.

"I'm sorry, what?" Averie asked, blinking her thoughts away.

"Haven't you been listening at all?" Sera groaned.

"Sorry, I didn't get much sleep last night," Averie hurried to explain.

Thane grunted, shoving the rest of his burger into his mouth.

"Oh, well, ah … I was wondering if you still wanted to go to prom together. I know we aren't together right now, but we already made most of the plans last month. I understand if you don't want to," Lucas said, tapping his fingers nervously against the table.

"Yeah, sure. I don't see why not," Averie answered, with what she hoped was an excited smile.

"Great!" Lucas beamed. "What about you, Thane?" he asked, elbowing Thane's ribs. "Any dates lined up?"

"Nope, I'm going stag," Thane said through a still half-full mouth. "I'll have more options that way."

"Gross. You are despicable, Thane Matthias," Sera sneered.

Thane smiled, winking. "You love me," he said, blowing a kiss.

Sera rolled her eyes, suppressing a smile. "Not even for a day."

"Hello. Sorry. I'm late." Silas smiled as he walked up to the table and took the empty seat beside Thane. Averie's prior bravado quickly dissipated as his voice slid across her skin.

"Hey, man, you okay?" Thane asked, turning to get a better view of Silas's face.

Averie looked across the table, immediately noticing why Thane had asked if Silas was okay. His hair was disheveled, and his eyes held dark circles underneath them, but the most alarming was the fresh cut that stretched across his cheek. His clothes were covered in what looked to be dirt, and at the moment, he was refusing to look anywhere close to Averie. Instead, he smiled and nodded his head. "Absolutely."

"Do you know you're bleeding?" Sera asked, tapping her cheek.

Silas's brow pinched together slightly as he lifted his hand to his face. He pulled back, slightly surprised at the red on his fingertips. "Well, would you look at that?"

Denial

Thane handed his napkin over to Silas, watching him carefully. "You look like you were in a fight."

Silas shrugged his shoulders, placing the napkin against his face. "Oh, well, I was helping Armand move some stuff around this morning."

"Who's Armand?" Sera asked, curious.

"He's my, ah, uncle. Him and his wife Cleo are my guardians," Silas explained slowly, as if testing the lie as it spilled from his lips. Averie's gaze narrowed, but no one else seemed to catch the blatant untruth.

"Why? Don't your parents want you anymore?" Lucas asked, his anger still present.

"They're dead," Silas answered smoothly.

Averie's eyes widened while everyone else's gaze shifted to Lucas, who shrank back into his seat. "Sorry, man."

"Not a problem," Silas soothed.

To say the remainder of lunch was anything but tense, awkward, and silent would be like saying the sun was anything but a bright, hot fireball ready to explode and destroy all existence. While Averie tried to catch Silas's eye, he did nearly everything possible to avoid her, going as far as turning so his back rested against the table while he gazed at the masses.

When the bell rang, ending their lunch period, Averie decided to take on her previous thought process. It didn't matter if Silas didn't want to see, look at, or even talk to her; it wasn't her problem. Anything that had been said, done, or seen last night didn't matter. Maybe it was all fake anyway. Sure, she hadn't figured out how he could have pulled the whole thing off, but that was what made magicians so great. Maybe that's all it was, just a street magician playing around.

As the teacher rambled on about … Well, Averie wasn't really sure what exactly she was saying. Instead, she was consumed once more with the events of last night as she stared down at the thin golden line that ran down her palm. She trailed the tip of her finger up and down the line, her mind replaying every second over, trying to pinpoint what had happened to make Silas act this way.

* * *

"Averie, Averie."

Averie was in a blissful state of in-between. That sweet place that you find yourself in just before you fall asleep or as you wake up. Completely comfortable, relaxed, and content, as if your body is flowing on a gently rocking sea. The sound of her name broke through her content state, and, however pleasant that voice may be, was rather like having your alarm go off on a Monday morning. Though you knew you needed to get up to shut it off, you would really prefer it just shut itself off and left you alone.

"Averie, come on, wake up, open your eyes," the voice called again. Averie felt herself sigh as her eyes fluttered open. It was a strange feeling to awaken in complete darkness. Averie frowned in confusion as she forced herself to blink, wondering if she was truly awake. Gradually, the small fuzzy lights glittered in the distance,

Denial

outlining a large shadowed figure leaning over her. Jerking herself back, she groaned as her head smacked against the hard ground with a resounding thud.

Averie watched the shadow hold its hands up in surrender. "Calm down. It's just me, Silas. I'm going to turn this light on, so don't freak out."

The light started low before growing brighter as she sat herself up. "What happened?" she asked, holding her head, hoping to stop her brain from rocking within her skull.

Silas knelt before her, the light illuminating his features and enhancing the worried frown on his face. "Honestly? I'm not quite sure. I've done this a couple of times before and never had anyone pass out," Silas answered, his eyes roaming her face.

"You mean ... you have mixed blood with other complete strangers?" Averie squeaked out.

"Of course, it's the only way to communicate important information during times of traitors lurking in our midst. Although I must admit we don't usually use daggers like this," Silas answered, wagging the blade through the air. "How do you feel? Do you remember any of what you saw?"

Though she hated admitting it, she did. The entire experience made her feel crazy, and for a moment, she almost entertained the thought. Then she remembered that so much seemed different about her, that this was just another piece to add to the ever-growing puzzle.

"Why was part of the story distorted?" Averie asked.

"What you saw were pieces from me. Things I thought you needed to see to understand. That is how this works. I can only show you what I have seen or done," Silas explained. "What did you see?"

Averie's brow furrowed as she remembered the first flash. "There was a dark-haired woman sitting in front of a fire, telling the story of how the Realm fell. She was crying."

"That was my mother," Silas whispered.

"Why was she crying?" Averie asked.

Silas hesitated. "When the Realm was divided, it wasn't smooth or clean. Families were ripped apart and sent across the galaxy. It was sudden, completely unexpected, and horrifying. Many people were lost that day, both to death and to the split. My father ... he was one of them."

"I'm so sorry," Averie whispered, taking his hand into her own.

Silas smiled a half-smile through his remembered grief. "What else?"

Averie's stomach twisted violently as a metallic smell tickled her nose. Turning sideways, she leaned over, fighting the urge to vomit as bile burned her throat.

"Averie! Are you alright? What's wrong?" Silas asked, his hands on her shoulders.

"There was so much blood. It was everywhere. I could taste it in the air," Averie explained.

"We are at war."

"There was a man. He was moving things, throwing them without even touching them." Averie's eyes widened at the memory of the tall, terrifyingly large man. His eyes glowed silver as he attacked without mercy. His movements were fluid like water, but as sharp and precise as a blade in a master's hand.

"That's Callen. He is our greatest fighter, aside from me of course," Silas bragged.

"He has ... abilities?"

Denial

Silas nodded. "As I said, more people are born with magic than without it in our Realm. Only most don't know who or what their ability is until their sixteenth year. It used to be a happy time, but with Marcus, people take their children, choosing to run before they age up."

"Why?" Averie asked.

Darkness shadowed Silas's face, and his jaw ticked with emotion. "If anyone is found to have an ability that could harm Marcus, or be used as a tool to harm him, it is stripped from their body and locked away. But your power, your ability, is a part of who you are. Most don't survive without it, and the ones that do ..." Silas shook his head.

Averie considered his words. She couldn't imagine doing something so cruel to anyone. "What exactly is Callen's ability?"

"He can move anything made from the Realm. He's one of the strongest people that have been born in generations," Silas answered, beaming with pride for his friend.

"Where is he now?"

"He leads the rebellion while I am here with you." Silas smiled.

Averie swallowed thickly. "Right, so um, what happens now?"

"Well, do you believe what you saw?"

"It's um, it's kind of hard not to. I mean, you used a magical dagger to cut me, we mixed blood, I saw hundreds of weird things that will take me years to sort out." Averie paused, licking her dry lips, and gave an apologetic smile. "I think I owe you an apology for calling you crazy."

"It's understandable. The longer I'm in this Realm, the more I understand why you believe what you do. Here, magic and differences

have been condemned and persecuted since the separation. Hiding your ability makes you feel safe."

"Though, I do have a question."

"Of course."

"This thing, the Heart, my birth mother put inside me, is that why I have been having such pain?" Averie asked, rubbing her hand against her chest.

"I am not sure how to answer that. It is part of the story that my mother used to tell, but there isn't really a way to say if it actually happened. However, if it did, it would make sense. The Heart was created to keep the Realm together as a whole, and since they are not, it only makes sense that it would try to pull the pieces together," Silas offered.

"Is there anyone else like me?" Averie questioned after a long silence.

Silas shook his head. "You are one of a kind. In a world full of magic, you are something truly special."

"So even in your Realm I'm a fr—" Averie closed her eyes against the word.

"No, never, Averie. You are the most important person in any of the Realms. You are the only person that has the power to fix everything. So I guess my only question is, are you brave enough to do it?"

Chapter Seventeen

The sound of the bell rang out, snapping Averie from her thoughts with a jerk that sent her books tumbling off of her desk. With a groan of resignation, Averie slid from her desk and onto the floor with more than a few choice curses slipping quietly from her lips.

"At least they didn't open," Silas noticed.

Averie spared him a brief glance before she turned back to collecting her dropped belongings, thankful that they'd indeed remained intact. She didn't have the patience for collecting sprawled papers. "So now you want to talk to me?"

"What makes you think I didn't before?" Silas asked, gathering scattered pens.

"You've ignored me all day," Averie pointed out.

"When did I ever say that I was?"

"It isn't about what you say, but what you do, Silas. You ditched me this morning, didn't answer any of my texts, showed up late, and have ignored me ever since," Averie pointed out, taking the pens with a snap from his hands.

Silas reached under the desk and collected her psychology binder as he considered his next words. "I am sorry if I made you think I didn't want to talk to you. That was never my intention."

"I don't need your help," Averie mumbled, snatching the binder from his hands.

"Averie, please. I didn't mean to upset you," Silas explained.

Averie looked at him and laughed. "What the hell did you think was going to happen after you blatantly ignored me?" she asked sarcastically. "Am I supposed to smile and bat my eyelashes and thank you for giving me your time?" Satisfied that all her belongings resided again in her bag, Averie flipped the bag shut, threw it over her shoulder and turned away.

Silas grabbed her arm and turned her toward him. "I want to talk to you."

Averie smiled sweetly. "Really?"

"Yes." He smiled in relief.

"Damn, 'cause I really don't want to talk to you." Ripping her arm away from his grasp, she stormed from the classroom to head down toward the front of the school.

"Averie—" A hand on Silas's shoulder stopped him.

Denial

"Just leave her alone. Trust me, you don't want to mess with her when she is angry," Thane offered.

"But she's not angry with me," Silas explained.

Thane's eyes widened. "Are you kidding me? Yes, bro, she is."

"I don't understand. I didn't do anything wrong. How do you know?" Silas asked Thane for his wisdom.

"Because I know Averie, and I haven't seen her this mad in a long time. I actually feel sorry for you," Thane admitted, running a hand through his hair.

"When was the last time she was this mad, as you say?"

Thane clenched his jaw, looking back at the door. "When we were in middle school, I did something I shouldn't have to her."

"What did you do? Why did she get so angry over it?"

"I lied to her," said Thane, his eyes falling to the floor, pausing for a brief moment, before looking back, giving Silas a blank stare.

"That's it?" Silas asked. "I understand being upset when someone lies, but this reaction seems … excessive. What was the lie?"

Thane shook his head. "Not important. What is important is that Averie can't stand lies. After Karen told her she was adopted, it became her thing. She rarely lies herself, and on top of that, we made a promise to never lie to each other, and Evie takes promises seriously. My lie ended up causing a lot of problems, and she was really hurt."

"You hurt her?" Silas asked in surprise.

"Everyone makes mistakes. It was a long time ago, but yeah. I didn't mean to, but I was young and stupid, and I didn't realize what I was doing. I was trying to get someone's attention and ended up hurting Averie in the process. It took a while, but she finally forgave me, and we have been inseparable ever since." Thane sighed and lead the way from the empty classroom. "Look, whatever you did, just apologize, *really* apologize, and move on."

Silas ran his hands down his face and gave a whole-body sigh. "You don't understand. It's not that easy."

"It can be. You just have to make that choice."

Silas stopped in the middle of the hallway, an epiphany lighting his features, while students grumbled, forced to move around him. "You're right, thank you." Silas turned and pushed through the crowded hallway.

"Si, where are you going? We have class!" Thane called after him. He was answered with nothing but the sound of a bell. He sighed. "Good luck, dude."

Silas pushed through groups of talking girls and laughing jocks as he made his way to the stairwell. He ignored the flirty smiles, fist bumps, and high fives, letting their stares and confused expressions fade into the background as he continued his search.

Running down the stairs as fast as he could, Silas was forced to restrain the urge to shove the slow movers out of the way. The bell sounded again as he stepped out of the stairwell. The already crowded hallways overflowed with rushing students and endless chatter. Just as he began to

Denial

doubt whether he would be able to find her, he spotted the flash of her dark red hair.

Averie was angry. She knew that she felt hurt and something akin to betrayal at Silas's cold shoulder, but what she didn't understand was why she couldn't seem to calm herself down. A chill prickled her skin as she thought of Silas. How could he do this to her? What had she done wrong? Had she completely missed something? Misread the situation? How was it that she had only known him for a day and a half and he had already managed to piss her off so badly?

Shaking off her guilt, she kept up her speed, attempting to clear her mind, when she felt the first pulse run through her. It was like touching a nine-volt battery to your tongue, the initial shock of energy shook her body before fading away, leaving a tingling feeling in its wake.

"Oh, no," she whispered, squeezing her eyes shut. *Breathe, Averie, just breathe.* She had done so well for so long, so why was this happening now? Averie's stomach rolled as if she were on a roller coaster climbing to the top, butterflies jumping inside as she prepared for the descent.

"Averie!"

Averie jerked at the sound of her name, her mouth opening as she hissed through her teeth. She felt like she was fighting a losing battle over her own control when her eyes collided with Silas's. Silas stopped momentarily, frozen in place by the sight before him, as blood rushed to his ears. Averie stood in the nearly empty hallway, panic covering her face, her hands shaking, and her eyes glowing with a golden hue.

Chapter Eighteen

"Averie," Silas breathed, the tremble in her lip sending him into action. With reckless abandon, he shoved people out of the way until he was at her side.

"Silas, I don't know what's happening." Averie's voice shook as she looked up to him for answers.

"It's fine. You're going to be fine. But we have to get out of here. Okay? Come on." Silas gave a reassuring smile, threw an arm around her shoulders and pulled her tightly against his side.

"I can't stop it," Averie's voice quivered with desperation and panic.

"Okay, Averie, I need you to listen to me very carefully, okay?" Silas soothed, his hands running up and down her arms as he wove them through the crowd. His face was carefully blank as his mind struggled to find a safe place nearby they could make it to.

Averie nodded against his chest, clutching her trembling hands tightly.

"I need to know what your primary ability is," Silas whispered.

"I-I don't know what that means," Averie admitted.

"What element acts the strangest when this kind of thing happens?" he whispered.

"Water."

"Where is the closest body?"

"Um, there is a small lake around the back of the school."

"Okay, hold on. Focus on breathing, Averie. In and out," Silas soothed, mimicking the action, as if coaching someone giving birth. Silas hastened his step, as he navigated them through the school and out the back door. He smiled at a few of the teachers that had passed them with curious looks, slightly surprised that they hadn't tried to stop them, and ignored the students who had already started to point and whisper as they passed.

Finally, they reached the end of the hall. Silas kicked the door open, slamming it against the brick outside, and hustled the pair out into the open lot. They rounded a small grouping of trees that nestled against the banks of the lake. Silas scanned the area, making sure there wasn't anyone following them or lurking in the darkness, before lowering Averie to the ground.

Denial

Taking her hands in his own, Silas struggled to get her to release her hold. "You need to put your hands in the water, Averie," Silas explained.

"Why?" she gasped, the static burning along her skin as it tried to escape.

"You have to let the energy out, if you don't ..." He stopped himself, regarding the desperation on her face.

It took moments for Averie to gather the strength to plunge her hands into the calm blue water. The relief was instant, the cool water seeming to pull the burning out of her. The relief, however, was only momentary before her body started to vibrate, the static becoming sharp and more incessant, the sting of tiny blades dancing up and down her arms. She couldn't have stopped the scream even if she had tried. Her scream echoed as she jerked against the assault, her hands melded into the rippling depths. The cool blue liquid melted into a shimmering gold glow that spread from her hands and stretched across the lake like ink falling into a cup of water. The ground beneath the pair started to quake as trees groaned in despair and a growing wind battered them.

Silas marveled in amazement and disbelief. He had seen many things in his time and in his Realm, but nothing like this, never like this. This was a magic that was beyond magic, and it was in a Realm void of it. The glow from Averie burst like tentacles out of her hands, crossing the lake before splitting through the tree on the other side. The water rose and fell, crashing against the shore in its torrent, throwing fish and rocks in every direction. The shaking intensified, the surrounding trees cracked in submission. Silas was forced to his knees, gripping the trembling ground for support as the wind ripped at his body.

Then, just as quickly as it had all started, it stopped. Averie slumped back against her heels, her hands hanging loosely at her sides and head falling forward. The wind slowed to a welcoming breeze, and the ground went still. The air around them emptied until the only noise was the whisper of the water slapping the shore and the occasional snap of broken branches falling from the trees.

Silas's heart slammed against his ribs as his breath came out in short, uneven puffs. He looked up to Averie in a combination of wonder and horror. She slowly started blinking, the gold fading from her eyes as she did.

"Are you okay?" Silas asked.

Averie nodded, visibly swallowing. "What's happening to me?"

"I don't know. I've never seen anything like that before. Have you ever…?"

"No, I've never felt like that before," Averie answered, her voice wobbling slightly.

"Have you ever lost control like that?" Silas asked gently.

Averie shook her head. "Never. It was always easy. After a few deep breaths, I was fine. But this time, it was different. It felt like I was going to explode."

The sound of a siren split the air. Averie and Silas exchanged a nervous glance before turning to the school. "It's the earthquake alarm," Averie whispered.

Denial

"Come on, we need to go." Silas rose to his feet, still reeling from the experience, and held his hand out.

"Where are we going?" Averie asked, taking his offered help.

"My house. We need to start your training now, before something like this happens again."

Averie followed in silence as they crept their way back around the school, before making a run for the parking lot. Averie watched as students filed out in neat lines while the teachers hollered over the siren, giving instructions. As they made their way down the stairs, Averie caught a glimpse of Thane, Sera, and Lucas standing together in a group. As if sensing her presence, Thane turned and gave a questioning look. Shaking her head, she turned away and climbed into Silas's car.

The car ride started off uncomfortably quiet, with Silas occasionally glancing over at her. "I think we need to consider the possibility that the stories are true. I think you have the Realm's Heart inside you, Averie."

"What does that mean?" she asked nervously.

"It means when we—what I showed you last night must have unlocked whatever seal your birth mother placed on it. I'm not an expert on this. I know someone who is, but from what I've heard it means you could have more abilities than anyone could imagine."

"So, what do we do?"

Silas shrugged, pulling onto his street. "We start today and hope it's enough. All we can do is try to figure this out together."

C.R. Rice

Chapter Nineteen

Averie lay on her bed, staring up at the ceiling as her mind played through the changes her life had undergone. It had been almost two weeks since she had started to sneak around behind everyone's backs, using one lie after another to cover her random and unlikely actions. Averie had never been much of a liar, favoring the painful truth over a helpful lie since the day she found out she was adopted. *It is to protect them. To keep them off of Marcus's radar.* Even as her mind whispered the thought, she knew she was lying once again, only this time it was to herself. It was one thing to believe in what she had seen and what she could do, it was another to blindly believe in some crazy story that sounded like it should be written in some fantasy novel and not lived in real life.

Sighing, Averie threw her arm over her eyes as the tap came at her door. "Come in," she called back.

Karen opened the door with a soft smile. "I just wanted to come in and say goodnight."

Averie peaked through her arm. "Goodnight."

Averie heard her mother's exhale as the bed dipped under her weight. "Averie, honey, is everything alright?"

"Of course. Why wouldn't it be?" Averie asked, slipping her arm behind her head.

Karen shrugged, pulling the blanket to cover Averie's chest. Averie smiled at the motion, remembering the countless times her mother had tucked her in over the years. "Thane said you haven't been to your kickboxing class in over a week."

"I've been busy," Averie deflected.

She watched her mom's rise and fall with a heavy sigh, her shoulders sagging under the weight of the world. "Is everything alright, Mom?"

Karen forced a smile and gave a small nod. "Yes, of course, honey. I just worry about you and Thane. I don't remember the last time you two spent so much time apart. You seem so distant with each other."

"We are apart all the time."

"In some ways, yes, but ever since the day I brought Thane into our home, you two have always been in your own little world. Even when he tried to get you to leave him alone, you were always there, his little Fox." Karen laughed softly. "You love and defend and take care of each

Denial

other in a way I have never seen before. I just worry when you guys seem to be growing apart."

Averie took her mother's cool hands in her warmer ones. "You don't have to worry. Thane and I will be fine. We're just growing up."

Karen frowned. "A mother's worry never goes away, Averie, no matter how old your babies get. Plus, just because you grow up, doesn't mean you grow apart. Goodnight, honey." With one last squeeze of Averie's hand, she stood and kissed her forehead.

"Goodnight, Mom."

As the clock ticked by the minutes one by one, Averie thought over her mother's words. Was she growing apart from Thane? Did he feel it, too? The echoing silence of her mother's television being shut off pulled Averie from her pondering. Crawling out of her bed, Averie grabbed her jacket and slid it over her arms. Her feet were silent across the carpet as she pushed open her window and slipped through, easily maneuvering to the nearby roof overhang.

She remembered back to just a couple of weeks ago and how careful she was. The same sneaky actions were now like second nature. Careful to keep her balance, Averie stayed low, moving quickly across the shingles to the overhanging tree and climbed down. With a premature, self-satisfied smile covering her face, she turned away, slipping on the dew-covered ground and hitting the side of the house.

Averie flinched and squeezed her eyes tightly, holding her breath. One, two, three, four, five. Silence. Exhaling her pent-up breath, she opened her eyes and steadied herself before daring to step away from the house. A squeal escaped her throat before she could clamp her lips shut, her heart thumping heavily against her chest as blood rushed in her ears. She watched in horror as a towering shadow rose from the ground and stepped into the moonlight.

"Thane?! What the hell's wrong with you?" She gasped, her hand clutching her panting chest. "You almost gave me a heart attack. What are you doing out here?"

"What am I doing? What are *you* doing, Averie?" Thane demanded, his arms crossing over his chest.

"I'm going for a walk," Averie claimed, unable to maintain eye contact as she picked at the hem of her sleeve.

"You're going for a walk?" Thane repeated.

"Yeah, Thane, a walk," Averie defended.

"Since when does going for a walk require sneaking out of your window? What the hell is wrong with you?" Thane asked.

"What do you mean?"

"What I mean is that ever since you met Silas, you've been acting like a completely different person! You sneak out every night, doing God only knows what. You barely talk to Sera or Mom anymore. You ignore me. You've been skipping kickboxing and barely functioning during school.

So, I am asking you again, what are you doing? Are you on drugs?"

Averie stood open-mouthed in shock before shaking her head. "Jesus, Thane, no, I'm not on drugs. How could you even think that?" she demanded.

Thane threw his arms out in exasperation. "What else am I supposed to think, Averie? You have barely spoken two words to anyone except Silas in weeks."

"I'm not ignoring anyone. I've been busy, Thane."

"Doing what? What's so important that you are cutting everyone out of your life?"

Averie stood silent.

Thane released a humorless laugh and ran his hands through his hair. "When did we start lying to each other, Fox?" he whispered. "We made each other a promise."

Averie flinched at the pain in his voice. "Thane—"

"No, Averie." Thane sighed. "I hope whatever he does for you is worth it." Thane turned away, stepping toward the back door.

"Thane, wait," Averie begged. "Please."

"Wait for what, Averie? What could you possibly say that's worth listening to? Because it sure as hell won't be the truth."

"Just give me a chance to explain." Averie watched Thane struggle with himself. "Will you just meet me tomorrow? At our usual place, right after school?"

Thane held his silence, his eyes piercing as they roamed her face before finally giving a slight nod before he turned and entered the house. Averie swallowed back a sob as she stared at the empty doorway. Forcing herself away, she sent a silent prayer to the night sky before stepping into a jog. She would make it up to Thane tomorrow, but tonight she had bigger things to worry about. They were running out of time.

Her feet were silent yet steadfast against the plushness of the fresh spring grass. Sidestepping various fallen tree limbs and roots, Averie ventured farther down the darkened path, her body moving on autopilot as her mind struggled against Thane's words, with her mother's quick on their heels. Had she really been hurting those around her without realizing it? She pushed herself faster, harder, determined to get away from her thoughts.

"You're late," Silas snapped, standing with his hands on his hips, as she broke into the clearing.

Averie slowed to a walk. "Yeah, and you're an ass," Averie retorted, shoving by him to move farther into the field. The ground was stained with the evidence of their training. Craters and scorched grass peppered the ground, leaving only a single, large wooden trunk untouched at its center.

"And just what have I done to deserve such endearing words?" Silas called.

Averie shook her head, shaking out her hands and twisting her neck one way and then the other. "Thane is upset with me."

"Why?" Silas asked, moving opposite of her.

Denial

"Oh, I don't know, Si, maybe because I have been lying to literally everyone in my life and ignoring them because I've spent every waking moment with *you*."

"So this is my fault?" Silas scoffed.

"Yes, actually, it is! Everything was fine before you got here."

"Maybe for you it was, but I can promise you everything was not and is still not fine where I'm from. Though you may have been able to contain yourself for a while, eventually you would have broken. You saw what happened at the lake. It was only a matter of time before that happened. I just sped it up some."

Averie hung her head in defeat. "I know, and I'm sorry, but I'm doing everything I possibly can to help them."

"I know," Silas said as he knelt on the damp ground and shoved the grass covering away to reveal a large wooden chest. Silas lifted the lid, releasing a loud creak, then peered into the assortment of various weapons tucked inside. He ran his hand over a few of them before withdrawing two long, glittering blades. He tossed one to Averie and held up the other in front of his face.

"I am telling Thane tomorrow," she announced.

Silas shrugged.

"That's it? A shrug?"

"I never said you couldn't tell anyone or everyone. That was your decision," Silas retorted, circling Averie, lazily spinning his sword side to side.

"What do you mean?"

Silas sighed. "Averie, I never said you couldn't tell anyone what our mission was."

"Yes, you did! You said that anyone that knew would become a target for Marcus."

Silas shrugged yet again as he came to a stop, taking his sword with both hands. "That is all very true, but then he may go after them anyway. If we don't stop him, he will have access to every Realm."

Averie took her stance and lifted the sword. "So what do I do?"

"Easy, you choose those you trust the most, the ones that you believe will stand and fight. The ones you think will be willing to aid you on this journey and who you share your truth."

Averie nibbled at her lip, shifting her stance. "And if I can't?"

"Then you lift that sword higher, train harder, and you do everything you can to protect them." Silas lowered his sword, his face losing its levity in seriousness. "But Averie, you have to remember, even your God has angels."

Chapter Twenty

Averie woke the next morning just as the sun began to rise. With only a few hours of sleep, she was surprised by how rejuvenated she felt. Her body was sore and tense, but her mind felt relieved. The feeling of freedom from lies began to take root. She would bring Thane into her inner circle and, by doing so, lift the pain and stress she had unintentionally inflicted upon him. Climbing out of her bed, Averie moved into the bathroom, flipped the shower on, and stood staring at her reflection.

She slipped into the steaming shower, quickly washed herself before toweling off, and reentered her room to dress in her standard tee shirt, jeans, and Converse. Tying the laces, Averie glanced up at the clock and smiled. Seven o'clock. By now, Thane would be grumpily fighting his alarm clock. Anxious to get a good start with him, she grabbed her backpack and rushed out of her room, tip-toeing down the hall to crack open his door. Her steps were light on the old stairs. Averie felt her happiness dissolve as her smile faded away. Thane wasn't here. His bed was still made, with his sweats folded neatly in the center.

"Where are you?" Averie whispered into the empty room. Turning, she searched the room for any sign of where he might have gone. The pale blue walls of his room were empty of any posters or pictures, while the fourth wall was nearly covered in the varying collages that Averie, Sera, and Karen had made for him. Each of them was carefully aligned in the clean and precise way that had always been associated with Thane. His desire for order and cleanliness bordered on the neurotic side at times. Averie took in the dust-free surfaces of his dresser, nightstand, and bookshelves before drifting to the carpet that still held the lines of his most recent cleaning. From the state of the room, it didn't appear that he had even entered into his room the night before.

Averie closed the door behind her, taking in the fresh, rich smell of her mother's coffee. She entered the large open space and sat heavily at the breakfast bar. Karen turned at the slight thud, watching curiously as Averie dropped her head against the cool stone counter, her arms thrown out wide to cover the remaining open space.

"Good morning, dear." Karen smiled, sipping the warm brew.

Denial

"Mmm," Averie mumbled into the cool granite countertop.

"Would you like some coffee?" she asked.

"Mmm."

Karen pulled down Averie's favorite constellation coffee mug and filled it with the warm liquid. Adding the cream and sugar, she took the seat across from Averie and placed the cup beside her head. Averie twisted her head to the side, her finger tracing the small bumps and lines that had been molded to look like the constellation Draco.

Karen released a heavy breath. "So, Averie, would you like to share why you are up so early?" Karen asked hopefully.

Averie shrugged against the counter. "Couldn't sleep."

"Is that right? No other reason?" Karen pressed, as she sipped her own steaming cup.

"I was hoping to surprise Thane," Averie finally revealed, sitting up.

"I see, and I suppose him not being home has caused all of this," Karen asked, motioning to Averie's hunched form.

"You know he isn't here?"

"Of course, I do. I'm his mother, and a mother knows."

Averie nodded at her words and though she didn't truly understand them, her mother did have the uncanny ability to know exactly what they were doing and when they were doing something they most certainly should not. "What happened to us, Mom? I thought we were fine and everything was going great and now it just seems so complicated."

"That's life, Avi. Things are great and smooth one second and the next you wonder if maybe they never were."

Averie lifted her cup to her lips and drank the warm caramel colored liquid, the sweet bitterness mixed together on her tongue making her close her eyes in satisfaction. "You always make the best coffee," Averie breathed, taking another deep drink.

"Yes, years of practice will do that for you. Is there anything else on your mind, Averie?"

Averie took her time swallowing, letting the coffee sit in her mouth as she stared into the cup. "Have you ever had to tell someone something that might change the way they look at you and because of that it makes you freak out to the point that you don't tell them, but by not telling them you have to make excuses and lie to them, like all the time, but you only do it because you are trying to protect them, because you can't imagine losing them even if the thing you are trying to tell and are kind of hiding is really important?" Averie's words had started in slow motion before spilling from her lips so quickly that by the time she had finished her rant she was panting.

Karen sat silently as she slowly dissected her daughter's words, and even though she wasn't quite sure what Averie had meant, she did know that whatever it was had been causing the tension and pain that she had watched grow in Thane. Being a mother meant any time one of your

Denial

children was hurting, no matter the reason, it hurt for you as well, and right now both of her children were hurting.

"Averie, Thane loves you. He has changed his whole world just so he could stay with you. Why do you think he waits to train until late at night or first thing in the morning? Why do you think he chose to stay back this year? He can't imagine moving forward with his life knowing that it would mean leaving you behind."

Averie's eyes widened at her mother's words. After Thane had lost his own, his schooling had taken a hit but over the years he had more than caught up and should have graduated. "Thane stayed back for me?" she whispered.

Karen took Averie's hands in her own as she smiled across the table. "Yes, Avi, he did. Thane could have easily graduated three years ago if he wanted to, instead he chose to stay with you. You two have been protecting each other since the first moment you met. I don't know what your secret is or why you feel the need to hide it, but what I do know is that Thane loves you, Averie. You are his best friend, his favorite person in the entire world, and nothing you say or do will ever change that."

Averie sat considering her mother's words, fighting to let them take hold and give her the strength to do what she knew she should.

"When someone truly loves and cares about you, it doesn't matter what you have to say or what you do, they will love you for who you are," Karen promised.

Averie gave her mother a large, comforting smile. "Thanks, Mom."

"Always, darling." Karen squeezed Averie's hand once more before moving to place her cup in the kitchen sink. "So, are you waiting for Silas? Or heading to school?"

Averie sat for a moment in shock, her mouth gaped. She wasn't sure how her mother knew she was still seeing Silas, considering she never let him come to the house or even mentioned him since the day he had brought her home. "What do you mean?"

"Oh, honey, you don't think I'm that oblivious, do you?" she asked, amused.

Averie cleared her throat. "He's supposed to come later to ride with me."

"Are things getting serious between you two?" Karen asked, leaning against the counter.

"Mom! It's not like that. I just broke up with Lucas a month ago, and Silas is just my friend."

"Mmm, a friend you sneak out to meet in the middle of the night."

"How did you …" Averie shook her head and slipped from her chair to put her empty mug in the sink. "It's not like that."

"I know you say that and you might even pretend to believe it but … you are not fooling anyone."

A knock on the door cut off anything Averie might have said. Confused at the morning visitor, she looked over to find her mother smiling over her mug. "Go on, don't leave the poor boy standing at the door."

Averie pushed herself away from the counter, taking her time as she made her way to the door. Straightening her shirt and checking her face in the nearby mirror, she ran a hand over her hair in an attempt to smooth down any strays, before taking one last deep breath and opened the door. Silas stood with an easy smile, his eyes glittering in the early morning light, like the first rays lighting the ocean. Averie watched his smile shift to a satisfied smirk. Silas wore a fitted black tee shirt with a pair of faded jeans and black boots. With his hair still wet from his morning shower, the early morning light cast him in a glow, giving him the appearance of a fallen angel.

"Good morning," Silas greeted happily. "I brought donuts."

Chapter Twenty-One

Averie's eyes fell to the gaudy, pink box he held in his hands. She wasn't sure how long she had stared in confusion and shock at his early appearance but knew it was long enough for Silas to clear his throat. "Are you going to let me in?" he leaned in to whisper.

"What are you doing here?" she whispered back.

Karen stepped up to her side with a smile. "I invited him for breakfast. Good morning, Silas," she confessed.

Silas flashed his dazzling smile. "Good morning, Mrs. Hale."

"I figured if you two were sneaking around, maybe it would make things easier if I just had him over so I could get to know him a little better. Oh, and you brought donuts! Give me those and you come on in." Taking the donuts from his hands, Karen made her way back toward the kitchen.

Denial

Averie stood locked in place as she watched the exchange between them. Her mind fought to catch up with the sudden switch in her morning, when Silas had stepped closer, his hands moving to her waist as he forced her to take a step back.

"Deep breath, Averie, it's only breakfast." Silas chuckled and followed Karen.

Averie shut the door with a shake of her head. "'*It's only breakfast Averie*,'" she mocked trailing behind. "Yeah, well it's only my foot up your ass for not warning me," she mumbled. Averie stood for a minute deciding if she wanted to follow him to the kitchen, or just run out the door and never come back. Both options had their own upside, but eventually she let the fantasy go and decided that dying of embarrassment was at least a quicker option.

"No, she did not!" Silas's booming laughter had Averie flinching at the potential stories her mother was currently sharing.

"She did! She would collect them and put them in her closet, then burst into tears when she realized they had died," Karen exclaimed, wiping tears from her eyes.

Averie groaned as she caught the end of her mother's story. She stepped into the kitchen and saw Silas leaning over the breakfast bar, just as she had done before his arrival, a steaming cup nestled between his hands and a chocolate donut half eaten on the napkin beside him.

Karen had reclaimed her normal seat, which put her directly in front of him. Her cheeks were slightly rosy from her laughter, and she was dabbing at her face with one of the napkins in an attempt to collect the fallen tears. Averie located the pink box nestled beside her mother. Stepping forward she pulled out a chocolate-covered, custard-filled, doughnut and took a large bite.

"So you tried to save the ladybugs, huh?" Silas asked, his eyes twinkling.

Averie choked at his words. Clutching her chest, she coughed, attempting to clear her throat. "I was nine, and Thane told me that birds were going to eat them."

Karen had started up another fit of giggles at Averie's explanation. "Oh, Silas, you wouldn't know it seeing them now, but when I first brought Thane home, he did everything he could think of to keep Averie away from him, but she just wouldn't hear of it. The pranks he would pull on her, you have no idea!" Karen shook her head, glancing at her watch. "Oh! I am going to be late. Averie, can you pick up for me before you two go?" Karen asked, jumping from her seat, she was already halfway down the hallway before Averie had answered.

"Sure, no problem!" Averie called after her.

Silas watched her closely as she moved to the sink, wetting a dish cloth, then carefully wiping down the counters, all the while refusing to meet his gaze. He watched the slow, concentrated circles as she tried to prolong the simple task in an effort to avoid confronting him. A slow grin spread across his face as he moved to the sink and placed the cup inside.

"Are you purposely ignoring me, Averie?" he asked.

Denial

Averie's only response was to shake her head as she moved to wipe down the bar. She sighed, realizing that she was, in fact, ignoring him. Silas tracked her movements as she moved to the sink, an inch away, to rinse the cloth, leaving it on the edge. Finally, she looked up at him.

"Tell me something about you," she blurted, jumping to sit on the counter.

"Well, let's see. I am from the Dark side of the Realm. I have no siblings. My mother died when I was nine and my father ..." Silas said as he stepped between her legs. "My father is my father. I was sent here in hopes of finding you and bringing you back to restore the Realm to its former glory."

Averie hadn't heard most of his answer, or more accurately she had stopped listening once Silas had gotten so close to her that she could feel his warmth seeping into her clothes. She wasn't sure when he had placed his hands on the counter, or when he had closed the space between them. Her muddled mind could barely remember his last sentence, let alone what she had planned to ask him as her eyes bounced between his impossibly green eyes to his slightly parted lips.

Silas had felt the pull from the moment he had woken this morning. The bond was growing faster than he had originally anticipated. It started like an itch under his skin, one that was never quite satisfied until he was close to her again. The moment he had pulled into her driveway it had finally begun to ease, even more so when he had parked his car and knocked on the door. Silas leaned forward until they were a breath away, his mind briefly wondering if she felt the same urge to be around him.

Averie watched Silas as inched closer, giving her ample time to pull away if she wished. She didn't. The moment his lips met hers it was as if she had taken three shots of espresso at once. Her eyes drifted shut as a rainbow of colors flashed behind her lids as something released itself in her chest. Images began to flash, of a dark-haired, green-eyed boy running through the fields, a bright smile on his lips and dirt streaking his face. Slowly, the image faded to the same boy crying over a bleeding woman.

"Averie! You are going to be late!" Karen called from her bedroom.

The sound of her mother's voice was like being doused in a bucket of ice water. Averie jerked back instantly, the back of her head smacking against the cabinet with a resounding thud. Groaning, she rubbed the spot and peaked an eye open to catch Silas openly grinning.

"I guess we should get going," Averie said.

"Sure." Silas leaned forward to place small light kisses along her jaw. "Would you like a ride home today?" he asked, suddenly stepping back.

Averie blinked several times attempting to take in her current situation. Clearing her throat, she shook her head and slid from the counter. "No, I'm supposed to meet Thane after school today," Averie explained, slinging her bag over her shoulder and leading the way toward the door. "Leaving, Mom! Love you!" Averie called.

"Love you more!" Karen called back.

Denial

Averie stepped into the fresh morning sunlight and smiled. Closing her eyes, she stretched her arms out wide, inhaling the cool, crisp air. "It is a beautiful morning. Don't you think?" she asked, stepping down the porch stairs to her car.

"It absolutely is," Silas whispered into her ear.

One moment she was reaching for her door handle, the next her back was against the car and Silas was looming above her. "What are you doing to me, Averie?" Silas searched her face for any sign of deception; in his world you could never be too careful. Where he was from, a best friend could quickly turn into a deadly foe in their wars.

Averie smiled, resting her arms around his neck, leaning closer. "I'm not sure what you mean."

"Ahem." Karen cleared her throat, looking down at the pair with a frown. "You two are going to be late."

Silas stepped back and gave a slight bow. "My apologies."

Karen shook her head and walked to her car. "Get going, you two."

Chapter Twenty-Two

Thane wasn't at school when they arrived, nor was he in his first or second class. By the time lunch had arrived and he still hadn't shown, Averie had to admit that she was getting worried. Between keeping her secret and training to go to a Realm she had never even dreamed about in hopes of defeating some boss level bad guy named Marcus, Averie was already having a hard time focusing in class. Add in Thane not being around and not returning any of her messages, she felt completely lost.

Her eyes watched the clock and her leg incessantly bounced against the floor as she waited for the final bell of the day to ring. Tapping her pen on her book, she felt like she would lose it if time didn't speed up.

"You need to calm down," Silas whispered, his fingers brushing along her back.

"Thane hasn't answered any of my messages. Did he answer you?" she whispered back.

Denial

Silas's silence was the only answer she needed. Shoving her books in her bag, she waited for the final minute to pass before she jumped from her seat and raced from the class, leaving everyone else still sitting in their seats.

"Averie, wait," Silas called, running to catch up. "Where are you going?"

"I told Thane to meet me."

"You think he will? He hasn't answered any of your messages, Averie. Maybe he needs time," Silas offered.

Averie shook her head. "He'll be there." Pulling her keys from the side of her bag, she fumbled with her key fob dropping it on the ground.

Silas reached down and picked it up, holding it out. "Slow down. It's going to be fine. You need to relax, otherwise you will have an incident."

Averie took a deep breath. He was right, she knew he was, but her heart was conflicted. In fact, her whole body was frantic with uncertainty. She needed to see Thane, that was the only thing she was certain about. She couldn't remember the last time she had gone this long without seeing him. Even when he was away at tournaments, she'd often tag along, and when she didn't, he would call, video chat, or at least answer her text messages.

"I know. I just need to see him," Averie said.

Silas took her hands and kissed the top of her head. "It's going to be fine. Do you want me to go with you?"

Averie shook her head. "No, I need to do this alone."

"How about I meet you there in an hour. Just in case?" Silas had meant for the offer to be light, but the meaning behind the words were heavy. They both knew she was taking a risk. She had gained a lot of control over the last week, with daily meditation and by focusing her thoughts, but she hadn't really been put under any strain.

"That sounds like a good idea. We will be at the park off Main."

Silas smiled, leaning down for a kiss when a fist landed hard against his face, throwing him against his car.

"Silas!" Averie gasped rushing toward him. Silas shook her off, his hand rubbing at his jaw.

"What the hell is wrong with you?" she demanded, shooting Lucas a disgusted look.

"Friends my ass!" Lucas seethed.

"For God's sake Lucas. We are *not* together! This is a prime example of why! You don't listen, ever. We haven't been together for a while and you are attacking the first person that comes near me!" Averie yelled as she shoved him in the chest, forcing him back.

"You are going to prom with me, Averie, that makes you mine." Lucas spat.

"Where I'm from, only a little bitch sucker punches someone," Silas said coolly, cricking his neck from side to side as he stepped toward Lucas.

Averie moved to stand between them, her arms pressed against their chests as she attempted to keep them apart. "Dammit, you two. Knock it off! Lucas, I am not yours; I am mine. You don't own me. and if this is about prom then 'e won't go together. You can find someone else

Denial

to deal with your bullshit." Averie felt Silas's chuckle against her hand. "You're not helping!" she snapped.

"I'm not helping? I'm the one that got cheap shot by this sad excuse for a man. What exactly am I supposed to help with?" Silas growled, his eyes never leaving the death glare at Lucas.

"What is going on here?" Sera asked, walking up.

"These two are fighting for no reason, again," Averie vented, quickly filling Sera in.

"I wouldn't say no reason." Lucas glared.

"Getting bitch-hit isn't fighting," Silas quipped.

Averie stepped away; her hands raised in surrender. "I don't have time for this."

"Where are you going?" Lucas demanded.

"Away from you," she shot back, opening her door.

Lucas reached over and grabbed her arm pulling her away from the door. Her annoyance finally reaching critical levels, Averie turned in his hold and slammed her palm against his chest with a deep and echoing thud. Lucas instantly released his grip, dropped to his knees and attempted to capture back some of the air that had just been shot from his lungs.

Sera and Silas looked on, both their mouths hanging open. Sera had known Averie for years, and even though she knew Averie had taken a variety of defense classes, she had never seen her use them on anyone. In fact, Sera had never even seen Averie hurt a fly let alone a person. Literally, on multiple occasions, she had watched Averie shoo them out nearby windows or do a catch and release.

"I can't believe she did that," Sera whispered.

"I can't believe I didn't consider it first," Silas whispered back, suppressing the deep seeded urge to kick Lucas while he was down.

As she climbed into her car, Averie threw her bag into the passenger seat and drove away. Huffing out a pent-up breath, she looked in her rearview mirror to see Lucas climbing to his feet and spoke out loud to herself, "I can't believe I did that."

Chapter Twenty-Three

A short drive later, she was parked in the empty lot of the local park that sat off Main Street. She looked at herself for a moment in the rearview mirror and smiled. It had been so long since she had been here, so long since she had had enough time to just do something that she had wanted to. She loved this place. She loved the way the trees swayed, the way the flowers smelled, but most of all, she loved that she could be at peace here. She felt at home where the trees were able to dance freely.

Averie sat down on one of the swings and slowly started to sway back and forth with the trees. She took deep, drowning breaths of the cool, crisp air. Winter was just about over, but it was still as chilly as it would have been if it were just starting.

Closing her eyes, she let the events of the past couple days flow through her mind. In the span of a week, she had discovered that she belonged to a world entirely different than this one, that she was not only a member of a royal family, but now she had to somehow manage to take this world back and right all of the wrongs that were being done. On top of all of that, she had just broken up with her boyfriend of almost two years and clearly had feelings of some sort for a new guy, one from another world, that she just met.

Suddenly, her intuition kicked in and she felt someone close to her. She knew that this person was not a threat, but that they were there, nonetheless. Opening her eyes, she turned in her swing to find Thane walking over. Her face lit up with a giant and loving smile as she touched the swing beside her.

"You came," she said.

"Of course, I did," Thane said, taking the swing beside her.

They sat together, silently swinging, for several minutes as birds sang overheard. Averie looked toward the trees and sighed. "I missed this."

"Yeah, me, too. I remember how we used to come and sit like this every day after school."

"Lucas messed that up," she said, turning slightly to stare at him.

Thane's lip twitched and he gently kicked the ground on the downswing. "Yeah, a little."

Denial

"Thane, can I tell you a secret? Something that I'm pretty sure you'll think that I'm crazy for telling you?"

Thane forced a slight laugh. "Fox, I've known you for a long time, and in that time, you've said a lot of crazy things."

"This is different though. This is something that sounds crazy but is true in every word."

Thane stopped his gentle swing and fixed his eyes to hers. "There is nothing that you can say that will ever make me think that you are crazy or doubt you in any way."

Averie's gaze fell to the ground and she sat silently for a brief moment before she could meet his eyes again. She took a deep breath and let it all out. "I'm not from here, not really. I am from R1 or the Original Realm, the Heart Realm. My mother and father were the king and queen when Marcus betrayed them. To save the Realm my father, the king, used his power to split the Realm into pieces, confining Marcus to one. Silas came here to bring me there to overthrow Marcus and bring the Realm back together."

The silence was agonizing. Everything held its breath, including Averie. Birds stopped chirping, the wind died down, and all Averie could hear was her heart slamming against her chest and the sound of herself blinking.

"I believe you," he said after a long and drawn out pause.

Averie was electrified by the shock of the simple confirmation. She had turned her neck so quickly she felt it pop. "You do?" she whispered in disbelief.

"Of course, I do, Fox. Haven't I always told you that you were special?"

"Why?" she wondered.

"Why, what?" Thane asked.

"Why do you believe me? Why do you not think that I'm lying? Or crazy or both?"

"Averie," he said, grabbing her hand and squeezing it. "You have never lied to me, ever. Yes, I've lied to you, and yes, I'm shocked, but why shouldn't I believe you? I've always known there was something different about you," he added.

"What? How?" Averie asked, releasing his hand and pushing her feet off the beaten ground, swinging herself higher, her gaze locked on the grass blowing in the wind.

"Do you remember when Karen first brought me home?" Thane asked breaking the silence.

Averie smiled, looking over to find him staring off into the clouds. "Yeah, you were eleven, shaking with tears and snot covering your face. You asked me what I was staring at."

"Do you remember what you told me?" he asked, looking down at her.

"That you were my brother."

Thane grinned. "You said that even though you didn't know me yet, you loved me and would protect me, so I never had to cry again. You slept in my bed for six months with me."

Averie warmed at the memory as she could see it playing in her head. Thane had been so strong even then.

"I knew then Averie. I knew you were different."

Averie wrinkled her brow. "How? I didn't even know then."

Shrugging he looked back to the clouds. "It was little things. I would shiver and your body would instantly warm up. I would start to sweat, and you would feel like ice against my skin. Then when we got older, I would catch you twisting water, in the air Fox. Do you know how crazy I felt? The flowers would grow when you touched them. It just confirmed everything I already knew. I was just waiting on you to trust me enough to tell me." His eyes shifted back to hers. "You are a protector, Averie. Always have been and always will be. I know this is all weird and hard and scary, but if those people need you, you have to help them."

"What if I'm not strong enough?" she whispered her deepest fear.

"Then you get stronger."

"And if I can't?"

Thane sank into a crouch before her and smiled. "You can and you will. You are stronger than you let yourself believe."

Averie snorted. "That's easy for you to say. You're a brick wall."

Smiling, he shook his head. "Have I always looked this way?"

"No."

"Do you know why I started MMA?"

Averie shook her head.

"I wanted to be able to protect those that couldn't protect themselves. I watched my mom die." Thane held up his hand at her tears. "No, Evie. It's done. If that day taught me anything, it is that I wasn't strong enough. I can't change it, God knows I would if I could, but I can't. I promised myself that day I would never walk away from someone who needs help. I wouldn't ignore someone in need. I have trained and fought and lost. Just as you will. But you can't stop. You can never stop. But I am going to be with you every step of the way."

Tears welled her eyes. "Thank you, for standing by me. For protecting me."

"Always, Fox."

"Forever, Bear."

Averie smiled and jumped from her swing to tackle Thane. Hugging him tightly, she felt him move so that he slammed against the ground instead of her. Laughing together they looked up to the clouds, watching them lazily pass them by.

"Everything is going to get very complicated for you," Averie said, his smile fading from his face.

"What do you mean?"

"Silas said that there are people that want me dead, and that's not including Marcus."

Thane moved so that he could see into her eyes. "I won't let anyone hurt you."

Averie flashed him a concerned look, "You're not going to be able to stop them, Thane. Even if I wanted you to, you can't stop them."

Denial

"Averie, look at me," Thane ordered.

She did, but she couldn't seem to keep the fear from her eyes.

"I won't let anyone hurt you. Do you understand me? Nothing is going to hurt you," he said slowly.

Averie couldn't help but just stare at him. So many things had changed in him during the time she had dated Lucas that she felt betrayed. "You've changed."

Thane gave a wide grin. "So have you."

Laughing, they both turned to look back at the sky. They were silent for a long time, perfectly comfortable in each other's company. Averie heard Thane take a deep breath. "So what happens now?"

"What do you mean?" she asked, unsure herself.

"Do we go to this *Realm* and kick this Marcus guy's ass or what?"

Averie sat up and hugged her knees close. "No, Silas says that I'm not ready to yet." She shifted, turning herself back to look at him. How long had it been since she really looked at her brother? Thane propped himself up on one of his elbows and lightly brushed some stray grass off his shirt. His eyes were a clear crystal blue, his brown hair streaked through with a lighter, brighter brown, his skin darkened showing that he was in the sun so much more now than he used to be. His facial features so much sharper than she remembered.

After a labored pause as she spoke again, "Soon, I am going to take back what is mine, and soon my people are going to be free."

Thane beamed and stood. Putting out a hand to help her stand, he hugged her close. "That's the Averie I know! I'm going to train with you. Anything that I can learn to help you, I'll do it."

"Then we better get started," came a familiar voice from behind them.

Averie turned to find Silas, a blank expression on his face. "Silas!" she exclaimed as she bounded over and hugged him. "I'm sorry," she whispered into his ear.

Silas stood stiff in her embrace for a long time before he finally loosened up and hugged her back.

"I didn't mean to hurt you today," Averie continued. "It's just that I was so mad about everything that I took it out on you, and Lucas."

"No, it was my fault. I shouldn't have let him get to me," Silas said, his voice not holding any anger.

"He punched you … in the face," Averie reminded.

Silas reluctantly pulled away. "Things happen. I'm sure eventually we will have the chance to sort it out properly."

"Thanks, Si."

"For what?"

"For coming for me and giving me time."

He took her hand and, smiling, bowed over it. "It was truly my pleasure, Princess."

"Princess, huh?" Thane chuckled. "So where do we go from here?" Thane asked, moving to stand beside Averie.

Averie's face darkened, a distilled look of determination crossing it as Silas started speaking to Thane. "If you are sure that you want to get involved in

Denial

this, then we begin by some simple training. I need you to understand what you are getting into. This is a very dangerous task that we are undertaking. Your Realm does not have magic, so you will see things you've always thought impossible. There will be people who want you dead and in Averie's case, many people who will want her dead at all costs. I will try my best, but I won't be able to protect you at all times." He finished, his last words coming as he looked deep into Averie's eyes.

"I go where Averie goes," Thane answered with simple resolution.

Silas wrapped his fingers through Averie's and turned toward the parking lot. "Then we better get going."

"Where are we going?" Thane questioned.

"To the field," Averie answered for Silas.

"Do you mean the abandoned field behind our house? That field?"

"Yes, that's the one."

"But doesn't some crazy old guy own that?"

"Nope, I do," Silas replied as he opened the car door and helped Averie in.

Chapter Twenty-Four

The next two weeks were nothing but a blur of school during the day and training at night. Nothing could have prepared Averie or Thane for Silas's unrelenting determination and pace. There were the morning workouts before school, fight practice after school, and a mixture of meditation and skills training deep into the night. Silas pulled double shifts, not only guiding Averie but also teaching Thane the basics of fighting with swords, staffs, and knives. It wasn't much of a surprise to Averie that Thane took to it naturally.

When the sun rose on the second Friday, Averie rolled over, slapped her alarm, and with a groan, pulled her pillow over her head. There wasn't school today and yet, instead of sleeping in, she waited for her upcoming wake-up call. "Five … four … three … two…"

Before she could reach one, her bedroom door flew open with a loud crash. "Rise and shine, Princess."

Denial

Again, she groaned. "Silas, it's five o'clock in the morning, on a Friday, give me a freaking break, will ya?"

Silas sighed and sat on the edge of her bed. "You know that we cannot stop. As you sleep, your people suffer at the hands of another. As you bury your head in your pillows, people are dying. As you—"

"Okay!" Averie sat up and threw the blanket off, revealing her long, slightly tanned legs. "I'm going!"

Since she was amid getting out of bed, she failed to notice Silas's sudden change in expression.

"I don't see why we have to get going this early anyways, even when we have school it wouldn't start for another three hours. Three hours, Silas! Do you know how nice it would be to sleep until six? Do you even realize how crazy it is that I am asking to be able to sleep until six in the morning?"

Silas didn't answer and Averie continued her rant as she walked out of the room.

"I mean, yes, I know everyone is depending on me and everything, but how am I supposed to help anyone if I am constantly tired and barely able to stay awake during my classes? Do you even *know* what will happen if I fail my senior year? My mother will kill me! And on top of that prom is—"

As she came out of the bathroom, she found herself barely a breath away from Silas. Taking a shaky breath, she looked up into his eyes and swallowed, biting her lip. The silence that filled the room was quickly replaced with the vibrations that radiated from the two of them.

"P-prom i-is tomorrow," Averie stammered leaning her back against the wall.

Silas ignored her spoken words. He couldn't help it. From the first moment he had laid eyes on her, she had captivated him. This time was no different. He had put his feelings on hold because she was already involved when they met, but now, as they had been training for weeks to save their Realm, he found himself lost in her essence.

"We are going to the fair tonight. Do you want to go?" Averie asked, her voice slightly breathless.

Silas shook his head, placing his hands on either side of her head. "Can't."

"Why not?" she asked.

Silas leaned forward until he was an inch away. "Thane wants to work more with swords."

Averie frowned. "I know this is important and all, but you can take a break."

Silas ignored her comment, he had no desire to continue to talk. He leaned forward and pressed their lips together. Averie's arms immediately circled his neck and pulled him closer. Silas moved his hands under her butt and he lifted her against the wall as she wrapped her legs around his waist.

"Are you guys—oh, hell no, absolutely not," Thane roared, stepping into Averie's room.

Averie snapped back at the sound of Thane's voice, her feet landing back on the floor. "Thane, what are you doing in here?" she asked, jerking her hands quickly from Silas's neck.

Denial

Thane narrowed his eyes at Silas, who was still looking down at Averie with a smile on his face that Thane was currently itching to remove. "You were supposed to meet me outside five minutes ago. Now, I know why you didn't show."

Averie adjusted her hair. "Calm down, Thane. I'm an adult."

"And my sister."

"So? Do you have any idea how many times I've walked in on you with some random girl having *se*—"

"Okay, enough, let's go," Thane demanded, eyeing Silas.

Averie shook her head, leaving the room with a smile.

Chapter Twenty-Five

The atmosphere at the fair was filled with insanity. Groups of people huddled everywhere, making it nearly impossible to pass while their excited voices created a deafening chaos. The rings and buzzes from the different games were so loud someone would have to shout to be heard clearly. Averie had left Sera and Lucas by the Ferris wheel before venturing off to find something to eat. The sun's rays were warm on her exposed skin, only alleviated by the occasional cool breeze that breathed through the masses of people.

"Thanks," Averie said, taking a large funnel cake smothered in chocolate sauce and powdered sugar from a fare vendor. She broke off a large piece and shoved it into her mouth, savoring the chocolate-covered fried goodness as her eyes wandered over the brightly lit fair. The bright colorful lights twinkled from the various rides while pulsing ones glowed from the games in hopes of drawing people in. The blaring sound of a local, live band clashed heavily with the game runners trying to entice patrons to come and try their skills.

Averie made her way through the ever-increasing crowd in search of Sera and Lucas, stopping now, then shoved another piece of deep fried sweetness into her mouth. As she wandered through the crowd her eyes drifted from one game to another, the sound of laughter as children hit their target or made a basket brought a smile to her face. Averie tore another piece off, promising herself that she would save some for Sera, and immediately regretted it. She turned a corner around a small lemonade stand and froze in horror. Standing before her was her best friend, embracing her boyfriend in a very passionate make-out session. *Ex-boyfriend*, she reminded herself.

"Are you kidding me?" Averie barked, in a knee-jerk reaction. As if feeling her shock, Sera jerked back from a confused and dazed looking Lucas. Blinking hard Lucas looked from Sera to Averie with a baffled expression. Sera wiped the side of her mouth with wide eyes. Averie turned on her heel with a huff and stormed away, tossing the funnel cake in a nearby trash can. Her appetite for the fried delicacy was officially gone.

"Averie, wait!" Sera called racing through the crowd. "It's not what you think."

Averie ignored Sera's plea, continuing toward the exit. She didn't care that Lucas had driven them. She would walk home if it got her away from the two of them. The feel of cool fingers wrapping around her arm set Averie into the next level of anger. A slow vibration began deep inside, the hair rising on her arms, transforming her anger into panic. She couldn't do this, not here.

"Please, Avi, I promise it's not what it looked like," Sera pleaded. "Just let me explain."

"Explain what, Sera? You're my best friend and I just caught you making out with my boyfriend," Averie snapped.

"Ex-boyfriend and you have Silas now," Sera reminded, flinching at her own words.

"That's not the point!" Averie snapped.

"I know that's not the point and I'm sorry, but I promise there is nothing going on between Lucas and I. He was just helping me out."

"How exactly does Lucas shoving his tongue down your throat help you, Sera?" Averie demanded, her anger flaring once more.

"This guy has been following me for a while now, and I told him I had a boyfriend. Only he didn't believe me, he said if I did why wouldn't he be at the fair with me, and Lucas walked up and … well, you saw the rest. I'm sorry, Averie, I really am. You know I would never do anything to hurt you," Sera said, her pleading eyes starting to well with tears.

The look her friend gave was giving Averie no reprieve. The air grew warmer around her as her anger morphed into rage. Sera was supposed to be her best friend, and even if she wasn't, there was still the girl code. The friend code.

Denial

"Averie? Are you okay?" Sera asked, her cool fingers brushing Averie's arm. "Jesus Averie, you're burning up."

"I have to go," Averie spit out between deep breaths. *Breathe. Just breathe,* she told herself. Even if she did believe Sera, and she really did, she couldn't stay here. She felt herself so close to the edge she didn't know if she would be able to stop herself either way.

"Avi, wait, please," Sera begged.

"Sera, just stop! I can't do this right now. It's fine, really. We can talk another time," Averie snapped.

"But Lucas… he drove us here," Sera said slowly.

"I'll figure it out. You two have fun," Averie said over her shoulder.

Sera watched as Averie slipped between the incoming crowd, disappearing into the darkness of the parking lot.

"Is she okay?" Lucas asked, coming up behind her. "Where is she going?"

"She's fine. She just needed some air," Sera answered.

"She looked really mad," Lucas pointed out.

"Averie will be fine, Luke. She's not your concern any more, is she?"

Though Sera had said it with a smile, Lucas frowned at her words. "She is still my friend, Sera, and yours. I care about her and I don't want her to be upset."

"She's fine, Luke, I promise. Come on let's get some funnel cake."

Lucas looked toward the parking lot, hesitating before turning and following Sera.

Chapter Twenty-Six

"So are you going tonight?" Averie asked, seemingly offhanded.

Silas sighed, lowering his sword. "I don't know Averie. Now will you please pay attention? Your movements with the sword are still slow."

"Why does it matter if I can use a sword anyways?" Averie asked, dusting the dirt from her torn jeans.

"There may come a time when you are unable to use your abilities without causing too many casualties, using a sword will allow you to kill the enemy you intend instead of bashing around hoping for the best," Silas explained.

Averie stood frozen, eyes wide, mouth gaped open. "What?! I'm not killing anyone, Silas!"

"Don't be ridiculous. Of course you will, Averie. You are going to be walking into a war. What do you think all this training has been for? A parade after the enemies all surrender at your cute little smile? You need to know

Denial

everything Marcus does if you hope to stand a chance against him," Silas said, lifting his sword.

Averie nervously nibbled on her lip. "I won't do it, Silas. I can't. I'm not that kind of person."

"You hold the Heart of the Realm inside you, it is your destiny to right Marcus's wrong. Your Realm is at war, and if you wish to save your world then you need to make difficult decisions. Including ending your enemy's life. They won't hesitate and neither can you."

"I'm eighteen, for heaven's sake! I can't just kill someone because you say so! They have families and children, Silas!"

Silas's eyes hardened as he stepped forward. "Yes, they do, and so did the men and women that they have already killed, tortured, and maimed. Do you think they hesitated when it came down to the moment of life and death?" he demanded. "You stand there condemning a Realm when yours does the same. Do you not send your children to war? To fight and to kill in your own wars?"

The horrifying images that shot through her mind were vicious in detail, she dropped her head, forcing herself to take slow even breaths like he had taught her. As much as Averie hated the thought of hurting, let alone killing someone, she knew deep down there were things that couldn't be avoided in war. "Okay," she agreed, swallowing the lump in her throat.

Anguish coursed through Silas at her pained expression. Averie was still so innocent, so unaware of the horrors that she was about to face. Rubbing against the pain in his chest he tipped her chin up to meet her eyes. "I am going to be with you every step of the way. I promise to protect you, 'til my very last breath."

Averie felt breathless, she knew what he was promising, so why did it feel like there was more to his words? Something that he wasn't saying and yet still promising? She watched his eyes slowly drift from her own to her lips. Closing her eyes, she lifted her face to his, the warmth of his breath brushing against her cheek.

Beep. Beep. Beep.

Silas cursed and stepped away. Dazed in wonder and disappointment, it took Averie a moment to understand where the beeping was coming from. "Oh! My phone." Pulling the device from her pocket, she sighed. "It's Lucas, he'll be here at eight …" Smiling, she looked up at Silas. "I'm going to tell him tonight, explain everything."

Silas said nothing, made no movements, his expression was vacant.

Averie's smile vanished. "Si, look, I know you're not his biggest fan but can't you just be a little supportive? For me? You said I needed to have a team of people I could trust. I trust him."

Silas fought against the flood of anger and jealousy that was threatening to overcome him. He wanted to tell her what a silly little girl she was, but more than that he wanted to even the score he had been keeping. Twice the sad excuse for a man had put hands on him. By his count, Silas owed him two in return and he was beyond ready to collect. Instead, Silas pushed out a half-fake grin and said, "Of course, but do you think it is wise to tell him?"

Averie smiled, placing a kiss on his cheek. "He has been one of my closest friends since elementary school. It's going to be just fine. I promise. Thane was fine when I told him and I need all the support I can get."

"Even after the other night?" Silas questioned.

"Sera explained what happened and I believe her."

"Then why not tell her over Lucas?"

Averie shrugged. "Sera is complicated and she tends to freak out when you give her too much information at once." Silence slipped in around them. "Are you coming tonight?" she asked again.

He shook his head. "No, I have no desire to see the two of you together. Besides that, I should stay here and prepare for our journey."

"Oh, yeah, sure. Well, I'll call you when I get home and let you know how everything went." Averie sighed. Pushing the loose hair from her face she shoved her hands into her pockets and found herself wondering when everything had gotten so complicated.

"You are going to be late." Silas said, tossing the swords back into the awaiting chest.

Sighing, Averie turned to the trail and ran. She ran from Silas, from the turmoil building inside her, from confusion and destiny that screamed for her and toward the simplicity of the excitement of her senior prom.

"I think you're growing soft." A harsh voice laughed.

Silas's body tensed as he turned and found himself face to face with an opposite version of himself. Where Silas had black, the figure had white, almost glowing hair. Where Silas's skin was tanned and smooth the figure had a waxy, dark gray complexion. Silas's teal eyes stared into the glowing orange ones that stared back at him.

"What are you doing here?" Silas asked stiffly.

Mirror Silas jerked slightly as it walked and wandered in a large circle around him.

"Just thought I would come and see how you were doing. From the looks of her, I would say the fondness you feel is mutual," Mirror said, its voice crackly and grating.

"I don't know what you're talking about." Silas glared; his fists clenched at his sides.

"Ah." Mirror nodded, his head twitching from side to side. "You don't see it then?" He moved closer, fascinated by Silas's teal eyes.

"See what?" Silas growled.

The pair then stood frozen, locked in a silent battle of wills.

"She loves you," Mirror said simply, breaking the silence and beginning to walk in slow circles around Silas. Silas stiffened at the words, there was no time to focus on something that was clearly being used as a diversion, when he needed to get far away from Mirror and get away quickly. Silas felt a twinge of electricity slowly crawl across his skin, his heart sinking as he knew it was already too late to escape. The shocks increased in frequency then also in

Denial

voltage, until suddenly they stopped, leaving Silas to catch his breath.

Mirror stilled, his eyes narrowing as he came face to face with Silas, the orange glow of his eyes reflecting in Silas's. "And you love her!" Mirror bellowed, his anger vibrating around them, sending sparks and cracks into the air. "That is why you have not finished it. That is why you have ignored your true mission."

Silas stood resolute in his silence, his glare unwavering, as Mirror's fury grew.

"You will finish your mission," Mirror seethed.

"No," Silas said firmly, daring to take a step closer. "I will show her your vulnerabilities, teach her the skills she needs to defeat you, and help her get the kingdom that you destoryed, back."

Mirror's fury visibly pulsed in the air, making Silas's hair stand on end. A mixture of pinks, purples, and blues arched through the air, burning the tips off the flowers under them. "You cannot do this!"

A hollow and dark grin crossed Silas's face. "You have no power here. You can't stop me. Now go back where you came from."

Mirror said nothing for a long time, just stared in silent rage at Silas. Finally, after what seemed like an eternity, Mirror flicked his fingers back and forth. In an instant Silas was engulfed in shocks, each one of them feeling as though it would burn the flesh from his bones. Silas fell to his knees in silent resolve, refusing to give the satisfaction of a cry. "She will not have you." Mirror laughed as it backed away, the rainbow of lights circling it like a cyclone.

"What does that mean?" Silas asked, pushing himself up to one knee, panting heavily.

Mirror gave a flourishing bow, as it faded away into the wind as quickly as it appeared.

"What does that mean!" Silas roared, racing forward, reaching out in an attempt to catch Mirror, but his hand fell through the fading figure like a bird flying through a cloud.

Mirror was gone, leaving Silas standing alone in the middle of the field, searching the trees for answers. "What does that mean?!" he screamed unanswered into the growing darkness.

Chapter Twenty-Seven

Averie stood before the mirror with a frown on her made up face. She had been so excited, just weeks ago, about this moment. She and Sera had searched through five different stores, gathering ideas and snapping pictures of the ones they liked to show her mother. The thought of getting dressed up in a beautiful gown and dancing the night away had held such appeal, now felt so empty and pointless.

"Honey, what's wrong?" Karen asked, concern laced through her words.

"Silas isn't going," Averie answered.

Karen moved to stand behind her daughter, their eyes connecting in the reflection. "You are growing rather fond of him." Karen stated, her fingers working the ties of Averie's dress.

Averie nibbled her bottom lip, the chalky taste of her lipstick stopping her. "I think so."

"Averie, listen to me, go to this dance and enjoy yourself. You only get one senior prom. You never know what will happen, Silas might even show up," Karen offered.

Averie's heart jumped at the thought. "You think so?" she asked, turning to face her mother.

Karen gave a small shrug. "You never know. Men can be a little slow at times, but they tend to come through at the end."

The doorbell echoed through the house. "I'll get that," Karen said, kissing Averie on the cheek. "You look beautiful, Avi."

Averie swallowed the lump in her throat as she watched her mother leave the room, her words echoing in her mind. Releasing a slow breath, she turned back to the mirror. Averie loved her dress, and the fact that Karen had spent her own time designing and making the dress made it that much more special. It was long, white, and flowing with tiny glittering golden stars all along the bottom, that became sparser as they rose up to her waist. Averie had wanted it to be strapless, but Karen had insisted on the inch wide straps that went over her shoulders. As she took in the full effect, she had to admit that her mother had made the right decision. The waist was tight while the neck line scooped down in an elegant way, revealing little while still accentuating the natural curves of her body.

Denial

Karen's favorite diamond earrings and necklace gave the ensemble a classic finish. Averie had spent hours watching make-up tutorials, practicing how to recreate Cleopatra's signature look on herself. The dark black eyeliner and gold accents served to bring the richness of her eyes out. Karen had carefully curled her hair, wrapping it in a variety of different braids and curls on her head. As she stared at her reflection, Averie had to agree with her mother, she looked beautiful, almost enchanting, but instead of being excited for the night ahead, all she could think of was Silas and the fact that he wouldn't be there.

"Averie! Sera and Lucas are here!"

Karen's announcement brought Averie into the moment, shaking her head in hopes of clearing away the disappointing thoughts she turned to the doorway. "I'll be right down!"

Giving herself one last glance, she turned and left the room, nearly floating to the stairs. No matter what happened, tonight was her senior prom. It was going to be a night to remember, and she fully intended to enjoy herself.

* * *

Averie stood at the top of the stairs, her hand resting lightly against the banister as she looked down to her friends. Thane leaned against the door frame in a black tuxedo with a black shirt, and black tie, his hair slightly disheveled, giving him a roguish appearance. Sera stood between Thane and Lucas. Her blonde hair neatly coiled to the side in loose curls against her porcelain face. Her dress was fitted, sparkling, and ombre pink, the waist was tight and the top strapless with a daring plunge. Sera had done her makeup to match her dress, which only made her blue eyes appear even larger. Averie chuckled to herself. She should have known her enthusiastic friend would take the phrase 'go big or go home' literally.

Lucas was the first to notice her entrance. "Wow, Averie." His eyes widening as his gaze slowly ran down the length of her body before lifting to meet her eyes. "You look … amazing."

Sera nudged her elbow into his side. "Don't act so surprised, Luke."

"Stop drooling, *Luke*," Thane glared.

"But he is right. You look incredible. That dress is amazing, Karen," Sera gushed.

"Thank you, Sera." Karen beamed at the compliment.

Averie smiled, her cheeks warming at the praise. "Thanks, guys, you all look amazing."

Lucas took a step forward and spread his arms wide. "Only for you, baby, only for you."

Averie couldn't help but admire his appearance, though still rolled her eyes at his annoyingly cheesy line. The midnight blue suit and gold tie accentuated his physic, while managing to maintain the classic appeal. He was stunning, but wasn't he always? With his all-American good looks and charming smile, it was hard for him to be anything but stunning and yet even as he stood before her, looking like he'd just stepped off of a magazine cover, her mind still wandered back to Silas.

Karen cleared her throat and waved her camera. "Come on, kids, let's get a couple pictures before you are all late." Karen snapped the pictures quickly, her motherly tone disappearing as she ordered them about like a general ordering her troops. She quickly moved them between couples and groups, girls and guys. When she had decided she was done, or that she had enough pictures to fill six albums, she nearly shoved them out the door. "Be careful!" Karen called, slamming the door in finality behind them.

"That was weird," Thane said, adjusting his jacket.

Averie shrugged as she took Lucas's arm. "Maybe she's just excited about having a night to herself."

"Alright, everyone, the limo has arrived!" Sera announced, clapping her hands and jumping in her excitement.

"Actually, I thought me and Lucas could go separately," Averie said, forcing a smile as Thane gave her a knowing look over Sera's head.

"Oh, okay." Sera frowned.

Averie's stomach clenched at Sera's disappointment. "Don't worry. After the prom we are going to have our own little after party in that limo driving around town."

Sera looked up through her lashes. "Promise?"

"Absolutely," Averie vowed, hugging her tightly. "You look amazing, Sera," she said, pulling away.

Sera flipped the loose curls from her shoulder. "Well, what did you expect?"

"Okay, ladies, let's get this going," Thane demanded, waving toward the limo. "I have ladies eagerly awaiting my arrival."

Sera made a disgusted sound while Averie shook her head.

After saying their goodbyes, they separated into the two cars and set out for their night.

Karen waited anxiously by the kitchen window, watching the teens talk. It took all of her willpower to not shout at them to get going. Finally, she watched Averie give Sera one last hug before they got into two different cars. *Curious*, Karen thought. Though that wasn't the problem she had at hand. As she watched the cars turn from the driveway and disappear down the road, she released her pent-up breath and made her way to the door. "Now for Silas," she said, closing the door tightly behind her.

Chapter Twenty-Eight

The car's uncomfortable silence was palpable. Mindlessly, she twisted one of the white frill layers of her dress before flattening it back down. She shifted slightly in her seat to get a better view of Lucas. As she drank in his all-American profile, she couldn't help but let her mind wander back and forth to 'him' in silent comparison. The rich golden hue of his shaggy hair to the short midnight locks Silas held. Lucas's sky blue eyes glistened in the sun, while Silas's teal ones seemed to create a light all their own. Even their bodies were at opposite ends of the same spectrum. Where Lucas embodied the cliché jock mold, as someone who only emphasized their glamour muscles, Silas had the body and build of someone that was molded by hard work and endurance.

"Hey, Luke?" she asked cautiously.

Hearing her tone, he turned the music down and looked at her. "What is it? Are you okay, Averie?"

Forcing a smile, she looked down at her hands nervously. Her mind flashed through the years they spent as friends. The summers they spent at the lake as children, the school field trip to the zoo. Her emotions sparked at the thought of that zoo trip. She remembered how she was flooded with sadness and broke down into tears at the thought of the animals being locked in their cages forever. She remembered her anger when the boys taunted her about her crying. Then the strange, unknown emotion when Lucas, leaving his friend, walked over to console her. He lightly rubbed her back and promised her that the animals were happy because they had their families with them. He then sat there with her in silence until she was content and ready to continue on with the trip, holding her hand the entire time.

Slowly, her mind drifted deeper into the time they had spent together as more. The day Lucas invited her to a picnic in the park when she was fourteen. Everything had been so perfect. The checkered blanket, laid out across the grass and flowers, holding a small wicker basket. He had taken the extra effort to learn her favorite chicken salad sandwich recipe, which had dried cranberry and celery. He even had her favorite chips and finished it with fresh pineapple slices, again, her favorite. All that effort was so he would have the best chance when he had asked her to be his girlfriend that day, and it absolutely worked. The

Denial

happy memories quickly melted into the bad ones. The constant fights they had over him flirting with other girls, his lack of attention with her, the heartbreak she'd experienced when she found him cheating on her, then their final fight in a parking lot.

Averie shook herself out of her memories and into the present. All of those times were behind them now, just fading thoughts and emotions. She hoped that, though she had endured the majority of the heartache, they could both mutually agree to move forward. Maybe Silas was wrong, though the realization that he rarely was pierced deeply. Averie still had hope that maybe Lucas and her could work it out. Maybe they really could be friends again through all this. She knew that Lucas really did care about her, but she also knew that what she had to tell him would change everything.

"No, nothing's wrong, but could we pull over somewhere? We need to talk, and I'd rather do it somewhere private…"

"Really?" The excitement in his voice made her flinch.

"Not like that, Luke!" she snapped.

"Okay, okay, my bad. No worries. No need to freak out every time, you know," Lucas mumbled.

Lucas slowed the car, pulling into the parking lot of the town square. He walked around the car and took her hand, leading her to a small, white, decorative bench near the fountain. As they sat, the sun started setting over the peaceful hillside outside of town. Its last dying rays, staining the sky in a foreboding red. Averie looked around and shivered. *Ominous*, she thought.

"Are you cold?" Lucas asked, shrugging off his jacket and with a warm smile, placed it on her shoulders.

"Lucas, do you consider us good friends? Regardless of how we ended?" Averie started.

Leaning his elbows on his knees, he looked out toward the fountain.

"Of course," he responded.

She read his face, as he struggled with his own thoughts. "Averie, I never meant for us to end the way that we did. I hate that my jealousy destroyed what we had," Lucas continued.

Averie nodded, her gaze focused on his face, trying to glean any idea of how the rest of the conversation may go.

"I know that we had promised to go to prom together but you really didn't have to. I would have understood. I know you and Silas—"

"I wanted to," she interrupted. "I know things between us have been strange lately, but I want my friend back."

Lucas nodded as they both fell into silence; the only sound between them was the bubbling fountain behind them.

"Luke, I want to share something with you, I-I just don't know how," Averie said.

Lucas shifted, so they faced each other. Taking her chilled hands in his warmer ones. He gently squeezed, then rubbed her hands to warm them.

Denial

"You can tell me anything, Averie, you know that," he said.

Nodding again, she bit her lip. "I know that, it's just that this, what I have to tell you, it's going to change everything. Our friendship and the way that you look at me."

"Never," he said firmly. "Never will anything that you say or do change the way that I see or feel about you." There was heavy meaning behind those words, and she felt it.

Taking another deep breath, she rushed through the words that had been trying to escape. "You know that Silas and I have been spending a lot of time together lately. I really just need to tell you why, and it's going to be really confusing, and difficult to explain. So I really just need you to bear with me and let me explain it all."

Lucas's entire body tensed at her words. "If you brought me here to say that you and Silas are sleeping together, just don't."

A moment of stunned silence hit Averie, as her mouth gaped open. "What?! No Lucas, this has nothing to do with sex!" Averie pulled her hands from him, stood silently and walked toward the fountain. A light music, barely audible, played in the wind, cutting the silence. She knew it was from the prom, a prom they would hopefully still be able to go once she finished her confession. Maybe it would be easier to just forget about what she planned to tell him, walk to the town hall, and enjoy the dance like every other girl her age. Unfortunately, she knew the truth.

She wasn't like the other girls her age, and as much as she wanted to pretend, she couldn't stop and walk away now. She needed to get this out, she needed to finally tell him, to get rid of the secrets that she was holding from him. The only way they could move on and rebuild their friendship would be if he knew everything.

She watched the sun slip farther down behind the hills and turned back to face him.

"Lucas, I need to tell you something but I think it would be easier to show you."

Lucas stood up from the bench and moved toward her. "Show me what? Averie, you know I hate when you don't just say what you need to and leave me guessing."

"Just watch and see, okay? Then everything will be easier to explain," she said.

Closing her eyes, she said a silent prayer, *Please let everything be okay.* Turning to the fountain, Averie gently ran her finger across the surface of the water. Small ripples echoed across the surface and up through the spout of the three-tiered fountain. The fountain's cascading water rippled as it fell, creating the illusion of the water dancing as it misted through the air. The water swirled back and forth, eventually drawing itself around her outstretched fingers. Averie, entranced by what she was doing, forgot that Lucas stood beside her in stunned silence.

As the sun finally disappeared behind the hill, she felt the power she was already channeling intensify. The water she was controlling whirled into the air, breaking apart into a fine mist that enveloped her and Lucas in a thin veil. The

Denial

sun's final ray bounced off the droplets, exploding into tiny rainbows around them. Smiling at the beauty of what she had created, she turned to Lucas. Her stomach plummeted, along with her smile, as she saw the pure horror frozen on his face. His body was shaking, yet at the same time was unmoving.

"Luke?" she asked as she stepped toward him. His body instantly unfroze as he stumbled backward. "Luke, I'm not going to hurt you. This is what I wanted to show you, this and so much more."

As she took a slow step closer, the droplets moved with her, following her with their iridescent glow, as if she wore a dress made of water and light. He threw his hands up defensively and shouted, "Stop! Please don't hurt me."

Averie stopped, stunned. "Luke, I would never."

"What are you?!" he shrieked.

"Luke, I'm Averie, the same Averie that you grew up with. The same person that you fell in love with, the same Averie that you have always been friends with."

He shook his head vigorously. "No, you're not. You're some type of freak! I've seen the stories of freaks like you all over the news! Weird voodoo witches that mess with everyone's head."

Averie took another step toward him, holding out her hand. "Please, you don't understand."

"Oh, I understand, don't take another step," he said. As he took another hasty step backward, he tripped over the bench they had been sitting on and fell.

Without thought, Averie threw out a hand, water jettisoning from around her, in an effort to catch him before his head hit the ground. As the water reached him, it crystallized into ice. Her stomach turned as the crack of Lucas's arm hitting the ice echoed through the quiet dusk. Tears welled in her eyes as Lucas lay on the ground, a thick, red pool of blood blooming on his shirt. This was not how the talk was supposed to go.

Chapter Twenty-Nine

Karen parked her car, walked up the stone walkway, and rapped on the thick, oaken door. She tapped her foot impatiently as she lifted her hand to knock again. A solemn looking Silas answered the door just before her knuckles reached for a second round. As Karen stood in the doorway, he forced a half-hearted smile.

"Karen, what a pleasant surprise. What are you doing here?"

She waved his words away, stepping inside and glancing around the foyer before turning to face him. "Why aren't you ready yet?"

Shutting the door, he gave her a confused expression. She stood in silence, hands on her hips, an irritated expression covering her motherly features. "I'm sorry? Ready for what?" he asked.

She let out a heavy sigh, her exasperation pouring to the surface. "The *dance*, Silas, why are you not ready yet?"

"I'm not going," he said simply.

"Yes, you are. Averie has been miserable for the past two hours because you told her you weren't going, and I refuse to let my daughter's senior prom be miserable because you are too stubborn to see that she wants you there."

Silas's face contorted into shock. "She wants me there?"

"Of course, she does!" Karen said.

A warm, glowing smile covered Silas's face. He had never thought that she would want him, especially so soon.

He paused for a moment in quiet contemplation, staring off into the distance, before he turned back to Karen. "I don't have anything to wear."

"Here," she said, handing him the large garment bag that she seemed to pull out of thin air. "I took the liberty of renting this for you. I figured you, being a man, would not have been prepared."

His dark eyes glanced, with a hint of uncertainty, from Karen to the bag and back to her. He took in the situation, his mind trying to process so much information in such a short period of time.

"Well? Are you going to shower or just stand there?"

Her voice snapped him out of his thoughts and back to the moment. He gave a small salute, grabbed the bag and raced down the hallway to the bathroom. Karen followed him down the hall, muttering about always having

Denial

to fix everything. Silas heard her words, but couldn't focus on what she was saying; his mind raced with much more important thoughts. Averie wanted him there. She was choosing him.

* * *

Lucas's wail filled the air as he pulled his arm to his chest. "What did you do to me?"

"No, no, Luke, I didn't mean to!" she stammered, her eyes wide with fear. "I was trying to help, to stop you from falling and hurting yourself. I didn't think—" she said, rushing to him.

"Stop!" he begged, his good arm pushing her away. "Get away from me, you monster!"

Averie backed away, his words cutting into her. Averie felt a part of herself crack. The fear and pain of what she had done, being pushed recklessly aside by anger. By rage. She stumbled back and collapsed onto her knees, fighting to get a hold of herself. "Luke, I'm still me. I'm still Averie."

Lucas shook his head frantically. "No, you're not! You're a monster! A freak!"

"Monster? Freak?" she said. "A monster. A freak," she repeated, this time, as a whisper. The water, that was still surrounding her, fell to the ground in a wave of sorrow.

As Lucas lay on the ground, staring at the girl he had thought he knew his whole life, the fear began to subside in him. This was the girl he knew. The girl he cared for and loved. This was not a movie or television show. This was real life he thought, standing up, the pain in his arm radiating across his body.

"Averie, I-I didn't mean it, I'm sorry. But you just can't—" Lucas started.

"Monster. Freak," Averie said. This time it wasn't a question, but acknowledgment.

As she sat there on her knees, repeating those two dreadful words over and over, the wind growing to a spinning torrent around them. The faster the wind spun, the warmer it got. Steam from the wet ground wafted into the air. Lucas swallowed deeply, his stomach twisting as pain shot down his arm. Something was very, very wrong.

"Averie, come on. I'm sorry. I didn't mean it. Let's go to the dance and forget this even happened. I'm sure my arm will be fine. I know you didn't mean to."

As he looked around at the steam rising in swirls around him, the roar of the wind picked up. All he could hear over it was Averie's laughter.

"Averie?" He moved forward, placing a hand lightly on her shoulder.

Her head shot up, her eyes glowing a rich gold. Her dark and broad smile sent chills down his spine. "I'll show you just how much of a freak I am," she said in a voice so unlike the one he knew.

* * *

Denial

Karen drove home with a wide, teeth-baring smile covering her face and a lightness filling her chest, making her feel as though she was soaring across the morning skies. She turned her music up, happily singing along, as peace settled over her. Her plan had worked and now it was up to the kids to do their part. As Karen sang along, a shiver of excitement ran through her as her mind replayed the last several minutes.

Silas stared into his reflection, doubt sparkling in his teal eyes. Twisting side to side, he eyed his appearance with a more than critical eye. Though the black suit fit him surprisingly well, accentuating his broad shoulders and bulging arms, maintaining a classic over flashy look.

"Is everything alright?" Karen asked from the doorway. Silas found her gaze in the mirror and gave a half-hearted shrug.

Silas sighed. "I look ridiculous."

Karen shifted from the doorway to stand beside him. "You look very handsome."

"She's right, Silas, you do look dashing. Averie will be so happy to see you." Cleo smiled; her hands clutched to her chest in excitement as she looked him over.

"Do you think so?" Silas asked, still unsure.

Karen and Cleo exchanged a knowing look as they beamed their smiles at him, their actions so contagious, Silas couldn't help smiling himself. Adjusting his tie once more, Silas turned to face them, his arms wide.

"So handsome," Karen acknowledged.

"Averie is one lucky girl," Cleo agreed.

"Time for you to get going. We wouldn't want you to be late," Karen said, rushing Silas from the room and out the front door. "Averie is wearing a white and gold dress. You can't miss her."

Silas tipped his head in understanding as he dug his keys from his pocket, watching curiously as they shook slightly. He was nervous. Such a strange and useless emotion. He couldn't remember the last time he felt this way. Day after day, he plunged himself into battle without so much as a quiver. But now as he stood. readying himself for a different sort of battle, he felt the trembling in his hands and met them with a smile.

"Nervous?" Karen whispered from his side.

Silas nodded, his eyes trapped on his quivering hands. He had waged countless battles and had never felt the worry he did now.

"Don't be. Averie adores you. She talks about you constantly, and she looked so sad when she said you weren't coming."

"Thank you, Karen, for coming here, for bringing this suit," Silas said, giving Karen a tight hug, before turning and doing the same for Cleo. As he pulled back, he watched the women dab at their eyes and sniffle their noses. "Is everything alright?" he asked, concerned.

Karen waved his words away and gave a small chuckle. "Don't mind us, honey, you need to get going."

Silas tipped his head and climbed into his car, waved once more and disappeared down the street.

"Do you really think she will be excited to see him?" Cleo asked, staring down the road.

"I have no doubt. Well, I'll be off, I got a full night of much needed relaxing ahead of me. It was great to meet you." Karen smiled, giving Cleo a small hug and moving to her car.

Denial

"Have a great night, Karen," Cleo said with a tight smile.

* * *

Karen parked her car and climbed out, her smile still clinging to her face as she danced up the stairs and into the house. The setting sun shined brightly through the kitchen window, bathing everything in its rich orange and yellow glow and creating long shadows from the appliances.

Karen smiled to herself as she opened the fridge and grabbed her favorite wine. Her daughter was going to be happy, fully and completely happy, in a way that she could never provide. She had always wanted to be a mother and when she had gotten the terrible news from the doctor that it would never happen naturally, her devastation had been too great.

Looking back, Karen realized if Averie hadn't been given to her that night, her life would have ended in another way. To this day, she couldn't remember the faces of the couple that had dropped the little red-haired baby off on her doorstep. The only thing she could remember was the desperation in their eyes and the warmth of the little one she had held in her arms. When they had given her the folder that held adoption papers, she had hesitated, but in her heart, she knew that they had saved her life in more ways than one.

Pouring the red liquid into the awaiting wine glass, Karen applauded herself for her accomplishments. It had been hard to pick herself up at first, even harder as she tried to figure out how to be a single mother, but in even the darkest moments, one glance at the smiling baby and suddenly she had known that this was what she had always wanted. To have someone to love unconditionally and have that love in return, there was nothing like it. To have a child and watch her grow into a beautiful woman had been the greatest gift that anyone could ever have given her.

Karen sipped from the glass and shook herself from the past as she turned toward her room. Now was not the time to get lost in memories, she had a sexy hot date with the latest romance novel and her bathtub. A small knock sounded, putting her plans on temporary hold. Another sip and Karen placed the glass on the side table before opening the door.

Chapter Thirty

There was no stopping the trembling in Silas's hands as he drove down the empty street toward the town hall. All he could think of was Averie choosing him, or Averie wanting him. What would she think when she saw him? Would she smile or be disappointed? Would it be a mix of both? His thoughts were racing. His mind shifted between wanting to drive faster and wanting to turn back. He couldn't remember ever being this nervous. He had fought countless battles, led men to war and yet this was something that threatened to bring him to his knees faster than any enemy. Something that could hurt him more than any sword or any arrow, but he drove forward, as any great warrior does.

He pulled behind a limo that was moving at an agonizingly slow pace. A group of excited high schoolers laughing and hollering from the sunroof. It took every fiber in his body to follow instead of recklessly pass them. No, he needed to be calm. Needed to be reserved. Needed the time to get his thoughts together, his feelings, so he knew exactly what and how to say what he needed to when the time came.

As he turned into the parking lot for the town hall, he took a deep breath, closed his eyes, and let his head rest against the back of his seat. He knew what would happen if he let himself go, if he let himself feel, truly feel. Was it worth it? Truly worth it? The risk of opening yourself up to someone on that level was something you ran the risk of never recovering from. Opening his eyes, he had made his decision. Yes, she was worth it. Everything he would lose would be worth it, if he could have her. A smile stretched his face as he pulled the keys from the engine and stepped out.

As the warm and humid air hit his face, Silas's stomach dropped. Something was terribly and irrevocably wrong. The sky swirled black and blue, red and orange as if someone had dropped a set of paints into a drain.

Slamming the car door, he sprinted up the stairs of the glistening white building and plunged into the mythically-themed prom. He ignored the futile complaints of the students he shoved aside as he scoured the dance floor in desperation. Flowered vines hung along the walls, and lights twinkled above, giving a soft glow to the otherwise

Denial

darkened room. Tables were spread along the side holding a variety of drinks and snacks. Three miscreants chuckled as one emptied a flask into the large punch bowl.

Silas continued his search, passed the fist-pumping DJ, bored teachers, and uncomfortable principal. Flashes went off all around him as friends and couples took photos to commemorate their night. All of their smiling faces, enjoying their pointless night, oblivious to the sick feeling consuming him, sent a pang of anger through him. Stepping into the throws of dancing teens and giggling girls he searched their faces, wishing to spot the one he knew deep down he wouldn't find.

He continued to shove his way through the growing crowd, desperate to find her. Where was she? She was close, that he knew, he could feel her. Their bond wasn't strong enough to pinpoint exactly where, at least not yet. Urgency and dread kept building throughout his body with every minute that passed.

The flash of blonde hair atop a pink dress was like water in the desert. "Sera!" he called to the small blonde.

She turned and smiled. "Silas! I was wondering if you were going to show up. What do you think? Can you guess who I am? Where's Averie?" she asked, looking around him.

With a sudden jerk, the ground began to quake beneath their feet. Screams and gasps flooding the air as the music screeched to a halt. Sera fell against Silas while he fought to keep them both on their feet. Glasses rattled and fell to the ground, smashing and spreading across the floor like confetti. After what seemed like an eternity, the earth stilled. Teachers rushed forward, cleaning the ground, while the principal moved to the stage.

"Alright, ladies and gentlemen, that was a little scary for all of us but let's get back to your senior prom! DJ, please." Nodding, the DJ started the music while students slowly slipped back into their roles as the chatter and dancing resumed.

"What was that?" Sera asked, releasing her grip on Silas's jacket to adjust her hair.

"Felt like an earthquake," he said.

"In May? Is that normal?" Sera asked.

Silas shrugged. "I'm sure it is. It's earthquake season, right? Now what were you saying about Averie?"

"I haven't seen her."

"You mean she isn't here?" he asked, clenching his jaw.

Her face faded to a frown as she shook her head. "No. I haven't seen her. I left first," she said. "She went with Lucas. She said she wanted to talk to him. Is everything okay?"

He forced a smile and nodded. "Yeah, no problem, just need to see her. If you find her first, tell her to come find me?"

Sera eyed Silas with increasing suspicion. "Yeah, sure." Sera nodded.

"Thanks, you look beautiful by the way." He smiled, brushing her arm.

Denial

Flipping her hair off her shoulder, Sera returned his smile. "I know. Now go find Averie, then save me a dance, okay?" she finished with a wink.

Making his way to the side door, he watched as the sky swirled. He could feel the energy pouring from the clouds. It was Averie, he knew it, could feel it seeping through their bond. Her anger and sorrow pulsated in the night air.

"Oh, stars, Averie, what are you doing?" he muttered aloud, taking off into a sprint.

* * *

"Averie, please, I didn't mean it." Lucas's eyes widened in fear.

"No? Are you sure?" she asked, smiling wide as she slowly stood. "I mean, I am, aren't I? Who else can do this?" Raising her arms, the ground began to shake, the wind ripping and tearing at his clothes.

"Please, Averie, I'm sorry!" Lucas gasped, the wind forcing itself into his lungs.

"Sorry?!" She stepped closer, sending quakes through the earth beneath them both. "Sorry for what? Shattering me with your hate and disgust? For the lies and deception or for calling me a freak?" Her words were ice, crystallizing the moisture in the air and turning it to tiny, frozen knives that sliced Lucas's exposed skin.

He cried out in agony as the blood streamed from his wounds.

"Shh." She placed a finger to her lips as she moved closer. "Don't worry, baby, this will all be over soon."

Her mind was trapped inside her own body, swirling in pain and confusion, reacting on pure emotion. She felt the power surge through her, the destructive rage bursting out into the elements around her. She couldn't control it. She couldn't stop it. The power she felt was controlling her body like a puppet as it tried to defend her from her emotional turmoil. The things she was doing and the words she was saying were coming out on their own, she couldn't temper them any more than she could swim through the pain she was feeling.

She watched Lucas, drowning in fear, the blood seeping from his face and arms. She didn't understand why, but something felt good about making someone else feel the pain, someone besides herself. It didn't matter if it was someone she loved or not, maybe it felt so good because it was someone she loved.

STOP! She screamed in her head. This wasn't right. This wasn't the way things were supposed to go. He was supposed to tell her that everything would be okay, that he would still be her friend that he would always be there for her. The hurt of that dream being shattered cut her deeper than anything she had ever felt before. Freak, that is what he had called her. That small little world caused more pain than anything she had ever felt before. Her mind bounced back and forth, hating what she was doing and hating that she didn't want to stop.

Denial

Her ears rang with the sickening sound of her own cruel laugh and her final words to him: "Don't worry, baby, it'll all be over soon."

"NOO!!!" Her scream exploded into the night.

Silas was close, he knew it but there was something pushing him away. Some force trying to keep him from getting to her. She was breaking, it was too soon, too fast. She wouldn't be in control. She didn't know enough yet. If she did know, he would lose her forever. She would do more than destroy herself, she would destroy everything.

Pushing past the fear that was gripping him, he urged forward across the courtyard. He could see Lucas's car. He knew she was with Lucas, so she must be close. His bones ached with her hate, her anger, her fear. He could feel it in his soul like it was his own.

"Averie!" he called out. He could see her now, her power and her anger swirling around her. Lucas stood pinned in the air, gripping at his broken arm, blood running down his face and arms. She couldn't see Silas. Couldn't hear him. Silas stood stunned at the scene unfolding before him.

He heard Averie's empty laughter, watched her lift her arms, preparing for a final blow on her defenseless prey. "Move, move!" his mind screamed at him. He pulled together every ounce of power he had left and threw himself forward. Suddenly the air went still. All sound and all movement stopped; the world seemed to pause.

Then an explosion ripped through the air.

The world had shattered around him. Silas felt the earth itself scream cry out in agony. A curtain of light, emanating from where Averie was, shot outwards in all directions. His body felt like it was on the verge of exploding as the light drew closer. Just as he knew he couldn't take it anymore, everything went cold. The blinding light blinked out existence and a deep, darkness flooded in. After a moment, Silas carefully opened his eyes to a disturbingly still and normal night. The moon hung high in the sky, the stars bright and shining in the clear sky. The ground around him was smooth and grass was blowing in the gentle breeze. Everything was again back to normal.

"Averie!" Silas called, searching for any sign of her.

A deep groan from behind him took his reluctant attention. "Oh, god, Lucas."

Silas had survived countless battles, watched limbs ripped from their owners and seen people die horribly before his very eyes. This was something different. Something he had never imagined even during his own torture.

Lucas lay before him sprawled on the ground, his clothes in tatters around his sliced and burned body. Strips of flesh lay at his sides, while his arm bone glistened with a red hue as the muscles tried to cling. His legs were both at awkward angles, and his nose was nearly gone. There was a large pool of blood under him, making Silas wonder if Lucas had any even left in his body.

Denial

"Stay here, I'll be right back." The words were useless to the unconscious man, yet they had felt necessary. Pulling the medallion from around his neck he ran for the trees, stopping suddenly when a long, golden light caught his eye. Looking toward Lucas, seeing his slow but steady breath, Silas turned toward light, letting the cool breeze clear his mind.

His heart hurt, his body ached, and his soul felt torn. Something was missing, and he longed to know what it was. The light started pulsing, getting brighter, as it beckoned him closer. He walked carefully toward it, wanting to pull away but not able to do so. The fear and thoughts of Lucas faded away as the light consumed his every thought. He reached the source of the light, it stood before him like a window. Peering inside, he felt his blood freeze. "Averie?"

The light reached up the trees like a shimmering cocoon. Silas couldn't help himself, he had to touch the light. His fingers graced the warm surface before electricity sparked up his arm bringing him to his knees. His whole body convulsed as the electricity worked its way down his body. He suppressed a cry, but he could not give up. He searched the cocoon for an opening, his eyes drawn again and again to Averie's shattered body.

He clenched his fist, the cold metal of the medallion snapping him back to reality. He looked at the cocoon of light one last time, then took off into the dark woods. One last look and he disappeared, the medallion held tightly in his hand.

C.R. Rice

"I'm going to save you, both of you."

Chapter Thirty-One

Silas dashed into the woods, as if the devil himself were at his heels, his heart thudding against his ribs as branches ripped and tore at his clothes. His mind rebelling as the horrors he had witnessed flashed through his mind. *What have you done, Averie?* A burn began to feather across his skin as he burst through the darkness to stop at an old ruin. Silas shook away his concern, his feet flying across the dew-covered grass with practiced silence. Shoving the crumbling door aside, Silas bound down the stone steps. "Callen!" The cave shook from his call.

Callen came running with four men, swords drawn. "Silas? What are you doing here? How did you find us?" Callen peaked curiously around his friend. "Did you find The Lost One?"

"I don't have time to explain. I need your help," said Silas, gripping Callen's shoulders.

"Of course," Callen agreed.

"What day are we on?" Silas asked, looking around.

"Thirty-four, why? How long has it been for you?" said Callen.

"Thirty days for me," Silas said exhaustively.

"Thirty days! But how?" Callen's scientific mind was reeling at the new information. He started doing mathematical formulas in his head, mumbling various formulas out loud as he tried to figure out the solution.

Silas waved him off. "That's not important right now. You!" He pointed to a tall burly man, in light chain armor. "I need you to get Maddox and quickly. Tell him I need him immediately and that he needs to bring all of the best healing concoctions he has. Then, find Radnar and bring him back here as well. Go!" Silas urged.

The man bowed slightly before turning on his heel and running out of the room. Silas turned his attention back to the curious Callen, who was still lost in his mathematics, and the remaining men as he took a deep, steadying breath.

"Silas, how did you get here?" Callen questioned again, his mind prickling with unease. "What is going on?"

Silas shook his head. "There is no time to explain. I need you and two of your most trusted men to come back with me, and it needs to be now."

"Now?" Callen asked, confused.

"Yes, now. Like *right now* Callen," responded Silas.

Denial

Callen nodded his head in dismissal to the men beside him. "What is going on, Si?"

"Averie, she's been … hurt, and I don't know how to reach her, and Lucas is dying, and if we don't hurry, the cops will be all over the place, and it will turn into a disaster," Silas said.

"Who are Averie and Lucas? What is a cop? And what kind of disaster? Silas what the hell is wrong with you? You are not making any sense, man," said Callen.

"There isn't time to explain! We need to go, now!" Silas snapped.

Callen held up his hands in surrender as Maddox, Radnar, and two other "standard" looking guards ran into the cave. Silas did not know the two random men, nor did he care to learn who they were.

"Silas, what's going on?" Maddox asked.

"Do you have everything I asked for?" responded Silas.

Maddox nodded tapping his large black bag. "I always come prepared. You know that," he said with a vague smile.

"Right, then, let's go," said Silas.

"Hello, to you, too, Silas," Radnar said, adjusting his belt on his hips.

"Hang on, this can be a little strange at first." Silas grabbed the medallion, distracting the group from the snapping of his fingers, and the world faded into a swirling mist. Within a moment, they were standing over Lucas's mangled body.

"By the stars!" Radnar gasped, as he heavily breathed in the cool night air.

"What happened here?" Maddox asked, leaning forward, pulling his large black bag open.

"What did you do Silas?" Callen demanded, his thoughts on more than just the mangled corpse before them.

The blond man leaned forward resting his hands on his knees. "Did that make anyone else feel extremely nauseous? Did it feel like you just got sucked through a giant straw? No, just me? Swell."

"There was an accident. Can you fix him?" Silas asked plainly, pointedly ignoring Callen's inquiry.

Maddox nodded, pulling a variety of bottles and bad smelling herbs from his bag. "It'll take time. It's a miracle he has enough blood in his body to beat his own heart with these injuries."

"How long?" asked Silas.

"An hour maybe to get him pieced back together, longer to fully heal," responded Maddox.

"Make it less," demanded Silas.

Maddox looked up aghast. "Do you realize what you are asking? This boy is lucky to be alive, let alone be rushed in piecing him back together. The pain alone would be—"

"Just do it, Maddox! We don't have much time before the cops arrive," responded Silas.

Maddox gave a reluctant nod. "I'll need at least one person to help, one who can stomach this mess."

Denial

"I'll help," the blond man stepped forward with his hand up.

"What is your name?" Maddox asked, crouching on the ground.

"Trite, sir."

"Get down here, Trite, we don't have much time," Maddox growled, not sparing the others a glance as he went to work.

"Good, let's go," Silas said, turning and racing down the hill.

"Where are we going?" Callen bellowed, trailing close behind.

"You'll see," Silas tossed over his shoulder, maintaining speed.

"What the hell is that?" Radnar asked when they finally reached another clearing.

Silas continued forward until he was forced to stop before the golden cocoon.

"This is the Lost One," Silas deadpanned.

"What the hell happened here Silas?" Callen asked, reaching forward.

"Wait!" Silas yelled, but it was already too late.

Callen dropped to the ground howling in pain, his arm clutched to his chest while his body rocked with tremors.

"You can't touch her!" Silas snapped.

"Well, that would have been great information to have, BEFORE, I touched it," Callen barked at Silas.

The group paused, looking from to the other.

"Dammit, Silas, will you stop this and just tell us what the hell is going on?" Callen beseeches from the ground.

Silas shook his head, desperation in his eyes. "Not now, we don't have time. These humans are not used to …" he motioned to the cocoon before them, "this. If she's still here when they arrive, we will be left in a complicated situation and may have to make some truly terrible decisions."

"By the stars, Silas! *We* are not used to this," Radnar noted, his arm motioning to the strange orb. "You will need to make time. We have all left from where we are needed, the least you owe us is a why." Radnar reached down, clasping Callen's forearm and helping him to his feet.

"It was my fault. I should have been there; I shouldn't have acted like such a child," said Silas distantly.

"Start at the beginning," Callen said, in a calming but stern voice.

With no choice, Silas did. He leaned against a tree, his back straight and eyes shifting slowly from man to man as he spoke of arriving in this Realm, finding his contacts, his discovery of Averie, and ending in the explosion that created the cocoon they now stood before.

"How is that even possible? To stop something like that, when it has already passed the point of no return is impossible. *Should* be impossible," Callen corrected himself.

Silas shrugged and shook his head.

Denial

"What can we do?" Radnar questioned, his arms crossed over his chest, eyes roaming inquisitively over the glowing encasing.

"We need to move her," responded Silas.

"How are we supposed to move her if we can't touch her? How do you even know if she is alive?" Radnar asked.

"She's alive," said Silas with a level of confidence that even surprised himself.

"How do you know, Silas? I've never seen anything like this!" Looking for confirmation, Radnar shook his head. "No one has!"

"I just know! Now we have to get her out of here." He looked to the three men standing before him. "Any ideas?"

"I might." A tall red-headed young warrior, that Silas didn't recognize, stepped forward.

"Who are you?" asked Silas.

"Beck," responded Beck.

Silas nodded. "Alright, Beck, what's your idea?"

Beck shifted his feet. "It is a theory, really. Something I read about." Beck looked up to see the urgency in the faces of the men before him. "It's risky, but we may be able to use the shifting power of the medallion to move it—her to a more secure location, but it's going to take a lot of energy, and if we don't have it…"

"If we don't have it what happens?" Callen asked.

"Well, essentially we would be ripped apart by the force of the move, part of us here, part of us there, and part of us wherever we pass through."

"Oh, is that all?" Callen asked, shifting his gaze to Silas. "Did you hear that, Si? We would be ripped apart. No big risk there."

"We can do it," Silas said firmly.

Callen threw his hands in the air. "Can someone please talk some sense into him?"

Radnar stepped toward the cocoon peering deep inside to find the smooth porcelain features and gasped. "Silas, how old is our Savior?"

"What does it matter?" he demanded through clenched teeth.

"How long have her powers been manifested?" Radnar asked.

Silas and Radnar's eyes locked in a silent battle, which ended in a draw as sirens echoed through the trees. "We don't have time to discuss this, the cops will be here any minute. We need to do this now," snapped Silas.

Moments later, Maddox and the large blond guard came running through the trees. "There are men closing in driving some weird metal things with annoying high-pitched noises." Maddox shook his head. "So inefficient."

"Yes, that is this Realm's version of guards. Cops as they are called," Silas explained, not bothering to look at Maddox.

The two newcomers slid to a stop, their mouths gaping open as they saw the cocoon shimmering before them.

"How is Lucas?" asked Silas, his gaze still fixed on the light.

Denial

Recovering himself, Maddox nodded. "He will survive, though his mind may not. I did not have time to change his memories. He's going to remember, Silas. All of it."

"It'll have to be enough," Silas answered.

Beck stepped forward. "We need to do this now. If my theory is correct, it will take a few precious moments for us to gather the energy we need, and with those cop-things you say are on the way, we may not have them."

"Do what?" Maddox asked, looking between the original group's conflicting faces.

"Oh, no one wants to tell them?" Callen demanded finally. "Allow me then. Silas needs to move this here Lost One, who may or may not be alive—"

"She is alive," Silas said adamantly.

Callen waved him off. "What we need to do is jump her to somewhere that Silas has, hopefully, already chosen and prepared. Right, Si? Got it all set? All ready to go?"

Silas's glare did nothing to sway Callen's tirade.

"Right. So we have nothing prepared, no location set and all of three minutes to decide before those siren people find us. Is that everything, or did I miss something?" Snapping his fingers, he let out a little laugh. "Oh, yes! Not only can we not actually touch the Savior but the bloody jump may rip us all to shreds, and I do not mean that figuratively, boys. I mean literally rip us to shreds. What was it you said, Beck? Leave pieces of us here, there, and everywhere?"

Radnar let out a roaring laugh, slapping his knee. "You two are just too much. Alright then, let's do this."

"Wait a minute, are we going to discuss the ripping to pieces part?" the blond guard screeched.

"No," snipped Silas.

"Time, time is of the essence, screw our safety, screw our lives. We have to be all about this 'Lost One' who may not even be alive right now." Callen glared.

"That is enough boys. Let's go." Radnar stepped forward. "Now how do we do this if we can't even touch it?"

Beck shifted his stance as all eyes turned once more to him. He forced a smile. "Well, that's the tricky part, see we are going to have to all touch it at the exact same time that the jump occurs otherwise it will be … well, everyone touches it at the same time."

A distant clamor of voices echoed through the trees.

"Now, do it now!" Trite said, jumping from foot to foot.

"Just so you know, this might hurt a bit," Callen mumbled, rubbing his arm in preparation for the searing pain once more.

Chapter Thirty-Two

Averie was floating, a warm wind chasing away the threatening chill that had filled her, leaving behind a feeling she couldn't quite shake. A soft sigh escaped her lips as the sweet smell of wildflowers tickled her nose. Her fingers twitched against the smooth grass beneath her. She felt herself relaxing into it when something rough and wet began lapping at her face. Jerking upright, her head swam at the sudden movement as she met a warm brown gaze.

Hot, panting breaths covered her face as the dog stared back, tongue hanging out the side of its mouth. It had a smooth, thick looking coat that shimmered somewhere between black and brown with its chest a glowing white. The dog tilted its head at her inspection, his face mirroring a bear with its broadness and ears that stuck straight up. Averie gave the beast a small smile sending its tail into a frantic wag against the grass.

"Hey, there buddy. What are you doing here?" she asked, looking around, a frown creasing her features. A meadow stretched as far as the eye could see, the only movement coming from the flowers as the wind traced across them. "Where is here?"

The dog barked suddenly, jumped up, and raced away. "Wait!" Averie called, climbing to her feet and chasing after him as though he held all of the answers in the world. Her bare feet slapped against the ground, the white flowing dress she wore tangled between her legs, sending her sprawling to the grass. As she hit the ground, all the air in her lungs was lost. She laid in the grass, gasping for breath.

She rolled to her side, her eyes scanning the horizon for any sign of her new furry friend. The dog, sensing she was not behind him, turned around then lunged from side to side playfully as though waiting for her. Pushing herself to her feet Averie twisted the gown to her knees, holding the hem tightly in her hand she gave chase, the animal darting away as soon as she started to move.

"Wait! Stop!" she called, pushing herself harder still as the animal became a speck on the horizon before disappearing completely, but still, she didn't stop. Her legs ached, her head swiveling from side to side as she ran, looking for a glimpse of the dog or a sign of where it went.

As the panic of being lost clawed its way inside her mind, a shadow appeared.

Denial

Averie slowed, her steps becoming unsteady as the figure became more distinguished. Shifting and changing as the dog danced in circles around it, the shadow settled smoothly into the silhouette of a woman. The light all around dimmed, a sudden and harsh wind twisted and roared, pulling the petals from the surrounding flowers until a rainbow of colors swirled around the figure. Averie pulled her arms to cover her face at the flurry of motion, and as quickly as it started, it stopped, leaving a small, smiling woman behind.

Averie took a tentative step forward. Her curious eyes wandered across the woman to the dog and back again. The woman stood proud; her hands delicately clasped before her. She had long twisted hair, held back neatly with silver leaves on either side of her head. Her skin seemed to radiate from somewhere deep inside, giving her an ethereal appearance. Averie noticed the woman wore the same white gown she did, but her eyes were held captive by the pulsing green stone that she wore on a thin silver chain around her neck.

"Averie." The woman's voice surrounded her, forcing their eyes to connect. The words not in the air around her but inside her head.

"How do you know my name? Who are you?" Averie asked.

The woman chuckled. "I brought you here. Don't you think I would know who you are before doing that?"

Averie considered the words. "Am I ... dead?"

The woman eyed her as she chose her words carefully, "Not exactly."

"What does that mean?" asked Averie.

"It means you are not quite dead but not quite alive," said the woman coyly.

"That doesn't even make sense," snipped Averie. "I can't be dead."

The woman gave a small smile. "Don't worry dear, it won't be for long."

"What do you mean?" asked Averie, her head beginning to throb with the circular answers she was getting.

"I brought you here to give your body time," the woman said.

"Time for what? Where am I?" asked Averie.

"I am afraid I can't share that information with you right now. What do you remember?" asked the woman.

Averie shook her head, frowning. "Nothing, I can't remember anything."

The woman gave her a small smile. "Do not worry yourself. You will remember soon enough. Even if in the end you will wish that you didn't. Come now, walk with me and we shall spend the rest of our time together with a little talk."

"Who are you?" Averie asked.

The woman turned, walking away. Averie only hesitated for a moment before rushing after her. "What do you see?" the woman asked casually.

Averie looked around confused. "A meadow."

Denial

"What else?"

"A dog, you, me," answered Averie.

The woman smiled her hand patting the massive dog's head lovingly. "That is very good, Averie. We have time for three questions, so choose them wisely. I do not know when I will be able to bring you here again, if ever."

"But you won't answer all of them," Avery said, a hint of contempt in her voice.

The woman shrugged, bending to pick up a fallen iris. "I may not, but with enough time, all questions are answered. Would a question even be a question, if it did not have an answer?"

"You know they always say that in movies, but it never really comes out until it is too late," Avery quipped.

The woman's musical laughter twinkled through the air, "Oh, Averie, it truly is all happy endings with you." Standing once more she nodded ahead. "We are running out of time."

"I don't know what to ask," Averie admitted, continuing forward.

"How do you expect answers if you do not know the questions? How about, to help instead, I tell you a few things, then you can ask your questions," the woman said with a warm smile.

"Okay," Averie agreed, nibbling at her lip.

"I must tell you first, that some of the things I say will not make much sense at the moment but will become clear as time goes on."

"Of course, they will." Averie sighed. "Go on then, what do you have?"

"That is your one, dear Averie."

Averie stopped. "But you said you'd tell me something first! You tricked me."

The woman shrugged, deeply inhaling the purple bloom. "I can only reveal what is asked. Come now, we don't want to be late."

Biting back the desire to ask her what they would be late for, Averie fell back into step.

"Things are different now. When you go back, things are going to be ... difficult, but you must remain strong. Do not let the darkness pull you under. Lean on those that lean on you. You are strong little, Avi, and you will be alright, especially in the moments it seems the least possible."

"Even though I don't remember what happened, I know I did something terrible. I can feel it right here," Averie whispered, pushing against her chest.

The woman nodded sadly. "You did alter the course of things, but we cannot change that now. We can only move forward and take the battles as they come. Even someone as powerful as you cannot change time."

"The power isn't mine though, is it?" Averie asked, stopping to grab a long branch and waving it to the dog. The dog barked and jumped happily into the air just as she threw the stick over his head, sending him bounding through the meadow as he gave chase.

Denial

The woman stared after the dog as he stopped and grabbed the stick. Shaking it back and forth before bringing the prize back to them. "Yes and no. Some of the power is yours, but not all of it. Some of it comes from the Heart that was placed inside of you as a child. It pulls from the magic in the Realms around it. It was made to keep the Realm together, so when it was torn from the Realm, it fell apart as well. At that juncture, the Heart's purpose had to change."

"Which is why I can pull power from almost everything around me," Averie mused. "Sometimes the power is so much, I feel like I can do anything, while others it seems to be gone."

"In some ways you can, but you must remember that the more you take, the more that must be given back. There is a balance to all things in the universe."

Averie nodded, half listening through her own swirling thoughts.

"Last question, Averie." The woman smiled, coming to a stop before the door.

Averie's brow furrowed, "That wasn't here a moment ago." Averie walked around the door; it wasn't connected to anything but stood in silent defiance of all logic.

"It means our time is up. Now ask your question."

"How do I save the Realm?"

"That, my dear, is the right question."

Chapter Thirty-Three

There was pain everywhere. It was a living, breathing, violence that had burned itself deep inside her body. There was a darkness weighing heavily that she couldn't quite place or even explain. She heard the groan escape her lips and felt the harshness of the sound as it tore out of her parched throat. Her eyelids felt like weights as she tried to force them open. *Why can't I move? Why do I hurt so bad? What the hell happened?* Her thoughts were interrupted by the lightning of pain coursing through her body.

Voices, she heard them getting closer. She heard a door open before shutting with a soft click a moment later. Footsteps echoed in the silence that surrounded her, the scraping of a chair against tile sounded like a glass window shattering in her head. Another groan ripped automatically from her dry, cracked lips.

"Finally," a familiar voice breathed. *Who is he? Where am I?*

Denial

Warm hands took one of hers. *Why am I so cold?*

Other voices whispered in her head incoherently. She had to fight to stay awake, fight to listen, fight to understand. Their words didn't make any sense and yet something inside seemed to register them. So much fighting. The darkness beckoned her, promising no more fights, no more confusion. She knew she could give in, allow it to take her away, to drift from the pain, from the sharpness of everything, only her mind wouldn't let her.

Releasing a strangled breath, she fought once more to open her eyes. The bright light burning like acid on her raw eyes. "Water…" she begged ruggedly, swallowing down another groan.

"Maddox!" she heard the deep voice call, grating against her aching head. The door swung open quickly as a man hustled in. He looked familiar, but her head ached with pain and trying to pull a memory was beyond her right now. "She's awake, and she wants water," the familiar one explained.

Another set of steps alerted her to the beckoned man. She watched him nod and put a large bag on the small side table. Quickly, he opened it, removing a variety of different colored vials and bottles, and began mixing something together.

"This should help her with the pain, though she's going feel a little groggy," Maddox said, as he continued his mixing.

"Why?" the other asked, his eyes locked on her pale face.

Maddox sighed, handing over the cool glass. "How would I know, Silas? I told you before I have never seen anything like what had happened before, but I can't imagine she is going to understand everything immediately. Be gentle with her."

Silas nodded. Taking the glass, he delicately cradled her head, holding it to her lips. Maddox watched for a moment, flashed her a quick, reassuring smile, and took his leave.

In her head, their words made no sense. She knew the meanings of them but as their meaning got close, they slipped away just as quickly.

"Here," Silas ordered, pulling her from the darkness and plunging her into the world of pain once more. "Drink."

Slowly, she parted her cracked lips, the tear of them separating sent a sharp pain along her mouth. Ignoring the throbbing, she greedily drank from the cool cup, the thick warm liquid coating her throat and giving her body new life as it eased the stiffness and radiating pain. Lifting her arm, she touched her head, rubbing at the pain in her temples. Prying open her eyes once again, she waited for them to slowly steady on the dimmed lights above.

Fighting through her constant pain, she turned her head, finding a set of piercing teal eyes staring back at her. She felt her heart speed at the look he gave her. "Mesmerizing," she whispered unwittingly.

She watched as his brows furrowed before moving to rest his hand against her forehead. "How are you feeling?"

Denial

There was such a heavy feeling in his words that it made her ache.

"Where am I?" She knew this man, but why couldn't she remember? It was like an itch somewhere deep in her mind.

He gently laid her head back on the soft pillow then sat the glass on the awaiting table. "My house." It was said simply as she fought through the fog in her mind.

"What did you do to me?" she asked.

Silas grimaced at her accusation before he shook his head. "Nothing. I wasn't able to get there in time."

"In time for what?" she whispered.

He eyed her carefully, as if taking great consideration in his next words. "You don't know what happened?"

Shaking her head, unknown tears filled her dry eyes bringing reluctant relief. "I can't remember."

He took her hands and kissed them gently. The simple comforting gesture sending lightning prickling across her skin. There was something important she was missing here.

"Averie, I need you to focus." *Averie? Is that my name?* The thickness of forgotten moments cloaked her. Clenching her eyes tight, she let his words flow through her.

"Focus on the richness of the flowers, the brightness of the lights, and the sound of my voice," he said calmly.

She slowly nodded, taking in the deep rich tone of his voice. She felt his words swirl in the air around her, dissipating the fog in her head. Her breathing picked up as memory and thought flooded back in, but there was something inside her desperate to stay hidden.

"Si?" she begged.

"Shh, it's okay, Averie, everything is okay." He ran his fingertips across her forehead and down her jawline. "Everything and everyone is fine."

More memories flashed at his words. She stood twirling before a standing mirror, her dress flaring slightly as she turned. "Prom, I remember." Opening her eyes, she bit at the inside of her lip. "What did I do?"

Chapter Thirty-Four

The four men sat in resolute silence on their high-backed bar stools around the crystal black bar. The sun cast its rays through the large oval windows, setting it alight. Their stares locked heavily on the man sitting at the end of the bar. A set of two plates were laid before him, a glinting silver fork ready in his hand, his gray eyes swiveled from one plate to the next. Finally, settling with the one to the right, he slowly pierced the spongy piece before bringing it to his mouth.

The men all leaned forward, watching his expressionless face as he chewed and swallowed. Lifting the fork again, he pierced the left piece's flaky crust before repeating the process beneath the men's intense stares. At last, the man placed the fork down with a soft click against the bar and pointed to the right.

"You have got to be kidding me!" Thane shouted, slamming his hands against the bar surface as the others exchanged smiles and handshakes.

Callen shrugged. "It tastes better."

"In what universe is cake better than pie?" pushing from his stool, Thane moved around the long bar to stand beside the smirking Callen and glared down the bar. "Which one of them put you up to it?"

Callen cocked a brow, a smile twitching his cheek as he struggled to hold back a laugh. "I'm sorry?"

Thane pointed to the three others and grit his teeth saying, "Which one of them told you to say something so ridiculous?"

Callen shook his head. "None. I tried the two you set before me and made my decision."

"That's a lie!" bellowed Thane.

Callen's eyes narrowed. "I do not lie."

"Well, then welcome to your first time because that is a complete lie. Cake is and never will be better than pie!"

"I feel as though you are overreacting," Callen said, leaning back slightly on his stool.

"Really? And just what is the appropriate response to someone choosing *cake* over pie?"

"Well, if you think of more than just the taste, you have the aesthetics, the more enticing flavors and varieties. You have frosting. It is quite incredible. Not to mention

Denial

the breakfast cupcakes. I mean, this Realm really perfected turning cake into a breakfast food."

Thane sat staring at Callen for a moment in disbelief. "You are choosing cake because you think muffins are breakfast cupcakes?"

"Are they not?" asked Callen.

"No! They are muffins!" responded Thane.

"What's the difference?" Callen asked.

"Well," Thane hesitated on his arguement. "One has frosting and the other doesn't."

"But breakfast cupcakes have glaze. Isn't that the same?" Callen responded.

"No!" barked Thane.

"They are both made from sugar, yes?" Called asked.

"That's not the point!" yelled Thane.

"Have you tried a cinnamon bun? You know those twisty cake things covered with *frosting*. Fantastic breakfast cake," Callen asked, knowing how to truly bait an enemy.

Thane glared, his jaw clenching over and over. "Pie has breakfast stuff, too, you know."

"Like what?" Callen asked, curiosity peaked.

"Like ... you know, those little pie things." Moving his fingers into a square, he looked to the group behind him. Beck, Trite, and Radnar looked from one to the other before shaking their heads.

Shrugging, Callen rested his elbows against the bar, lifting the fork once more to pierce the cake.

"Don't you do it. Don't you even do it," Thane gritted, his fists clenching at his sides.

Maintaining eye contact, Callen lifted the forkful to his mouth and took the large bite with a smile.

"You son of a—" Throwing himself forward, both he and Callen tumbled to the ground, landing with Thane on top. "Say you lied! Say pie is better!"

Callen shook his head but couldn't stop the chuckle from escaping. Beck rushed forward, Trite on his heels, as they each grabbed one of Thane's shoulders, pulling him from Callen and stopping him from shaking the man. Radnar approached lazily shaking his head.

"That is enough, boys," he said, exhausted. "We did what you wanted, Thane. He tried both of them. It is no one's fault that he does not agree with you."

"He's lying!" Thane screamed.

Radnar sighed and pulled the pie closer before lifting it with his hand and taking a large bite. The fresh, plump, cherries bursting with flavor over his tongue. "I like the pie."

Thane shot a triumphant smirk in Callen's direction. "See. At least someone here has some brain cells left."

"But…" Radnar continued, picking up the last piece of cake and shoving it into his mouth. The buttery cake and rich chocolate frosting were satisfying in an entirely different way. "The cake is just as good. I like them both."

"What!" Thane raged, pulling at Beck and Trite's grip. "You can't do that!"

"Why not?" Radnar inquired. "I enjoyed the pie, but the cake was delicious as well."

"Ha! I told you cake is better," Callen taunted.

Denial

"You shut your mouth!" Thane bellowed pointing at Callen.

"What is going on here?" The chilled voice broke through Callen's impending retort as they turned to find Maddox standing in the entryway.

Thane ripped his arms from Beck and Trite's grip, straightening his shirt, before nodding toward Callen. "He said cake was better than pie."

Maddox's brow rose. "Are you serious right now? All of that shouting and bickering was over pie?"

"It's something important to know in a friendship," Thane growled.

Maddox shook his head, dropping his bag to the ground. "Averie is awake."

Chapter Thirty-Five

Silas continued to speak, slowly drawing out her memories. He reminded her of her training with him and Thane. Her getting ready with her mother for her prom. Lucas picking her up, the pain that flared at the mention of his name, caused something to snap inside her head and she was thrown back, her memories taking her captive.

He had called her a freak, and she felt herself retreat into the protection of the darkness. The pain of someone she loved and cared about seeing her as something wrong had been more painful than she had thought possible. She watched like an outsider as she became someone, no, some*thing* more. She felt herself fill with an amazing rage until it was all she knew. She stood by, watching herself pull Lucas into the air as though he was nothing. She felt herself slice into his flesh, watched as her eyes traced his life's blood making trails down his skin.

Denial

She had retreated further and further away from herself until there was nothing she could do but stand by and watch as the darkness inside tore him slowly to pieces. The blood poured from him, filling the air with a sickening metallic smell. It all played out like a nightmare as her arms lifted him higher and higher into the air. The sound of her sinister chuckle, the thought of simply waving her hands and tearing him into pieces.

She watched frozen and useless within her own body as the power grew greater, felt the smile form while her fingers rose ready and willing to deliver that final blow. Suddenly Silas was there, her heart raced in a different way. He didn't think she was a freak. He didn't think she was anything but her. Suddenly she was thrust back into control of her body, yet her mind raged in darkness and she had no way to stop it.

Fear and anger had gripped her. She couldn't stop; it was too late. Someone was going to die, and that someone might just be Silas. She cried out against the strain, pulling the power back inside, forcing it down, and that's when the light burned through her.

"Where am I?" she repeated, her eyes clenched tight.

"You're at my house."

"How did I get here?"

Silas shifted in his seat.

"Silas, tell me, please."

"You were dead, Averie." His voice cracked as he looked toward the ceiling.

"How is that even possible?"

Silas shook his head. "I'm not sure. None of us are."

"Us?" Averie asked.

"I had to call in reinforcements when you…"

"When I what?"

Silas ran his hands over his face before leaning to rest his elbows on his knees. His gaze seemed lost in a far-away place when he spoke next. "After it happened, you were locked in a ball of your own energy. We couldn't even touch you. I didn't know what to do, and Beck had this crazy idea about how to move it, but the timing and the pain…" His words trailed off as his body shook at the memory. "Stars, it took so much to get you here. We were worried at first, but then we saw …" Silas paused for a moment, trying to come up with the right words.

"What did you see? Who is 'we'?"

Silas looked away, seemingly fighting with himself. "You were hurt really bad, Averie. I brought you here to clean you up before…"

"Before what, Silas?!" Her impatience grew with every delayed word.

Silas nodded. "After we brought you back here from the field, things began to change. We could touch you, but only barely. Maddox, he is an excellent doctor back home, I brought him here to help you and Lucas, but then cops were everywhere, and everything went wrong so fast. When I came back to the room, well…"

He looked back at her, still fighting with himself. "You stopped breathing, Averie, for a really long time. I tried everything I could but—" He pushed away from the bed

Denial

and started to pace. "I tried everything, Averie. Every spell, every incantation, every medical concoction that I could get Maddox to mix together. Everything that I could think of to try to bring you back. I even found nonsense from what you call the internet, but none of it worked. *Nothing* worked. I lost it, Avi, I was afraid you were really gone. It took Callen, Maddox, and Radnar to pull me out of your room. Your body was nearly ripped apart! Pieces of you were scattered throughout that entire damn bubble!" He stopped turning back. "Whatever you did to stop that last blow," Silas paused, taking a deep breath, then continued, "it ripped you to pieces."

Averie shook her head. "That's not possible. I'm here. I'm right here. I'm sitting right here," she said, pushing at her chest.

Silas ignored her words, too lost in his story. "A few hours passed, and your cocoon changed again. Maddox went in to prepare you for the passing ceremony, and it had grown so large he could barely enter the room. That's when Callen pulled me from my pit, dragged me back, and we watched you put yourself back together." He was deep in his memories as his mind raced. "It was like nothing I had ever seen before, ever *heard* of before. Threads had appeared out of nowhere stitching you slowly, so damn slowly, back together. A day passed and you were here, your form more recognizable. Then we saw it. Your chest fluttered and life returned." Silas stopped his pacing, eyes wide, almost frantic. "Do you know what that means, Averie?" he asked, his eyes shrinking to normal.

Averie shook her head, still trying to process his story.

Silas knelt beside the bed, taking her head in his hands. "It means you can't be killed. At least not by magic. You are unstoppable, Averie!"

Averie nodded at his words while her mind was lost in a single thought. Fighting tears, she turned to him once more. "Is…" She swallowed stiffly against the lump that had lodged itself inside. "Is Lucas…"

Silas tightened his grip on her hands. "He was fine when I left but…" She felt the hesitation in his words.

"But what?" she demanded, searching his face. It was the first time she really looked at him, and she realized how gruff he was. His hair was in complete disarray, deep, dark shadows surrounded his eyes, and his cheeks were sunken in as though he hadn't eaten in days.

"No one has seen him since that night, Averie. When we left, he was stable but…" He shook his head.

Confusion swirled in her mind again. "Si, how long have I been here?" Averie asked as the numbness slowly left her body.

"Three days."

Averie's eyes exploded with shock. "Jesus, three days! My mother is going to kill me," she said, her voice shaking in nervous laughter.

Silas flinched at her words.

"Si? Is everything alright?" Averie asked.

"Everything is fine. You're fine."

"Except Lucas is missing." Averie nodded, biting her lip.

Denial

"Yes."

Sitting in stunned silence, Averie could feel her energy returning with renewed force. The ache and tiredness that had weighed her down dissipated. The realization of the time passing, of Karen's worry, of Lucas missing ... it was all getting to be too much. She felt the urge to fix what was wrong and to do that, she needed to pull herself together.

"I need to go; I have to talk to my mom before she officially loses it."

"Averie, wait."

"Wait for what?" she asked, looking back to Silas.

Pity masked his face, his hands dropping to his sides. "Avi..."

"Wait for what, Silas?" Averie demanded as she shoved off the bed, her eyes scoring the pained look covering his being. "Wait for what? Why can't I go? Why do you keep half answering and stammering?! What are you telling me?!"

The door swung open, slamming against the wall with a resounding bang. "What's going on?" Thane questioned, his eyes swinging from a desperate Silas to a fuming Averie.

Averie turned, her chest heaving, as panic seeped in. "Why can't I go see Mom, Thane?"

Thane visibly stilled, his breath halting in his lungs, as the blood drained from his face. "Avi..."

"No, why do I need to wait, Thane? Where is Mom?" Averie's voice was verging on hysterics.

Thane's eyes filled with tears as he took a careful step forward, lifting his arms toward her, his eyes pleading. "There was an accident. Karen, she didn't—"

"No." Averie shook her head. "Don't say it. Don't you dare."

Thane's arms dropped to his sides. "She didn't make it, Averie."

"No." Her voice cracked. "No, you're lying. You're all lying!"

She turned to Silas as she dropped to her knees, taking his hands into her shaking ones. "He's lying, isn't he, Si? This is just another one of your tests. You're just trying to see if I have control now, and I do. See, I have control." Her voice was on the brink of breaking. "Now, tell him. You tell him that he can stop this. He can tell me the truth that Mom is just at home, and she's pissed at me for being gone so long."

Silas shook his head slowly, his eyes misting, a tear already starting down his cheek. "I am so sorry, Averie. This isn't a test."

Averie jerked back like she had been slapped. "No, please no. Not her." Averie climbed to her feet on trembling legs. Turning back to Thane, she saw two other strange men standing in the doorway, pity etched into their faces. "When?"

Thane shook his head, his breath catching.

"When, Thane?!"

"Prom night."

"How?"

Denial

Thane looked past Averie, locking on Silas before shifting back.

"Fox."

"It was me, wasn't it?" Averie breathed.

Thane's silence was her answer. A pained sound escaped her lips.

"It wasn't your fault," Thane assured.

Averie shook her head. "Oh, God, it was. It was me. I'm going to be sick."

Thane took a cautious step forward, approaching her as he would a wounded animal, he lifted his hand slowly to rest on her arm. "Averie—"

Ripping herself away, she looked through a watery gaze to each set of eyes. They all held a truth that she couldn't bear. Anguish tore through her body. "I have to go," she whimpered through gritted teeth.

Thane and Silas jumped to their feet. "Now isn't the time."

"I have to see her, Thane. I have to make sure she's okay."

"Averie, she isn't—"

"No! She's fine! Now let me through."

Thane stood, firmly planted. "I can't do that, Averie."

"Let me through!" Averie demanded.

Thane shook his head at her and the other men stepped forward, flanking him on either side in solitude.

A ringing was starting in her ears as her harsh breath echoed. "Let me through, Thane."

"No."

Averie lunged at him, landing with a heavy thud as her palms collided with his chest, but Thane stood unmoving, taking on her assault as if the blows could mend the fracturing she felt inside. "I don't want to hurt you," Averie raved.

"Then don't," Thane said, devoid of emotion.

"Let me go, Thane. Please," she pleaded.

Thane looked down at the girl he considered his sister. Her large green eyes filled with such turmoil he sucked in a breath. "Now isn't the time."

"Don't make me do this," Averie threatened.

"No one is making you do anything, Averie. I need you to trust me. I need you to stay here for a little longer," Thane begged as he stepped forward and pulled her into a deep hug. Averie sagged against him, her tears tracing burning pathways down her cheeks as her broken sobs filled the small room as reality finally took hold.

Her mother was gone and it was all her fault.

Chapter Thirty-Six

Two days. That's how long they made Averie sit in the house. She wasn't allowed to use the phone or leave the house. Food was brought to her along with a disgusting cocktail that Maddox had whipped up twice a day. She spent her days pacing the halls or staring at the bedroom walls, her mind tormenting her as it forced her to relive that night endlessly.

On the morning of the third day, when she was sure she was teetering on the brink of insanity, Averie marched from her room and into the kitchen ready for war. Silas, Thane, and Callen sat around the bar, each with a large bowl filled with a mixture of the three cereal boxes that sat in front of them.

"Good, right?" Thane asked around a mouthful.

"It is not bad." Callen shrugged, filling his own mouth.

"That's bullshit, and you know it. Fruity Pebbles, Lucky Charms, and a dab of Frosted Cheerios is the best mixture you can make. Tell him, Silas," Thane urged.

Silas shifted his head side to side. "It's not bad, but the Fruity Pebbles with Frosted Cheerios and chocolate milk is better."

Thane and Callen exchanged a look before leaning over to look in Silas's bowl.

"Where did you get chocolate milk?" Thane demanded.

"In the fridge. There's chocolate sauce and milk. Mix them and boom, magic."

"Take me to my house," Averie demanded, slamming her hands against the counter to get her point across. She succeeded in not only thoroughly interrupting their breakfast banter, but also in making them all jump in their seats. Thane jumped so hard he knocked Silas's cereal bowl off the counter, throwing a rainbow of colors crashing to the ground. Averie refused to let the sting and throbbing pain in her hands show as she held her glare on the boys.

"Jeez, Averie, good morning to you, too," Thane chided, shoveling another bite into his mouth.

"I want to go home, Thane," Averie repeated.

"I heard you," Thane acknowledged.

"And?" she asked.

"Okay," he answered, slurping milk from his bowl.

"Okay, what?" Averie slowly asked.

Denial

Thane sighed, dropping his spoon into the empty bowl. "What do you want me to say, Averie?"

"Start by explaining why it's fine *now*, when it wasn't two days ago?" she demanded.

Thane pushed back from his seat and moved into the kitchen, Averie close on his heels. "You needed to rest," he explained, turning and accidentally running into her. With a deep and deliberate sigh, he took a step back. "What are you doing?"

"Making sure I get an answer."

"By being right on top of me? Have you lost your mind? I could have knocked you over."

Averie rolled her eyes, crossing her arms. "In a way, yes, I have. I've been trapped in this house with my own thoughts and …" Averie shook herself. "When can we go?"

"When do you want to?" Thane asked.

"Now," Averie said.

"Fine," Thane grunted.

"Fine?" Averie asked.

"Yes, Averie, fine." Thane slowed his words.

"Okay, I'll go get dressed." Averie smiled in triumph.

"Fine," Thane sneered, his annoyance clearly growing.

"Fine!" Averie called over her shoulder.

The sound of snickering brought Thane's attention to the grinning Silas and Callen. "She is absolutely the most annoying person in the entire world," Thane ranted.

Silas and Callen nodded in agreement.

"She is! You saw her. Coming in here, interrupting breakfast, demanding stuff, and insulting me for trying to keep her safe."

"Of course," Callen agreed.

"You two are no help, just sitting there letting her act like … well, you saw," Thane said leaning against the counter.

"I think she just wants to see it, to know that it is real. She needs this, Thane. Haven't you heard her crying at night?" Silas asked.

Thane clenched his jaw. "Of course, I have."

"Sometimes the only way to get past things we have done, is to confront them head on," Callen offered. "Maybe that is what she wants to do. Confront her mistake so she can move on."

"It wasn't Averie's fault!" Thane roared. "And even if it was, do you think seeing it somehow would help someone move on from killing their own mother?!"

Callen looked to Silas who shook his head. "Neither of you are willing to admit that she played a role in this?" Callen asked, bewildered. "You can not be serious! Silas, you told me what happened. You were there."

"All I know is what was done to Lucas. There is nothing to show that she is responsible for what happened to Karen. Now drop it," Silas ordered, rising from his seat and leaving the room.

* * *

Denial

"Averie?" Silas called, knocking on her door. "Can I come in?"

"Yeah, sure," Averie answered.

Silas opened the door and took in the disheveled state of the room. Blankets and pillows were twisted and falling off the bed. Scattered books lay half opened, covering nearly every open inch of the floor. Averie sat on the edge of the bed, Cleo standing before her, their conversation halting at Silas's entrance.

"Is everything alright?" Averie asked, noticing his silence.

"Yes, of course. I was just coming to see if you were sure this is what you wanted to do. Have you been sleeping?" Silas asked, motioning to the destroyed room.

"Yes," Averie answered, trying to believe her own lie.

Silas stepped forward, shutting the door behind him. "Are you sure?" he asked, studying the dark circles under her eyes.

"Is this what you came in for? To do a health check for Thane?" Averie clipped.

"No, Averie, I came by to see if you were coping with everything and to make sure this was something you really wanted to do."

"I am fine, Silas, and yes, I am sure this is what I want to do," Averie answered firmly. "We are burying my mother tomorrow, and I have to see …"

Cleo reached forward and took Averie's hand in her own. "You can't blame yourself."

Averie cleared her throat and held back the ever-lingering tears.

"You don't have to do this Averie," Silas said.

Averie stood from the bed. "I don't? And why is that, Silas? Why is everyone trying so hard to stop me from doing the one thing I want. The one thing I need?"

"Because you—" Silas slammed his mouth shut.

"Because what? Because you think I'll lose control again?" Averie snapped. "Well, I'm not."

"You don't know that."

"No, Silas, you don't know that. I do. I have already paid the price for being what I am once. I refuse to ever pay it again. I'm going with or without your approval."

"Fine, but I'm going with you," Silas relented.

"Fine. Why don't you wait for me outside? Thank you, Cleo." She smiled, dismissing them both.

Silas stood resting his back against the polished wood, hands shoved into his pockets taking deep slow breaths as he waited for Averie. "Is she really alright?" Silas asked Cleo before she could disappear once more.

Cleo sighed. "Physically, yes. As incredible as it is, she's fine. But mentally, it will take some time."

"Do you think this is a smart thing for her to do?"

Cleo eyed the younger man before nodding. "She needs this, Silas."

"Let me know if anything changes," Silas ordered.

Cleo nodded once before starting back down the hall, stopping half way, she turned back. "You're running out

Denial

of time, Silas. The longer she is away from our Realm, the more unstable the Heart will grow."

"I know."

Cleo looked over the tired looking young man once more before continuing on her path.

Silas knew he should be thankful that Averie was here, alive and functioning, and yet as he watched her over the last several days, it was obvious that the fire that had once burned deep and bright inside her eyes had been doused by the consequences of her actions.

"Silas, how is she?" Thane inquired, strolling toward him.

Silas shrugged. "She's getting dressed now."

"What's wrong?" Thane asked, taking in Silas's distressed expression.

"I don't think she has been sleeping." Silas frowned.

"Understandable." Thane sighed. "I've barely slept myself."

"She's been consumed with going home."

"She is not the only one," Callen interjected.

"What's that supposed to mean?" Silas questioned.

"We need to get back soon. We left the rebellion with nobody to lead. Marcus's attacks have grown more powerful, taking larger tolls on us and our men than ever before. We have to move the camp before he figures out where we are."

Cleo was right, they were running out of time. The rebellion couldn't go on much longer without them, even just a few days could mean the end of everything they had fought so long and hard for. Silas tipped his head in agreement. "I understand. What's your plan?"

Callen sighed. "Maddox is working on a way to get us all back. He believes we can go back through where you came through. The trick is getting the portal to cooperate."

"Portal?" Thane inquired.

Callen nodded. "In our Realm, we do not have the same modes of transportation you do. The Realm used to be covered in portals that would send you where your mind requested," Callen explained.

"Efficient," Thane agreed, seeming to take the impossible in stride. Though after what he had seen and heard over the last couple weeks, nothing seemed impossible anymore.

"So what's his plan?" Silas repeated.

"His father was a traveler, so he has some idea of what he is doing. Though I must admit, it was a lot more appealing when it was you going through the portal with the potential of getting ripped to pieces, then it is for me."

"I'm sorry, did you say ripped to pieces?" Thane chimed in.

Silas ignored his questions and pushed forward, his mind running over countless possibilities. "Will this portal be able to take you anywhere?"

"I am not sure, to be honest. I am really just hoping to make it home in one piece," Callen admitted.

"Good," Silas agreed. "What about the Rebellion? Do you have any idea where you will go next?"

Denial

"The northern caves, but, Si, when we get back, I have to tell them something. Our people are losing hope."

Silas sighed, rubbing the back of his neck. "Tell them I will be back with the Lost One soon."

"What is soon, Silas? Many have spoken of the Lost One since childhood, it is more of a myth at this point."

"Give me a week. I will meet you then."

"You can't be serious." Thane choked. "We are burying our mother tomorrow and you want to ship her off in a week!? She isn't ready for that, Silas!"

"We don't have a choice, Thane. The longer she is here, the worse things will get," Silas tried.

"Worse for who? You or her?" Thane challenged.

"For both."

Thane glared at Silas, shaking his head in disbelief. "You can't be serious."

"We are running out of time, if we don't act first, the decision will be made for us."

"I don't care about them! I care about my sister who is falling apart, while you two sit here willing to send her into something that she isn't ready for."

"She isn't the only one falling apart. Our entire Realm is hurting, dying. Mothers, sisters… She's our only hope to end our suffering."

Thane scoffed, shaking his head as he knocked on Averie's door. "I won't let you get her killed," he growled over his shoulder as he pushed her door open.

Chapter Thirty-Seven

Averie stood, eyeing herself in the full-length mirror. Her eyes tracked the subtle changes that had taken place in such a short amount of time. Her already long hair had grown almost double its length. The soft, dark auburn hue had changed to the deep, burnt red of old blood. Her skin was a sickly pale, her cheeks slightly sunken and her eyes held more gold then green now. Her eyes drifted lower to the bandages wrapped neatly around her arms and chest. She had been contemplating over the last three days to remove them but feared the possible horror underneath.

Averie lifted a trembling hand, as she slowly unraveled the white fabric. As they untwisted, they revealed thin, intricate lines of gold that weaved themselves around the heavy pink forming scars. The design was mesmerizing as it shimmered and swirled under her gaze. Averie ran the tip of her finger across a

Denial

deep gold line on her forearm, intrigued as it began to glow and shake at her touch.

A knock at the door jerked her from her inspection as she fumbled to grab the black t-shirt from her bed and cover herself before someone could see her. She pulled her hair in a quick bun, slid her jeans over her bruised legs, and turned toward the door.

"Come in," she called, sitting on the bed, trying to look casual.

Thane walked in giving her a weak smile. "Hey," he greeted softly.

"Hey." She forced a smile back. Reaching down, she grabbed her black Converse and slipped them on, tying the laces in a swift, efficient knot.

"Silas said you wanted to see the house to prove something to yourself."

Averie cleared her throat, whipping her damp hands against her legs. "I have to."

Thane sat down on the open spot beside her. "This isn't your fault, Avi."

Averie let out a humorless chuckle. "No? You know someone else that caused a county-wide earthquake that night?"

Thane frowned. "I'm not going to sit here and lie to you Averie. I did blame you. Initially."

Averie swallowed against the lump in her throat. "What changed?"

Thane gave a small smile. "You."

"What do you mean?"

"I've known you for years. You are the little sister I never wanted but can't imagine not having. I know you better than you know yourself, and I know that if you had been yourself that night, you would never have hurt anyone. Not Lucas and definitely not Mom. I don't blame you, Averie, and you shouldn't either."

"I don't know how not to. If I would have—If I could have…" Averie's voice broke as she hid her face in her hands.

"You can't change it. No one can. The only thing we can do is move forward and live our lives in a way that would have made her proud. You can't sit here and dwell on could have, would have, should have. You need to move forward, we both do. Mom wouldn't want us sitting here like this." Thane stood, holding out his hand. "Come on, if you still don't get it and need to go, let's do this."

With a confidence she didn't feel, Averie stood tall and took Thane's hand and let him lead her from the room. As they stepped into the hall, Silas and Callen, who had been huddled in a hushed conversation, turned to face them. Callen gave her, what she assumed he believed to be a reassuring smile and dipped into a small bow.

"Hello, I do not believe we got to properly meet before. I am Callen of the Heart Realm. It is an honor to meet you."

"Please don't bow," Averie flinched.

"I don't know, Fox, seems pretty awesome to me. Someone needs to teach 'Mr. Cake is Great' here what is right and wrong." Thane laughed.

Denial

Callen straightened with a genuine grin. "I see someone is still upset that I did not agree with their view on desserts."

"Oh, no, you like cake better than pie, don't you?" Averie gasped.

Callen pushed out his chest and smiled. "I do indeed."

"Poor Thane," she mocked.

"Yeah, well, now you can order him to change his mind or at least tell us who put him up to it." Thane glared.

"That is ridiculous, Thane. You can not demand someone change their opinion just because you happen to disagree with it," Callen snapped.

"I can if it is a stupid opinion and wrong," Thane mumbled sullenly.

Averie sighed. "Guys, I appreciate the temporary distraction, but I need to go and see where it happened."

There was a sense of pride that went through Averie as she watched two of the strongest people she had ever known, and one stranger that looked like he could break through a brick wall, nod in silent agreement with her decision. With Silas on one side and Thane on the other, she felt as though she could take on the next chapter of her life and she knew she was about to need that strength.

* * *

Averie stood before her childhood home, a strange feeling raising the hairs on her arms and prickling across her skin. From the front, it was as if nothing had happened. Flowers still grew from their hanging pots on the porch. Three chairs sat neatly organized around a small glass table, and the brightly colored, summer wreath her mother had purchased still hung on the door. Everything was just as it was when she'd gotten into the car and headed to the prom.

"Do you want to go in?" Thane asked from beside her.

In lieu of answering, Averie climbed up the porch steps and twisted the doorknob. As the door slid open, Averie entered the house, carefully stepping as though the floor may break under her weight. Contrary to what she had expected, the house smelled and looked the same as she left it. The sun drifted in through the cracked curtains. Her mother's coffee mug sat ready and waiting by the coffee pot. Everything felt as though she would walk through at any moment demanding to know where she had been.

Tears burned at Averie's eyes as she turned to make her way down the small hallway. Every step brought trepidation, the prickling on her skin increased to a buzz, blood roared in her ears. It didn't make sense, her mother allegedly died here three days ago and yet the house was still the same, not a single piece out of place. Nothing was broken or pushed from its perch, the floors still creaked in the same places. It was still home. Averie took the stairs two at a time, rushing to her mother's door and throwing it open.

Denial

Her breath echoed in the air around her, as she took in the sight. The room was nearly intact, the only thing out of place was where her mother's bed normally lay. Averie stared at the remaining chunks of large tree the fire department hadn't removed. Her mother's bed was nearly crushed through the floor, the pink and purple floral blanket she had loved so much stained a dark red. Averie remained transfixed on the blanket, as her mind replayed the memories of late-night movies and sneaking into her mother's room after a nightmare. The countless hours spent tucked in when she hadn't felt well or when she needed her mother's advice.

The warmth of Thane's hand seeped into her arm, ripping her from her reverie. "Averie? Are you alright?"

Averie closed her eyes in shame. "How many others?"

"Six homes on this street, all sustained minimal damage. Mostly fallen branches or picture frames. Down the road, Mrs. Johnson lost one of her angel figurines," Thane answered.

"Deaths?" she whispered, preparing for the guilt.

"Just one," Thane declared.

Averie's eyes popped open in surprise. "What? How is that even possible?"

Thane ran his fingers through his hair, looking over their mother's room. "I don't know."

"How is the entire house fine, except for this one spot? Not a single picture fell from the walls, there isn't any broken glass or dishes from the cabinets. It doesn't make sense, Thane."

"Averie, please, don't do this to yourself. That tree was ancient. Branches fell all the time."

Averie released a heavy breath, her shoulders trembled as she struggled to bite back the sob.

"I think we should stay with Silas tonight. I called Sera. She said she can come over tonight, too, if you want. Does that sound okay?" Thane asked.

"Yeah, sure."

"We need to get a few things for ourselves and pick something for tomorrow. If you can't do it, I can."

Averie shook her head. "No, I got it. You go get your stuff, and I'll meet you at the car."

Thane watched the mask slip over Averie's face as she attempted to compartmentalize what she had done with what she now needed to do. Taking her in his arms, Thane hugged her close as if he could give her the strength she needed and kissed her forehead before resting it against his.

"I'm here for you, Fox."

"And I'm here for you, Bear."

Chapter Thirty-Eight

Sera had been ready and waiting for them when they returned to Silas's house. As the car pulled up the long driveway, she burst through the front door, with enough force that it sent the screen door slamming into the side of the house. Sera reached Averie, just as she stepped from the car, and pulled her into a hug which instantly shattered Averie's newly erected emotional barrier. Averie squeezed her back as Sera's body shook with silent sobs. The two stood in the driveway long after the boys had disappeared inside, to give them privacy, as they attempted to regain control of their sorrow.

Sera was the first to pull away, wiping the tears from her friend's eyes, she gave a reassuring smile. "I am here for you, Avi. Always. No matter what."

Averie smiled, her first *real* smile since waking. "Thanks, Sera," she said, squeezing Sera's hands.

"Now, come inside. I came bearing gifts of the carb and sweet variety, and I just know those boys are going to eat everything before we get the chance. By the way, who are they?" Sera asked, looping her arm through Averie's.

"I think they're Silas's relatives." The lie felt like ash on her tongue. In the years they had been friends, Averie could count on one hand the number of times they had lied to each other.

Sera frowned as they entered the house, as if sensing the untruth. Thane and Callen stood bickering over which desert was better while Silas was explaining what appeared to be a variety of different dips to Maddox and Beck. The sudden shout of hooting and victory chants echoed from the living room, revealing that Radnar and Trite hadn't stepped away from their game since before Averie had left.

"You know those snacks are supposed to be for everyone," Sera snapped, snatching the bag of chocolate-covered pretzels from Thane.

"Hey! I was eating those." Thane pouted.

"They are for Averie. They are her favorite, which you would know if you stopped inhaling everything," Sera scolded, shoving the bag into Averie's hand.

Averie shook her head, as a ghost of a smile tugged her lips, earning a real one from Thane who immediately made a grab for the second bag that Callen held. Callen shoved a handful in his mouth, moving the bag just out of reach.

Denial

"You can share, you know." Thane gave a pointed glare.

"No," Callen grumbled, his mouth still full.

Thane reached again, the bag slipping through his fingers once more. "Last chance, Frosting," Thane warned.

"Bring it on, Filling," Callen taunted, waving the bag like a red flag.

Thane lunged, grabbing Callen around the waist and sending them both to the floor, knocking hard into the table. Silas jumped to the side, attempting to avoid the thrashing bodies, dropping the container of salsa in the process.

"What the hell, guys!" Silas sulked, looking down at the spill.

Maddox and Beck grabbed the table, sliding it forward as Thane and Callen's scuffle brought them closer. The sound of wood scraping wood snapped Trite and Radnar from their game, as they exchanged an excited glance and jumped over the couch. They entered the room with broad smiles as they looked down at the pair, while Averie shook her head as one by one, they started cheering for one side or the other.

"Animals, all of them." Sera shook her head in disgust as Thane and Callen wrestled over the remaining bag. "Come on, let's go put on a movie and order pizza. It looks like the half a grocery store I brought won't be enough."

As they moved into the living room, Sera popped in a movie. Together she and Averie settled onto the couch. Just as the movie began, Thane and Callen joined them in the living room, covered in salsa and sweat but sharing the remaining crumbled bag of chocolate-covered pretzels.

"I don't think so, boys. Shower," Sera ordered, shooing them off.

"Aww, come on, Sera, it's not that bad," Thane teased, opening his arms for a hug.

"Thane, I swear to *God* if you touch me right now, I will wax your eyebrows in your sleep." Sera glared, slowly rising to stand on the couch.

"Bring it in, Sera," Thane smiled, refusing to back down.

"Averie!" Sera shrieked, running across the couch.

"Sorry, Sera, you know this is my favorite movie." Averie laughed as she watched Thane chase Sera across the couch and into a corner where he caught her, making sure to rub his salsa covered face along hers.

"I missed that sound," Silas said, taking the seat beside Averie. "I've known Callen a long time and I don't know that I've ever seen him act this way."

"Yeah, well Sera and Thane have a way of making anyone laugh, no matter how they feel on the inside," Averie replied with a genuine smile as she watched Callen mimic Thane's assault.

Setting his arm across the back of the couch Silas turned Averie's face to his. "You are going to get through this, Averie. You're not alone."

Averie nodded.

"You two are so gross!" Sera shrieked, unable to contain her own laughter as she finally broke free. "Some

Denial

best friend you are." She gave a mocking glare. "I think I deserve a hug since you abandoned me."

"No, I'm good, not much of a hugger," Averie said, slowly rising from the couch as Sera, Thane and Callen set their sights on her.

Silas reached up, pulling her into his lap, effectively trapping her.

"Let me go, Si!" She giggled, struggling against his hold.

"I think it is important that you give your friend a hug, you did abandon her after all."

* * *

Later that night, after they had all showered and cleaned the room from the impromptu food fight, their bellies full of pizza and ice cream, the boys had moved every mattress in the house into the living room. The night had been filled with movies, shared stories, laughter, and popcorn, but now, long after everyone had drifted off, Averie lay awake as sleep continued to elude her. The tick-tock of the clock taunting as it slowly drifted around its face. Bodies lay around her, their soft snores creating a chorus to the random household sounds.

Averie lay, with silent tears streaming down her cheeks, as her mind ran wild with memories. Some happy, filled with hot chocolate and days spent playing in the snow, camping with s'mores by the fire and late-night scary stories. While others were angry, like the time she had told her mother she hated her for grounding her, after she snuck out with Sera. Those were the ones that hurt the most, the ones ripping her apart from the inside. The angry moments outweighed the happy ones when you were the one responsible from the death of your mother. A living hell you had to face until you died and went for real.

"Are you awake?" Sera whispered into the darkness.

Averie quickly wiped her cheeks and turned on her side to face her friend. "Yeah."

"Can't sleep either?"

Averie shook her head in the darkness. "No."

"I don't know what to do, Avi. I want to make this easier for you," Sera whispered. "But I don't know how."

A small sob escaped Averie's lips, bringing a hand to cover her mouth she squeezed her eyes shut. "It's all my fault, Sera."

"No, Avi, that's ridiculous. You couldn't control when that tree decided to fall. It was older than this town," Sera explained. "It wasn't your fault."

"Sera, you don't understand," Averie sobbed.

"Understand what?" Sera asked.

"I—"

"Avi? Sera? Are you guys, okay?" Thane's deep, sleepy voice cut through the night.

Averie cleared her throat, wiping the tears away. "Yeah, we're fine."

Denial

"Go back to sleep, Thane. It's just girl talk," Sera added.

"Mmm," Thane responded, rolling back over.

"You should too, Averie," Sera said.

Averie nodded into the darkness. "Goodnight, Sera. Thank you."

"For what?" Sera asked.

"For tonight, for being here, for always being there when I need you."

Sera squeezed Averie's hand. "Always, Avi. Now, go get some sleep."

Averie rolled to her other side, resting her hands under her chin, her eyes colliding with Silas. "Hey," she whispered.

"Hey, are you okay?" he asked.

"No, not really," she replied.

Silas reached forward and pulled her into his embrace, kissing the top of her head. "It will be okay, Averie. Get some sleep." Averie snuggled closer, her head resting lightly against his chest, as she let herself get lost into the sound of his beating heart, allowing herself, if only for the moment, to forget and sleep.

Chapter Thirty-Nine

The morning was too bright and the sun too comforting for what was happening. Averie couldn't understand how the day could be so beautiful when there was nothing but darkness ahead. The scent of freshly cut grass and sweet flowers clung on the wind, bringing the calming scent to her nose. Averie shook her head against it; she didn't deserve its calming embrace. She didn't deserve the beautiful day or the warmth of the sun against her skin. Her mother did. Averie's heart rebelled against the memories of what her mother would be doing on a day like this. She kept her eyes down, watching her black clad feet crush the spring grass beneath them.

Thane held her hand, his grip tightening ever so slightly as they approached their destination. Averie didn't have to look to know they were close, she felt it in every step she took. As the gleaming white chairs came into view Averie's heart broke a little more. There was

Denial

only one reason anyone ever used these chairs, and it was for that reason that they were here today. Death.

With Thane leading, they made their way down the aisle and took the seats in the first row. The moment Averie sat, like a moth to a flame, her eyes were drawn to the casket. Her mother's rich white casket sat on a high table, white and pink lilies cascading like a waterfall down its edge. Averie sat numbly, oblivious to her surroundings, as the chairs began to slowly fill. She watched as the sun rose higher, highlighting her mother's casket and giving it a lustrous glow, before touching her mother's photo to give it a fitting halo.

People whispered behind her as the priest moved to the podium. His long black gown still had press lines from the morning's ironing. His white hair was neatly combed and parted to the side, while his face, lined with memories and time, held a sad smile as he gazed at the gathering.

"We are gathered here on this beautiful morning to remember a beautiful soul that was taken much too soon," the priest started, bringing the first round of quiet cries and sniffling noses, but Averie heard nothing. Her gaze had slipped from the casket to her mother's memorial photo. Thane had chosen the perfect one to capture her spirit. It was the day of the community picnic. She was smiling wide, her hair blowing in the wind as she fought to keep hold of the large bouquet of flowers she was holding.

Averie felt a tear drip from her eye and slide down her cheek. Silas took her chilled hand in his own, while Thane took the other and gave her a reassuring squeeze. Her heart beat violently in her chest as she watched person after person fill the air with their happy stories and words of love, each word another hit, driving a dagger deeper into her heart, searing them into her soul, until finally Thane stood and walked to the podium.

He stood strong, proud as he looked around, meeting everyone's gaze before settling on Averie's. "Karen was one of the bravest, most loving women I have ever met. She would help anyone, any day, anytime. She would always say that she had never met a stranger, only a friend she didn't know the name of. Over the years, I have been fortunate enough to have seen her kindness and felt her love more times than I could ever count. She was a second mother to me. Karen took me in and raised me as her own when there was no one left to try. She taught me and loved me. She believed in me when I didn't, and she gave me the strength to move on when I had given up. She never gave up on me. She watched over me and protected me. Now that she is gone, I will continue to pay that love and belief forward."

Averie's chest burned as her body refused to take in the much-needed air. She knew Thane hadn't meant to hurt her, but she felt the sting of his words. She couldn't take it anymore; she felt like she was about to burst. She jumped from her chair, her breath coming in quick pants. The crowd around her gasped, their eyes drilling holes as Averie tried to gain control of herself. Sera and Silas exchanged a worried look, slowly rising from their chairs.

"Averie, honey, sit down," Sera whispered reassuringly.

Denial

Averie's breathing grew louder, more frantic, her heart slamming against her ribs like a caged bird fighting to get free. Her eyes searched for an escape.

"Averie?" Silas called.

Averie sent Thane an apologetic look. The sorrow in his eyes was the last straw. She turned and ran from the whispers, the pity, and the tears. Her feet slammed against the ground as she ran through the cemetery, her heels catching and digging into the soft, dew-covered ground, sending Averie slamming into a large crying angel. Tears filled her eyes, her body wracked with silent sobs. Pain, anger, self-loathing, it filled her to the brim. She had lost her mother; she was gone because in a single moment she had lost all control. Her mother's love and light would never grace the world again, because she had been too weak, too careless.

Averie shoved the shoes from her feet, blood smearing down her legs, highlighting the large gashes on her palms. Rising to her feet, she shoved away from the angel. She would never feel anything but this wrenching pain from her mother's loss, the surge of pain in her palms paling in comparison. Averie plunged into the woods, branches pulling at her hair and clothes as she attempted to run from it all. She pushed herself harder, faster, further. She just needed to get farther away from the cemetery. She couldn't be here. It was all too real. Her mother's death, Thane's pain. She didn't know where she was running to, only what she was running from.

Averie burst into a small clearing, her foot catching on a hidden root, sending her stumbling once more to the ground. Her heart thundered against her ribs. Her breath came in quick, shallow pants as she openly sobbed. Forcing her tired body into a sitting position, Averie hung her head in shame. "I am so, so sorry, Mom. I should've been there. I should've done better, been better." Tears streamed down her face as a sob caught in her throat. "I should have been there to protect you." Every word tore a little more at her heart as her mother's smiling face popped into her mind.

An anger so raw, so volatile, filled her body as she began slamming her fists into the ground. She slammed harder, each collision bringing her pain and relief.

The scent of her mother's favorite perfume tickled her nose as they rode in the car together, the sound of her laughter echoing on the winds as she chased Averie as a child. The taste of her favorite blueberry pancakes turned to ash in her mouth at the thought of never tasting them again.

"I'm nothing without you," she whispered to the winds. "I'm scared, Mom. I need you." Her voice broke as the tears continued down the red trails on her face.

"Averie?" Thane's voice sounded from behind.

"I can't do it, Thane. I can't go on without her," Averie's voice broke.

"Yes, you can. You already are."

Averie shook her head, her tears coating the grass, mingling with the dew.

Denial

Thane crouched before her, taking her hands into his own. "You can do anything, Averie. I know you are hurting and that you can't see past that pain right now, but it won't always be this way. I never thought I would recover when I lost my mother, but you and Karen showed me that I could."

"And I took her away from you," Averie sobbed.

"No, Averie, stop that. You need to stop blaming yourself."

"The pain." She shook her head. "It's too much. I can't breathe."

Thane lifted his hand to wipe her tears away, pulling her gaze to his. "Pain is fleeting. You have so much more than that. You have love, hope, and memories. We will get through this, together. You are not alone. I am here, and so are Silas and Callen and Sera. We are all here for you."

"I'm so scared."

Thane smiled. "We all are. Everyone here and in the world. Everyone is afraid. But you, you're full of strength and nothing will stop you. Just because she isn't here anymore doesn't mean she isn't still with you. You are stronger than this, Fox. Mom raised you to be stronger than this. You might not see that right now, but don't give up. Not on me or yourself. Don't let this pain make you helpless. Don't let it take away the light and surrender yourself to the dark."

"I have scars that will never let me pass this. Every time I look at myself, I see them. I see that I wasn't strong enough to stop this," Averie cried.

"No, you weren't, but you will be. Every day from this moment on, you do everything you have to, to make sure this doesn't happen again. I will give you one more day, Averie. One. Then, you are going to pull yourself together and fight. You are going to do everything you can to make Mom proud," Thane promised.

"I miss her," Averie sobbed.

"I do, too, but we can't let this consume us. Mom wouldn't let us if she were here. One day this pain and hurt won't be as bad. You will stand again and feel the strength that she gave to you. We both will. Every beat of my heart feels like it is breaking into pieces, but I'm not hopeless. I know that she is here, and even though I am hurting, I am full of strength. Even though this will scar my soul, you are my light, Averie. The light that always brings me home, even in the darkness that I have gone through. So now, let me be yours."

Chapter Forty

Three weeks had passed since anyone had seen or heard from Lucas. Three weeks since Averie had lost control and nearly torn him to pieces. Three weeks since she had lost her mother. Three weeks since her view of the world around her had shifted so drastically. Three weeks since something deep inside had shifted irreparably. Three weeks since the numbness had taken hold, with no desire to vacate anytime soon.

Thane had to nearly drag her back to school, three days after they had laid Karen in the ground. Since then, it had become common practice for him to use their adopted mother's words against her.

"You know Mom didn't like it if you skipped meals like this, Averie."

"Mom wouldn't want you hiding from life like this, Averie."

"You know how disappointed she would be if you didn't graduate, Averie."

Sera was practically living with them, surrounding Averie and Thane with an overwhelming amount of attention. She had quickly stepped in with a purpose. She would arrive before they woke, helping around the house, doing the chores, and having meals sent over. She had even gone as far as keeping the cops, who had been questioning everyone about Lucas's disappearance, from pestering them too much.

Averie stared blankly ahead. The sterile white walls of the classroom pressed in around her, suffocating her, and bringing a wave of nausea. The flickering fluorescent lights hummed, creating an unpleasant cacophony with the rhythmic ticking of the wall clock. Tapping pencils would chime in, driving the already uneven pattern to an even more erratic tune. It was all driving her mad.

As the erratic tune grew to a crescendo in her mind and the tickle of irritation crept along her skin, the class door opened, stopping the teacher's lecture mid-sentence and severing all noise. All eyes turned to the door to find the principal standing there, scanning over the class. "Averie, if you would come with me."

Every head in the room snapped in her direction. Averie rolled her eyes as she shoved free of the tiny, uncomfortable desk. While Thane and Silas sat a little straighter, their attention glued to her lazy stride. The principal stepped aside and lifted his arm to motion her outside. The click of the door echoed in the empty hallway as he led her to the office.

"Is something wrong, Mr. Hyatt?" she asked.

The man cast a small smile in her direction and shook his head.

Averie released a heavy sigh and followed dutifully behind, her eyes taking in the scuffed tile, old lockers, and chipped paint dotting the walls. Eye-popping blue and yellow posters were sporadically and strategically placed, covering the walls in an attempt to boost school pride and morale while also hiding the deep cracks in the walls.

As she rounded the corner, Averie's gaze landed on two men in cheap black suits. One was younger and blonde with his hands shoved into his pockets as he leaned against the wall while the other held his phone in one hand and the other on his hip, revealing a holstered gun and glistening golden badge.

Fantastic. Averie sighed. *Cops.*

"Gentlemen," the principal greeted with a tip of his head, pushing the glass office door open. The men eyed her cautiously before motioning her forward.

"What is this about? Do you have information on my mother's case?" she asked dryly.

The men exchanged a look. "If you would just step inside, we have a few questions for you."

"About?"

"Lucas Parker."

Averie stopped walking and crossed her arms, glaring at the two men. "So you have just completely dropped my mother's case in favor of someone else?"

The younger cop rolled his eyes. "Miss Hale, there are many cases going on at any given time. It is our understanding that your mother committed suicide."

For the first time since seeing her mother lying in that casket, something flared to life inside her. "Suicide?! She dropped a tree on herself? Or are you saying she staged it to look like an accident? That she pushed a tree over into the house, climbed under it, and then what? Waited patiently for it to crush the life out of her? Are you cops or morons? Or both?"

"Averie," Mr. Hyatt interrupted, "if you would come into my office, these men just have a few questions for you."

"And if I don't want to?" she argued.

The blond detective arched a brow, his face twisting with arrogance as he looked down at her. "We could always take you to the station until you decide to cooperate."

"Am I in some kind of poorly written cop show I don't know about? I guess you're the bad cop and Mr. Silent there is the good one?" Averie fumed, days of pent-up anger pouring from her lips. "Why not just ask me if I want to do this the easy way or the hard way?" she ended, rolling her eyes.

"Miss Hale, Averie. Please come in, it'll just take a few moments." Mr. Hyatt smiled.

Denial

With a stiff nod and a slight scowl at the one she now thought of as Mr. Bad Cop, she entered the stuffy office and dropped into one of the wooden chairs before the large desk. Awards and family photos decorated the carefully stuffed bookcase shelves. The large desk before her held only a tangled corded phone, computer, keyboard, mouse and name plate. The uneven layout of the decorations bothered her, as if there was a subtle dissonance that she couldn't quite grasp.

Mr. Hyatt entered, stepping around the desk to settle into his cushioned office chair while the two detectives stood off to the side. "I believe introductions are in order," Mr. Hyatt started, folding his hands lightly atop the polished surface. "Averie Hale, these are detectives Morrison and Humphry."

Morrison was the blonde one who had been casually playing with his phone, his razor-sharp features reminding her of a hawk. A predatory being that stalks its victims endlessly. Taunting and playing with it, until finally ending it all with an abrupt and brutal drop to the earth. An instant distrust coiled deep in her stomach. Her eyes shifted to the one called Humphry. His hair was dark red, giving it an almost brown appearance if not for the sun cutting through the blinds behind him. He had warm brown eyes and a trusting air. As she took in the scene, she grinned to herself. They really did look like a cliché buddy cop film pair.

"You were the last one seen with Mr. Parker, correct?" Morrison questioned unceremoniously. "Approximately one month ago, on prom night, is that correct? And you were also the only one who has received a call since that night, isn't that also correct?"

Averie sat, letting silence consume the space as she eyed him carefully. "Yes." No explanation, no elaboration, just the simple and honest truth revealed in one word.

"And just what did Mr. Parker say during that three-minute and twelve-second phone call?" Morrison scowled.

Averie narrowed her eyes. "What are you implying, *Detective*?"

"Just looking for the truth," Morrison glared back.

Humphry stepped forward and grabbed the empty chair to her right, pulled it forward and took a seat. "Miss Hale," he began with a soft, fatherly smile. "I know you have been going through a rough time, and I apologize if my partner is coming off a little brash," Humphry threw a glare over his shoulder, receiving one in return. "But we have a missing boy out there, and his parents are very worried. We are not implying anything. We're just checking to see if he's told you anything that would help us find him."

"Lucas is eighteen. And to be honest, I'm surprised his parents even noticed he wasn't home."

"What's that supposed to mean?" Morrison demanded, taking a weighted step forward.

Averie ignored the man's attempt at intimidation and kept her eyes on Humphry as she spoke. "It means I've known Lucas for over ten years, during which I could count the number of times I have seen his parents on one hand. Lucas wasn't raised by his parents, only created by them. They barely knew he existed."

"Miss Hale, Averie," Humphry smiled. "May I call you Averie?"

Averie dipped her head in a reluctant nod.

Humphry smiled. "We have heard that you spoke to Lucas after prom from multiple sources, but what we need from you is to tell us what the two of you spoke about that night. Did he tell you that he was leaving? Did he share where he might go?"

Averie's mind drifted back.

Silas stood clutching the bar, his jaw ticking. "Why are we doing this?"

"Because it will buy us some time. We know that Lucas couldn't just get up and walk away. But by making it look like he is still contacting his friends, it will give us more time to find him," Thane explained, powering up the thin black device.

"I don't like it," Silas breathed.

"I don't either, but we don't exactly have any other choices. Unless you have an idea?"

Silas crossed his arms. "Fine, who is he calling?"

"Me," Averie declared.

Silas and Thane exchanged a worried glance. "Why you?" Silas asked.

Averie released a humorless chuckle and ran a hand through her loose tresses. "Which reason works best for you? The fact that we dated for over two years, or that anytime Lucas ever ran away he would call me, or that we have been friends for over ten years. Take your pick, but the answer will remain the same. We have Lucas call me," she finished with finality.

"He called to say goodbye. He said he couldn't take being in town anymore. That the pressure was getting to him and he needed a break. He wanted to get away for a while," Averie shared the lie with indifference.

"It took him three minutes to say that?" Morrison glared.

Averie met his gaze unflinchingly. "You know, just because you're playing bad cop, doesn't mean you have to be a dick in everything you say. I tried to talk him out of it. Told him he couldn't just run away from graduation or from his problems. He said his parents were putting all this stress on him and he couldn't focus anymore. He said he needed some time to think things through. This isn't even the first time he's left! Did his parents tell you that?"

The detectives shared a confused expression.

"I didn't think so. Lucas leaves once a year, minimum. But he always comes back."

Averie dropped her head back and stared up at the ceiling. How quickly she had taken to lying to everyone. Until now, she had always considered herself an honest person, and until recently she was. But over the last couple of months, she had become a master of lies. Then again, she couldn't tell the exact truth here. It wasn't like she could just casually explain to the police that she was from another world and that Lucas was only gone because she had completely lost control of her ever-growing abilities, accidentally ripped him to pieces, and after some magical

Denial

healer pieced him back together, got distracted by the need to hide her cocoon and now they couldn't find him.

"Are you sure that's all he said?"

Averie lowered her gaze and sighed again. "Yeah. I told him that I understood. I mean, we're teenagers graduating in a month, where we will go from having to ask to use the bathroom to making every decision by ourselves while trying to figure out what to do with the rest of our lives. Add in the constant stress and pressure to do everything perfectly from his parents, and it seems pretty understandable to me."

"Lucas had a troubled relationship with his parents?"

"What teenager doesn't?" Averie retorted.

The principal shot her an angry look.

"Look, Lucas was really good at acting like he didn't care that his parents were never home. He buried himself in sports, schoolwork, and the more than occasional party. He is impulsive and sometimes unstable, but he always comes home."

Silent glances passed between them as they looked at each other, the tension thick in the air.

It was Humphry who finally broke the silence. "Okay, Mrs. Hale, you are free to go back to class. Thank you for your time."

"Ah, thanks. You are free to go back to looking into my mother's case." Averie stood and turned for the door, her hand reaching for the doorknob when the next grating words reached her ears.

"But, Miss Hale?" Morrison called.

"Yes?"

"We'll be in touch."

Averie barked out a laugh. "You really just can't help yourself, can you?" She threw the door wide, a smile cresting her lips at the *thump* it made against the wall.

"Finally," she mumbled as she stepped into the empty hall. She was going to leave, but she was definitely not going back to class, not with Lucas's betrayal and what she had done so raw in her mind.

She was tired of the constant looks and continuous need to lie. God, the lies felt like quicksand, constantly shifting, pulling her under as each one slipped effortlessly past her lips. What she needed was a long talk with her mother. She needed the warmth of her hug and the taste of her amazing warm cookies as she reassured Averie that everything would be okay. That would never happen though, ever again.

The familiar pain she had managed to suppress for the last few minutes crept back in. They say it gets better, but how could that be possible when the searing burn of emptiness never goes away?

Her steps echoed off the empty halls around her as she wandered lazily back to the classroom. Her departure was imminent. The only flaw in her quick disappearance was the knowledge that she had left her bag and keys behind in the classroom. She turned the corner leading down the final hallway when a figure caught her eye.

It stood like a phantom grinning at her, clad in black. The sun leaked around him from the window, its rays unable to penetrate the thick darkness that emanated from him. The air left her in a gasp. Her heart thumped ferociously in her ears, and her body went cold.

"Lucas?"

The bell rang, and the doors swung open as students and teachers spilled out around her. Averie pushed through the crowd, dodging and side-stepping as she tried to make her way to the end of the hall. Whatever she saw had disappeared. She searched the group for him, her body twisting from side to side as searched faces.

A hand gripped her shoulder and without thought, she shot her palm out directly into the assailant's chest with a deep, echoing thud.

"Jesus, Avi!" Thane gasped, his breath coming in short bursts. He leaned forward with his hands gripping his knees as he fought to catch his breath.

"Thane! I'm so sorry, I thought you were…" her words trailed as she continued to search the thinning halls as students made their way to their next class.

"That I was who? Who in the world would you want to hit like that?" Thane asked, straightening himself as his breathing regulated.

"Is everything alright, Averie? You look like you've seen a ghost," Silas asked, holding out her bag, his eyes drifting from Thane to Averie.

"He was here," Averie whispered. "He was standing right here!"

Silas and Thane watched as Averie began to pace back and forth, her fingers running through her hair.

"Who are you talking about?" Silas asked, his eyes scanning the hall as he lowered her bag to his side.

"Lucas!" she hissed. "He was here. Standing right here."

"When?" Thane asked.

"Just a minute ago! I was coming back from the office, and he was standing right here ... smiling at me."

Silas and Thane exchanged a worried glance.

"Fox—" Thane's attempt was cut short when she lifted a hand, her head shaking in vigorous denial.

"I'm not crazy, Thane. I know what I saw. He was—"

A light clinking drew their attention toward the window. The sun was shining brightly on this clear summer day, bringing immediate attention to the darkly dressed figure that stood waving below them.

"Holy shit," Thane breathed.

Lucas smiled, his wave turning into a beckoning motion.

Averie's response was immediate. In an instant she was running, her steps slamming against the old tile as she raced down the hall and threw the door to the stairs open.

"Avi, wait!" Thane called closely behind.

Ignoring his plea, Averie gripped the railing and used it to propel her forward as she rushed down the flights of stairs. She came to a skidding stop against the door leading to the courtyard when a hand wrapped around her arm and spun her around, trapping her against the wall.

Averie's heart was racing, her chest heaving with frantic breaths. "Let me go."

Denial

Silas shook his head. "This could be a trap, Averie. In fact, I can almost guarantee you this is some sort of trick."

"Averie, you're not thinking clearly. We need to be smart about this," Thane added, catching his breath as he dropped from the last step.

She knew they were right, but she couldn't get it to process properly in her mind. The only thing she could comprehend was that Lucas was in fact alive, and that he was just outside that door waiting for her.

"I have to see him," Averie explained.

A long look passed between them before Silas nodded. "Fine. But we are going with you."

Averie bobbed her head in frantic agreement. She took a deep breath and turned from his hold and pulled the door open.

Lucas was leaning casually against the old brick building, patiently awaiting their arrival. His hands were tucked into his pockets and his head tipped up to the sun. Averie stopped just outside the door in disbelief. For weeks, she had thought the worst, and yet here he was, alive and well. Averie frowned at the thought and looked over his profile. His skin was slightly paler than the last time she had seen him, his hair more disheveled than she had ever seen, and a thin layer of scruff covered the lower half of his face. Faint red lines zigzagged across his arms and neck, tainting his otherwise smooth skin. The sound of the metal door closing behind him had Lucas slowly lowering his head and opening his eyes. Revealing indisputable proof of change.

Averie couldn't mask the shocked sound that left her mouth in that moment. If by some miracle she had managed to go back in time to cover her mouth and smother the noise, it would have been felt. When Lucas turned to face them head-on, his usual charming smile morphed into something more sinister, accentuating the angry claw marks that marred the left side of his face. Though the more alarming and unsettling change lay in his once vibrant and laughing ocean eyes, now the color of snow. Dead and devoid of any life, as if something dark burned deep within them.

"Hello, Averie."

Chapter Forty-One

The group recoiled as his voice screeched—a sound like nails on a chalkboard, raw and unpleasant, made their skin crawl. The musical lilt he once had a distant memory compared to the piercing quality it now held.

The scene before her defied Averie's understanding. "Lucas … how…?" she breathed. Her mind raced, a whirlwind of disbelief and confusion, as she tried to reconcile what she saw with her emerging belief.

"How am I alive?" Lucas taunted, pushing from the wall. Averie watched, fascinated, as he moved toward her, his steps jerky and uneven, like a marionette with tangled strings. Stretching his arms out wide, he turned in a circle, his face marred with its sick smile. "I know this must be quite the shock to you. After all, you did a damn good job of trying to kill me. Though not good enough as it seems." His smile grew as he wagged his fingers animatedly at her.

Averie shook her head. "Luke, I didn't ... I wouldn't... I never wanted to hurt you."

Lucas waved her words away. "Nonsense, you did me a favor, little Avi. I am more alive now than I ever was. I am more now than I ever would have been."

"How are you here, Lucas?" Silas inquired, his eyes narrowing behind his tensed stance.

"Just ask what you really want to know, Silas. How am I alive when you left me alone to die in that field that night?"

Silence descended. Averie and Thane turned identical confused, disbelieving looks on Silas. Silas stood tall, his eyes tracking Lucas's every move.

"What's he talking about, Silas?" Averie asked.

"I saved you," Silas glared.

"You left me broken and bleeding in that field!" Lucas bellowed.

Silas shook his head. "Maddox fixed you, if you recall. We only left when the police were close enough. We had to get Averie out of there."

Lucas began to pace back and forth in front of them. His heavy, rough steps crushed the grass, creating a quickly widening trail. He shook his head, his hands weaving into the short strands of his hair and pulling.

Denial

"Where did you go, Luke? I searched everywhere for you. Checked every hospital, called everyone we know. I went to every hangout," Thane said, taking cautious steps toward him, as though he were approaching a wild animal.

Lucas stopped suddenly, smoothed his hair back, and let out an exaggerated breath as if the moment of chaos hadn't happened. He stopped with a wide smile and pointed toward them. "Fine! I'll tell you, but then, we get down to business, okay?"

Averie nodded. "Okay."

"Well, it was a nice spring day. The sun shining and the birds singing. All was cheery and right in my perfect little world. I thought I was going to go to prom with my on-again-off-again girlfriend like we had planned, but then this …" he stopped to sneer at Silas, "*guy* showed up and started messing everything up. I was actually surprised she had agreed to go with me at all, considering she had barely spent more than five minutes with me in weeks. But that is neither here nor there," he pressed on, waving the thought away. "Then, as we were driving to prom, this girl asks me if I would pull over so we could talk about something. Color me shocked when I found out it wasn't code for a quickie, but was actually about her showing me that she was some type of—" He stopped his pacing with a sly grin. "Well, we don't want to say that word again now, do we?"

Averie stepped forward, her voice barely a whisper, "Lucas—" Thane grabbed her hand, stopping her attempt to get closer. Averie looked to Thane, attempting to shake off his tightening grip when the slight shake of his head told her more than his words could have. *Something's wrong here.* Though she tried to ignore it, it hung heavy in the air.

Lucas's cold eyes slipped to Averie. Dread pooled in the pit of her stomach. "Don't be rude, Avi. I'm telling a story here." He smiled and his lifeless gaze slipped from hers. "Now where was I? Oh! That's right, the demonstration. She shows me she's a ... tad different. Then when I, understandably I might add, flip the hell out and need a moment to process what she told me. That's when she has me smashing into the ground and bam! Broken arm!"

"That isn't what happened! You fell, and I was trying to help!" Averie protested, fighting against Thane's death grip.

Lucas stopped and quick as a snake, pulled a long, black blade from behind him. It's glinting tip inches from her face. "You, stay right there, Missy. I am telling this story. I won't remind you again."

Averie froze, eyes wide in shock at the smoking blade. The longer she stared, the more it seemed like something, some*one*, was moving from within. "What is that?" Averie was captivated, as though it spoke to her, drawing her in. Without her knowledge, her free hand had drifted up and reached forward.

Silas snatched Averie's arm, yanking her back. "Don't touch it."

"What is it?" she whispered.

"You like it?" Lucas smiled. "It's my new toy. Enchanting isn't it?"

Denial

Silas shrugged. "It's just a dagger."

Lucas rolled his eyes. "It's not just *any* dagger, Silas. We both know that."

"Silas, what is it?" Averie asked.

Silas only shook his head, his eyes locked on Lucas and his body poised for action.

Lucas released an exaggerated sigh. "So full of secrets, aren't we, Silas?" he asked, motioning the blade toward Silas. "This lovely thing here, my dear, is called a Soul Blade. Designed to trap the souls of one's enemies deep inside, giving the wielder more power with every vanquishing. Or so I'm told."

"Lucas, what do you want?" Thane demanded, dragging Lucas's attention from Silas to him, as he and Silas worked to get Averie behind him.

"Well, I was *trying* to tell a story, but she keeps interrupting me!"

"On with it, then," Thane demanded.

Lucas's eyes narrowed as he wagged the blade inches from Thane's face. "You always were so demanding. Such an irritating trait to have, Thane."

"Why don't you finish your story, Luke?" Averie asked softly.

The sneer dropped from his face, replaced by the ghost of his old smile. "Of course, my dear Avi." He tapped the blade against his chin, smoke rising from where it met his skin. "Where was I? Ah, yes, you broke my arm."

With her mouth open to speak, Averie felt Silas's hand close around hers; a slight shake of his head, coupled with the firmness of his grip, instantly halted her words.

"So there I am, laying on the ground, in complete agony, my arm a complete and total mess, when I am hoisted into the air and my bones begin breaking piece by piece, over and over again until I can barely breathe. Then just when I think I can't possibly take any more, that death is right there, waiting to claim me, I hear something beginning to tear. Color me shocked when I realize that tearing is coming from me. Averie is literally tearing the flesh from my body."

Averie closed her eyes against the roaring nausea twisting her stomach. Lucas continued his story, his movements becoming more animated and jerkier with every word. "Oh, how I screamed and begged. I screamed so loud I could feel my vocal chords popping as they were ripped apart." Lucas heaved a sigh. "Much of it becomes a haze from there."

"What do you want, Lucas?" Thane asked again.

"Wow, just wow, Thane. I don't even get a 'That sounds terrible', or 'Gee, that sucks.' Hell, I would even take a 'Dang' at this point. But I get nothing from you, do I, Thane? You always love to brush off the important stuff, especially when it comes to perfect little Averie. She always gets a pass."

"I'm sorry, Lucas. I never meant to hurt you. I lost control, and I didn't…" Averie choked back a sob, her

Denial

vision swimming with unshed tears. "If I could go back and fix it, I would."

Lucas stood silently staring at her for a long time before finally shaking his head. "No, I don't think so. You stood there, promising that you wouldn't hurt me, that you were still the same person, blah, blah, blah. Then we hit the first bump in the road and you just slice and dice to your heart's content. You are not a good person, Averie. You're only masquerading as one."

Averie's mind rebelled at his words. She knew what had been done, but it was as if she had been a bystander to the entire event. Trapped within her own body as something else took over, something dark and merciless. A small part of her mind also injected the fact that it was him that caused her to close control.

"But alas, my story isn't over yet because the good part didn't come until much later. Just as the sweet relief of death was coming to claim me, there was a burning light, and two people I have never seen before poured some type of smoking liquid over my body. I was already so far gone, I couldn't even scream as it seared its way across my mutilated body. But just as suddenly as they arrived, they were gone, and I was left alone on the cold, hard ground. Forgotten. I could hear the sirens coming, but I didn't care. I just wanted to die. I wanted to escape the pain. But as you can see, that wasn't in the cards for me. Just as the ambulance lights entered my field of vision, a figure ... let's call it, I don't know, *The Shadow*, appeared over me." He smiled, giving a long and drawn out pause. Averie felt

Silas stiffen at her side and sent him a confused look before turning back to Lucas.

"The Shadow?" she asked.

Lucas's smile spread, pulling at the scars across his face. His eyes bouncing excitedly between Silas and Averie. "Ah. I see. You're not the only one keeping secrets then. Would you like to tell her? Or shall I?" he asked Silas.

"Tell me what?"

"Oh, poor, naive Avi," Lucas tsked. "The Shadow is something not even you can, with all of your infinite power, stand a chance against. Not when it knows your darkest desires and the deepest fears that feed your insecurities and doubts. The Shadow is the very thing that gave Marcus the power to take the Realm. The same power he used to kill your birth father."

"I don't understand." Averie's mind turned his words over again and again in her mind. But no matter how she looked at it, it didn't make sense. If there was something darker than Marcus, more cruel and powerful, why would Silas keep that to himself?

"The Shadow is your real enemy." Lucas stepped closer, his snow-white eyes taking hers captive. "Marcus is just a puppet, and The Shadow is his master."

"Finish your story, Lucas," Silas ground out through clenched teeth.

Lucas broke their connection with great reluctance to eye Silas. "The Shadow saved me. Offered me the deal of a lifetime. Gave me the *kiss* of life, you might say. It broke me down to the very foundations of myself before

Denial

building me back up. Making me stronger, faster, and more determined than ever before," he spread his arms wide, twisted excitement stretching his smile wider. "Turned me into what you see now."

"What deal?"

"That's not important now, but what I say next is. This is your second warning, Averie. Do not leave this Realm. Do not enter the Heart Realm, or the next payment will be harsher than the first."

"You're not making any sense, Lucas. What warning? What payment? Why would I listen to something that calls itself 'The Shadow'?"

"Why don't you ask your mother?" He smiled, tilting his head as though listening to something. "Well, I must be off. Thane, good to see you again, Averie, pleasure as always, and Silas..." He shrugged before bowing and vanishing before their eyes.

The group stood frozen, the silence punctuated only by their ragged breaths, as the enormity of what had happened sank in. Thane's hands clenched as he glared at the spot Lucas had vanished from.

"The Shadow killed my mother." The words rushed from her mouth of their own volition. "But why? I didn't do anything! I didn't even know The Shadow existed!" A cold dread seeped into her consciousness, dragging her eyes to Silas. The weight of the revelation pressing down on her. He stood tall, his body tense, though his face held a calm that unsettled her. "But you did, didn't you, Silas? You knew, and you never told me."

As if in slow motion, Silas faced her, giving the slightest of nods. "I did."

The sound of her smack cleaved the air. Averie's anger vibrated off her. She held nothing back when she hit him. His head twisted to the side, a red hand print already blistering his face.

"Averie!" Thane lunged forward, capturing her in his embrace while she kicked and smacked wildly.

"You knew! You knew, and you never said a word! She's dead because of you!"

"Calm down, Fox, we don't know that," Thane whispered against her ear, an arm wrapped firmly around her waist, the other running up and down her arm reassuringly.

"Well, speak up, dammit! Did you know?" she demanded.

Silas nodded. "Yes, I knew about The Shadow."

Averie stilled. Wondering and knowing were two very different things. It was easier to wonder if something terrible could have been prevented, but nothing compared to the truth of knowing that it easily could have been. While the wonder was like an annoying fly that you can't seem to shoo away, the knowledge was like a knife slowly pierce into your body and ripping your heart from your chest.

"You son of a bitch!" Averie was dropped on the ground as Thane charged forward, his fist slamming sickeningly against Silas's jaw. Silas dropped to the ground. Thane was atop him in an instant, raining down blows like

Denial

a turbulent storm. Silas held his arms up in an attempt to defend himself.

"Thane! What are you doing?" Averie turned, finding Sera's shocked, pale face standing in the doorway.

Thane didn't halt his assault at the sound of his name. Anger burned through him like a flame descending on oil, slow until contact. His mind blurred into memories of Karen's smiling face, of her taking him into her home, raising him as her own. The hours she spent helping him with his homework, the time she took him to his first defense class, the moments she spent cheering louder than anyone when he got his first black belt.

"Thane! You're going to kill him!" Sera screamed, tears in her eyes. Her words finally permeated Averie's shocked brain. A quick flick of her wrist, and Thane was tossed from Silas's immobile one. Thane climbed back to his feet like a raging bull. Averie stepped in front of him, her eyes flashing in warning. Thane fought against his desire, his chest heaving, hands bruised and bleeding.

"Don't stand there and defend him!" Thane thundered.

"Take a walk," she ordered.

"Silas! Silas, you have to wake up!" Sera twisted to Averie. "Avi, he won't wake up! What do we do?"

Averie's mind continued to race with every step. "Get the nurse while I try to wake him up."

Sera nodded, frantically jumping from the ground and racing around the side of the building. Averie knelt down, taking in Silas's bloodied and bruised face, the shaky rise and fall of his chest causing her to worry at her bottom lip. Laying a hand on his chest, she took a deep breath, closed her eyes and imagined the warmth of Karen's life enveloping her. As the tingling took hold, she rested her other hand against the ground, sending a silent request of aid, the current of life trickled through her.

A minute passed, and the tingling eased away as Silas's hand covered hers. Slowly, she opened her eyes, peering into his less swollen ones.

"Thank you," he whispered.

"You deserved everything you got and more."

He nodded, wincing as he shifted into a sitting position.

Averie fought the urge to help him. "Why did you lie?"

"Averie, I—"

"Silas!" Sera squealed, rushing forward. "I was so worried! I came out and saw Thane…" Her words stopped as she looked around. "Where is Thane?"

The nurse stepped forward, kneeling beside Silas. "Are you alright? Sera said that you were in a fight and unconscious."

Silas gave a small smile. "Just a misunderstanding."

The nurse frowned. "We don't permit fighting on school grounds. Are you hurt anywhere? Where did all this blood come from?"

"We were just horsing around and things got out of hand. I'm fine, and no, it's clay, see?" he explained, pulling some of the dirt from the ground and rubbing it on his shirt. "Mixes and looks like blood when it gets wet."

Denial

The nurse shook her head. "Really, now?"

"Yep." Silas smiled, standing. "See all good."

The nurse rolled her eyes, then rose to her feet. "No more fights, Silas," she ordered, before turning away and leaving.

"Why didn't you say something?! Thane could have killed you, Silas," Sera demanded, stomping her foot and crossing her arms.

"There was just a misunderstanding." Silas grunted.

"What are you doing here, Sera?" Averie asked as Silas stepped toward her. "Aren't you supposed to be in class?"

Sera's eyes narrowed as they moved between them. "Yeah, actually, I am just like you two."

"I'm going home," Averie announced.

Sera frowned. "Are you sure? You have already missed so many days since…"

Her words trailed off and her face flushed.

"Yeah, I'm sure. I'm already caught up on the work I missed and got an exception letter from the principal."

"Is it because of the detectives?" Sera asked, concerned.

"Part of it," Averie answered.

"Lucas will come home, Avi, you just watch," Sera promised, wrapping her in a tight hug. "I will get whatever homework I can for you and drop it off before I head home tonight."

Averie returned her embrace and smiled into her hair. "Thank you. I don't know what I would do without you."

Pulling apart, Sera smiled and flipped her hair over her shoulder. "You would fall completely apart and probably wear the same Converse for the next ten years."

Averie gave an honest laugh. "That's probably true."

After saying their goodbyes, Sera disappeared back into the school, leaving Averie and Silas behind in a tense, awkward silence.

"Averie," Silas started.

Averie held up her hand, shaking her head. "I don't want excuses, Silas. I need to find Thane."

"If you would just let me explain."

"Explain what exactly? How you lied about who or what the real threat was? How you knew what really happened to my mom and just let me go on living with the crushing guilt of thinking that I was the one that killed her?"

"I didn't know, Averie. Not really. The stories of The Shadow are like the ones of your boogieman. They are told to children at night or when they don't listen. No one knew if they were real or not."

"Like me? Like how your entire Realm didn't believe I was real? How none of them knew for sure yet they still clung to the stories, to the possibility?"

"Averie, that's different. Radnar was there at your birth. Everyone knew of the princess; no one knew what happened or if you had survived the separation, but people had seen you. The Shadow has never been seen."

"I don't have time to play games with you," Averie called over her shoulder, leaving Silas to stare after her.

Chapter Forty-Two

It hadn't taken Averie long to find Thane. He was a creature of habit, and when he was angry, he could always be found in the gym. Averie took her time crossing the thickly padded room, every step bringing her closer to the tangible pain that shrouded Thane like a cloak. The sound of his fists pounding against the large blue bag echoed in the empty room, only broken when Thane released a grunt or thundering roar.

Averie hugged her waist and stopped a foot away. Her stomach clenched at the mixture of fury and pain on her brother's face. She watched him attack the bag with a ferocity that was rarely seen outside of the wild. Like a starved lion battling for the final scraps, Thane slammed his fists again and again until his chest heaved and sweat poured from his body.

Averie felt another piece inside snap when he finally rested his head against the rough blue leather, silent tears streaming down his cheeks like a broken dam. Averie closed the space between them and wrapped her arms around his sweaty back, clinging to him tightly while he unleashed his silent sorrow.

"I'm leaving, Fox," Thane announced, breaking the silence.

Averie's breath caught as her heart stuttered, her arms falling to her sides. "What?" she whispered, praying to the gods she heard him wrong.

Thane unlatched his gloves and slowly unraveled his taped hands, letting the bandages spool on the floor before he finally faced her. Lifting his shirt, he wiped his face free of the salty mixture of sweat and tears. "I spoke with Callen. He said that Maddox found something called a traveler's portal. He believes that it will be easier than using Silas's old one. I'm going with them."

"You're leaving me?" she whispered.

Thane watched her for a long, silent minute. "No, Fox. I'm not leaving you, but I need to get out of here. I can't stay here with him."

"I'll come with you. I've been hiding here for too long, anyway."

Thane gave a small smile and a shake of his head. "Not yet. As much as I hate it, you and Silas need to work out whatever it is between you two and reach a place where you can work together. We all do."

Denial

"He knew it wasn't me. How can I trust someone that made me think I killed my own mother?"

"He had his reasons."

Averie and Thane turned at the sound of a new voice entering their space. In the dimmed light, Callen stood like a shadow. He moved silently forward, his hands shoved deep into his pockets and his shoulders rolled back.

"He had his reasons?!" Thane demanded. "He killed our *mother* and let Averie think she had done it. What possible reason can someone have for doing something like that?"

"First, he did not kill your mother. There is nothing any of you could have done if The Shadow was coming for her. Second, he was not sure whether The Shadow even existed," Callen defended.

"But he did have an idea?" Thane asked, stepping forward.

Callen heaved a sigh, giving a slight nod.

Thane gave his friend a narrow gaze. "How long have you known?"

"Thane," Averie's fingers tightened in his shirt.

"Not until just now. Silas called, speaking gibberish about finding you and Averie. Mentioned The Shadow and I put two and two together. I know that it hurts you to think that he kept something like this from you, but I have known Silas a lot longer than you. He would never do something to intentionally hurt either of you," Callen answered, stopping a few feet away.

"How can you defend him?" Thane demanded.

"He is my friend. I thought he was yours. I know you have rage, but you must focus it on who has actually committed the evil deeds, not who may have known who did it," Callen answered simply.

Thane trembled in his new rage. His hand clenched at his sides as he stared at Callen's peaceful expression. Thane stepped forward, then a cool hand wrapped around his wrist. Looking back, he saw Averie staring at him, her face neutral, almost devoid of emotion, like a solemn painting.

"Doesn't this bother you, Avi? He let you think it was you. He let you blame yourself for *weeks*!" Thane thundered, the empty room making his words reverberate and scream back at them.

Averie flinched as Thane's harsh words slapped against her. "Of course it does, Thane."

"Again," Callen interjected. "He did not *know* anything, for certain"

Thane threw his head back and released a humorless laugh, ignoring Callen and focusing on Averie instead. "Sure as hell doesn't seem like it. Or are you too wrapped up in his pretty words to care that he lied to you?"

"Did *not* lie," Callen whispered.

Averie dropped Thane's wrist like it suddenly caught fire.

"Thane," Callen warned, his voice low and deep.

Thane twisted to sneer at his friend. "How can you follow a man that would let someone torture themselves like she has? You sent him here for her."

Denial

"In war, there are decisions that have to be made in a moment and sacrifices that we all must make. Silas would never intentionally hurt Averie, and you know that. You are just too lost in the situation and too deep in your emotions to see that right now," Callen said pointedly.

Thane turned back to Averie. "Don't you care, Fox? He let you believe that it was you. How many nights did you stay up haunted by what you thought happened? How many times have you cried yourself to sleep or awakened from a nightmare because of what he did?"

Averie shook her head, swallowing thickly against his words. "It doesn't change a thing. She's dead because of me. The Shadow wanted to teach me a lesson."

"It changes everything! You act like you don't even care!" Thane's voice boomed throughout the space.

"You think I don't care?" Averie whispered. "I care, Thane. Every part of me cares, but I can't do this. I can't go to a gym and release my anger and pain on a punching bag, because if I do, this whole damn place could come down! The whole town could be destroyed. So yeah, I may look like I don't care, but inside I am screaming and I am fighting to stay in control of myself."

Thane deflated at her words. He couldn't imagine what she was going through, never being able to fully express yourself without the fear of what may happen. To have to hold back everything, no matter how painful or angry you felt. The thought of it all made Thane feel like he was suffocating.

"Fox, I'm so sorry," Thane whispered, pulling her into his arms. "I can't imagine what you're going through, and I'm sorry for yelling."

Averie stood in his embrace, letting his strength seep into her before returning the hug. "You know you stink, right?" Averie said into his chest.

Thane chuckled, his chest and shoulders shaking.

Callen cleared his throat. "I hate to break this up, but we are leaving, and if you are coming, Thane … the time is *now*."

"Now?" Averie asked, pulling from Thane.

Callen nodded in confirmation. "Maddox found the traveler's portal. They tend to move around and we do not know how long this one will stay put."

"How long?" Thane asked.

"Twenty minutes at the most, and that is pushing it. We should have gone immediately," Callen answered.

Averie watched Thane battled against himself. Taking his hand in hers, she smiled. "It's okay, Bear, you go. I'll be there soon."

Thane's expression pinched in pain. "I can wait until you're ready."

Averie shook her head. "No, you were right. I have to sort things out with Silas."

Thane pulled her in and pressed a light kiss to her forehead before he turned to Callen. "I need five."

Callen and Averie watched Thane disappear into the shower, each lost in their own thoughts. Averie shifted her

Denial

feet and sent a warning looking to Callen. "If anything happens to him, I will kill you."

Callen looked down at the small woman, his brow arched in amusement. "He will be fine."

"I know Silas said you are supposed to be some badass magic guy, but you have no idea the hell that will rain down if you don't protect him."

They stared at each other for a long moment, locked into a battle of wills, before Callen finally nodded. "Nothing will happen to him," he promised, holding his hand out to her.

Without breaking their gaze, Averie took his hand and let the prickling on her skin flow into him. A smile tugged at her lips when he flinched back in shock. "I will hold you to that."

"I'm ready," Thane declared, as he swaggered out of the steam cloud that hid the bathroom door. His shirt was plastered against his chest as he ran his hands through his dripping hair.

Averie frowned. "You could've hollered for a towel."

Thane shrugged and threw his bag over his shoulder. "I'm dry enough."

"Do you have everything?" Callen asked.

Thane nodded, motioning toward the bag.

Callen gave Averie a small smile. "I will give you a moment to say goodbye." Then he disappeared out the door.

Averie released a heavy breath before she could look at Thane. "I'm going to miss you, Bear."

Thane smiled and pulled her close. "I'll miss you too, Fox."

"Stay safe. Don't do anything reckless or let Callen talk you into doing something stupid."

"Never," Thane promised, resting his chin atop her head.

"And make sure you're there when I come through, okay?" Averie continued.

"Of course."

"I love you, Bear," Averie whispered into his chest, her words muffled by his tear-stained shirt.

"I love you, Fox."

These questions are for reflection and discussion after reading Denial

1. Which characters did you like the most?
2. What would you do if you were Averie?
3. Would you go to the Heart Realm?
4. What did you think of the story's pacing?
5. Which character would you like to meet in real life?
6. What scene would you point out as a pivotal moment for Averie?
7. Was there a scene that stuck with you? If so, which one?
8. How did you feel about the ending?
9. Would you want Thane as a big brother?
10. What is your impression of Silas?

About the Author

Prepare to be pulled into realms unlike any other. C.R. Rice masterfully fuses fantasy, dark noir, mystery, romance, and sci-fi within her sprawling Realm Series. These aren't just stories; they're high-stakes odysseys where true consequences keep readers relentlessly on the edge of their seats, utterly immersed in every twist. Her pen first hit the page from a burning need for escape—a journey into worlds she couldn't find—and now, she fiercely invites you to join that thrilling quest. Driven by the literary brilliance of Terry Pratchett, Scott Westerfeld, and Clare B. Dunkle, C.R. Rice is on a singular mission: to deliver the most powerful, immersive escape imaginable. Off the page, she's navigating adventures of her own, traveling, enjoying life with her husband, and valiantly attempting to keep her delightfully daring golden retriever, Tyr, out of delightful trouble.

https://www.authorcrrice.com
https://www.facebook.com/authorcrrice
https://www.instagram.com/authorcrrice

C.R. Rice

More From C.R. Rice

Continue the journey through the Heart Realm — a world of danger, mystery, and destiny. Each book dives deeper into a universe where choices shape worlds… and nothing is ever as it seems.

Explore the Complete Series, now fully available:

Novels:

Denial
The beginning of a cosmic war and the awakening of hidden powers.

Anger
Tensions rise and loyalties are tested in a realm on the edge of destruction.

Bargaining
Choices must be made as secrets surface and destinies collide.

Depression
Darkness deepens, and the cost of survival becomes painfully clear.

Acceptance
The final confrontation that will determine the fate of worlds.

Denial

Novellas:

Broken Beginnings
The story of Thane and the events that shaped him.

Sins of the Father
The journey of Silas, his truths, and the burdens he bears.

Shattered Start
Sera's story and the making of the Shadow.

Honorable Darkness
The tale of Hex and Snip, showing how far brothers will go.

A Love Lost
Radnar's story: how a lost love forged a warrior.

Each tale delves deeper into a universe where choices shape worlds… and nothing is ever as it seems.

Made in the USA
Coppell, TX
18 January 2026

67245391R10203